THE ORGAN
GROWERS

Also by Richard Van Anderson

The Final Push: a short story of surgical suspense

The Organ Takers: a novel of surgical suspense

THE ORGAN GROWERS

A novel of surgical suspense

Richard Van Anderson

WHITE LIGHT PRESS
SEATTLE

Cover design by Visual Quill.

This book is a work of fiction. References to real people, events, establishments, organizations, or locales are intended only to provide a sense of authenticity, and are used fictitiously. All other characters, and all incidents and dialogue, are drawn from the author's imagination and are not to be construed as real.

Publisher's Cataloging-in-Publication Data

Anderson, Richard Van, author.

The organ growers : a novel of surgical suspense / Richard Van Anderson.

Seattle, WA : White Light Press, 2017. | Series: McBride trilogy, bk. 2.

LCCN 2017917775 | ISBN 978-0-9907597-3-7 (hardcover) | ISBN 978-0-9907597-4-4 (pbk.) | ISBN 978-0-9907597-5-1 (ebook)

Subjects: LCSH: Physicians--Fiction. | Transplantation of organs, tissues, etc.--Fiction. | Tissue engineering--Fiction. | Medical fiction. | BISAC: FICTION / Thrillers / Medical. | FICTION / Thrillers / Suspense. | GSAFD: Medical novels. | Suspense fiction.

LCC PS3601.N54486 O73 2017 (print) | LCC PS3601.N54486 (ebook) | DDC 813/.6--dc23.

For Kathleen.
Thank you for your unwavering love, support, and patience.

Author's Note

Surgery is a technical endeavor. As such, this story is laden with surgical terminology. Taken in context, the meaning of these terms should be clear. If, however, you are interested in expanded definitions, photos of surgical instruments, and X-rays and CT scans of pertinent pathologies, please go to rvananderson.com and click on the Glossaries tab. I strongly encourage you to take a look. Gaining familiarity with the subject matter will enrich your reading experience, and the glossary is interesting in its own right. Thank you, and enjoy the story.

I absolutely see a day where you'll walk into a manufacturing facility somewhere, and there will be jars of kidneys, and jars of livers, and jars of lungs, whatever it is you need.

—Dr. Doris Taylor, University of Minnesota

- 1 -

Confucius said before you begin a journey of revenge dig two graves. It has also been said revenge is more efficient than justice. In addition, it is generally believed the most dangerous man is the man with nothing, for he has nothing to lose. Dr. David McBride was that man. He had lost everything—wife, unborn child, freedom, future—by the hand of another, and he did not trust the justice system to respond with the swiftness or severity such an egregious injustice demanded. So he had taken the matter into his own hands, and on the second floor of a dilapidated meatpacking warehouse in lower Manhattan Dr. Andrew Turnbull lay strapped to a gurney with four-point leather restraints, naked from the waist up, covered by a blanket from the waist down. EKG leads coursed from his chest to a cardiac monitor on a small table. A bag of intravenous fluid was infusing into his right arm. Razor thin surgical incisions ran just below the ribs on each side and curved around the back. The color had drained from his face. He was drenched with sweat. He looked terrified.

McBride inserted a syringe of succinylcholine into the IV tubing and depressed the plunger with his thumb.

"Please, David," Turnbull pleaded, "at least think about the impact this will have on thousands of lives."

McBride pushed harder. "Maybe you should think about the impact you've had on a handful of lives."

Turnbull pulled against the restraints. His face contorted with the pain of fresh incisions under tension. He groaned, fell back and lay there motionless, eyes squeezed shut, the heart monitor beeping furiously. "David, I beg you," he said, struggling to find the breath to form words. "Please don't do this."

David continued to push.

"You'll rot in Hell for—"

Turnbull's mouth kept moving, but he couldn't finish the sentence. And then he began to twitch—arms, legs, fingers, face. The succinylcholine was depolarizing his muscle cells, every muscle in his body now paralyzed, except for the heart. The monitor showed a normal rhythm. Andrew Turnbull was suffocating to death while fully conscious, his brain still receiving blood.

The plunger stopped, the syringe empty.

Turnbull lay motionless on the gurney, his chest no longer rising and falling, his eyes wide with fear. David put his mouth to Turnbull's ear and yelled at him the way the French screamed at decapitated heads during the revolution: "You can't take away everything from a man and expect to live!"

The alarm on the cardiac monitor sounded. A jagged line replaced the regular procession of spikes and dips. The heart had used up its oxygen supply and was fibrillating, dying along with the other organs, the organism, the man. David waited to feel something—satisfaction, relief, horror, guilt—but he felt nothing. He had just murdered the man who'd become a father figure to him as his own was consumed by Alzheimer's disease. He had intentionally inflicted pain on a man he had once admired and respected, and the only thing he felt was indifference. He was now dead inside. The ordeal of the last five weeks had stripped him of his humanity.

From up in the sky, the sound of a chopper, coming closer, hovering. From down on the street, cars pulling up, screeching to a stop, doors opening and closing. Through the dirty windows, lights flashing on the building façade across the street. David grabbed his coat and walked toward the freight elevator, passing through burnt-orange swatches of early morning sunlight that had penetrated the grime on the glass and filled the second floor of the warehouse.

He exited the elevator and crossed to the middle of the ground floor where ten days earlier he had discovered a drainage trough covered by steel plates laid end-to-end. He lifted the plate covering the drain outflow and lowered himself into the hole. The opening was barely large enough to admit a thin man, and he couldn't feel the bottom. He pointed his toe and kicked around for something other than empty space.

A massive boom erupted from the metal door on the front of the building, no more than forty feet away.

His feet found concrete. He was able to stand.

Another boom echoed through the warehouse.

He bent his knees slightly and slid the plate over the opening.

A third boom. The door slammed into the wall. Boots scuffled overhead. "NYPD!" rang out repeatedly.

David tried to crouch deeper into the pipe, but there wasn't room to fully bend his knees, so he braced his back against the wall and slid down to his butt, keeping his legs straight out in front of him as they extended into the horizontal aspect of the pipe. What sounded like an army of cops thrashed around above, presumably checking every nook and cranny of the warehouse. He needed to get moving before one of them thought to check the drain, but he had no way to turn around, no way to swap head for feet.

Using his heels and hands, he inched deeper into the drain until he cleared the bend and lay flat on his back. Should someone remove the plate and look into the hole, they'd be unable to see him, but he took no comfort in this. The top of the pipe was ten inches from his nose, he'd moved from low light into near darkness, and he had little room to move his arms or bend his legs. The sense of constriction was unnerving and quickly edging toward full-blown panic. He wiggled and writhed, twisted himself from supine to prone position and started working his way down the tube, moving feet first and dragging his coat behind him.

Every inch gained cost him a layer of skin off his elbows and knees. The short-sleeved scrub shirt and thin cotton scrub pants offered no protection against the rough concrete. Pain radiated from the eleven-day-old gunshot wound in his right thigh. He could not lift his butt to get on his knees or raise his head to relieve the strain in his neck. All he *could* do was shift from side to side, elbow to elbow, toe to toe.

Before long he was enveloped by absolute darkness and silence. He closed his eyes to hide the blackness and stopped trying to lift his head and butt so as not to remind himself that he was confined to a space no larger than a coffin, but it didn't help. His heart was racing. His breathing shallow and erratic. The air was becoming increasingly dank, making it harder to fill his lungs. He stopped, folded his arms under his chest and rested his forehead on his fists, took deep breaths and tried to relax, but he couldn't. His heart kept pounding. His lungs demanded more oxygen. He had to get out of the pipe. He tried to visualize the distance from the center of the warehouse floor—where he had climbed into the drain—to the street. He figured the drain followed a straight line to the sewer and guessed the sewer ran under and parallel to the street. In his mind's eye he pictured a distance of sixty to seventy feet. He had covered less than half that.

He started moving again, everything hurting, the heat rising. Good thing he wasn't wearing the coat. He'd be burning up in the heavy canvas with no way to slip it off. He felt the pocket for Turnbull's Blackberry and Rolex. Both were still there.

He developed a rhythm, rocking from hip to hip, using his forearms and toes to push and pull, covering about four inches with each effort. He counted three moves, figured he'd traveled a foot, counted the next three, another foot, and by focusing on his progress instead of the fact that he was confined to a stenotic cylinder six feet under street level, he brought his anxiety level from acute-panic-attack into the realm of might-actually-live-through-this.

Twenty minutes later his toes lost their grip of the concrete and touched nothing but void. He'd reached the end of the drain-pipe. Unable to turn his head and look, he had no idea of what lay beyond. He knew he was intersecting the sewer system—he'd been breathing in the feculent odor for the last ten minutes—but he didn't know if there was going to be a drop of five feet or fifty. He inched backward, now bending at the waist, legs dangling, and still no contact. He moved a few more inches, then a few more until he was hanging from the lip of the hole by his forearms, the way a kid rests on the side of the pool. His head now free of the pipe, he looked around but saw nothing, the tunnel untouched by light. He did get the sense that the surface below was moving, and as he trained his ears to listen, he heard the faint sound of gently roiling water, but he had no way to judge the depth, and the extent of the slime layer beneath. With his hold on the edge slipping, the only choice was to let go and hope for the best, which meant taking the brunt of the landing with his good leg.

His feet hit water, then a slick, angled surface. They skidded out from under him, his knees slamming into brick. His right knee flexed, putting the torn thigh muscle under extreme tension. The pain was excruciating. He wanted to scream but stifled it. The sound would carry up the drainpipe and into the warehouse.

Carefully he stood, leg on fire, elbows and knees burning, balance sketchy, wet from the waist down. The surface under his feet was not flat but concave and slippery. He was standing in a round pipe. The water, warmer than he would've expected, hit him at knee level. The air was fetid, thick with the smells that come from decomposing human excrement, wastewater from bathroom and kitchen sinks, and the grime washed from the streets and gutters of the city. He wondered if the fall had torn open the freshly healed bullet wound in his right thigh. The bulk of human fecal matter consisted of bacteria from the colon—E. coli—and coliform bacteria were no friend to the open wound. If it had opened, he'd be facing a rampant infection deep in his thigh unless he could clean the area sometime soon. He started walking, following the current and taking care to maintain solid footing on the slick surface.

- 2 -

Thirty minutes later, David was slogging his way up Tenth Avenue—his wet feet numb from the subzero temperature, his right leg throbbing after climbing a ladder up to and out of a manhole, his elbows and knees stinging from lack of skin.

At the corner of Tenth Avenue and West 16th Street he stopped, moved clear of the stream of morning foot commuters, and studied a Google map on Turnbull's Blackberry. Four more blocks would bring him to West 20th. A right turn on 20th would take him to the 10th Precinct. Or he could punch in Tyronne's number. Either way, it made no difference. The calculated action of thumb on syringe had snuffed out the last vestige of his humanity. His life as a caring member of the human race had come to an end, and just as he was indifferent to the act of taking a life, he was now indifferent to the course of his own. Confucius was right—seek revenge, dig two graves. He slipped Turnbull's phone into his pocket and headed up Tenth Avenue.

Half a block later a black Mercedes sedan pulled over to the curb. The front passenger door swung open. David was told to get in. He did, and he let his head fall back against the seat, and he closed his eyes. "So…this is how it ends," he said.

"No," Mr. White replied. "This is how it begins." He held out his hand. "I need the Blackberry."

David handed it over.

Mr. White turned it off as the Mercedes sped up Tenth Avenue.

They rode in silence, David staring blankly out the window, Mr. White navigating the heavy traffic. After they had covered ten or eleven blocks, David looked over at Mr. White. This was the third time David had been in the physical presence of the man, but it was the first time he had seen him without the scarf and hat. He was fair-skinned and sandy-haired, with a few wrinkles across his forehead and at the corners of his eyes—maybe late forties in age. Otherwise his features were well proportioned and unremarkable. Turnbull would have lumped him in with the gray people.

Mr. White glanced at David. "What happened to your knees?"

Blood had soaked through the wet scrub pants. No doubt the inner lining of the coat sleeves were bloody, as well. "I crawled down a drainpipe and waded through the sewer to escape the warehouse. The NYPD had it surrounded."

"Thus the source of the unpleasant smell."

"Yes."

"Where were you going just now, when I picked you up?"

"Not sure," David said. "Maybe the 10th Precinct, maybe not."

"If you were going to turn yourself in, why the daring escape?"

"Self-preservation, I guess, but then I found myself on Tenth Avenue in the midst of the morning commute, watching all these people scurrying along the street—people who think they control their fate. You know? If I work hard? Do the right thing? I can get what I want? And I thought, what bullshit, nobody controls their own fate."

David paused as an ambulance crossed the intersection ahead. Once the shriek of the siren receded, he continued.

"I used to think I had control of my destiny. If I studied hard, worked hard, played by the rules, I would achieve my goals. And even after getting fired I was rewarded with a second chance. But then you came along—you and Andrew Turnbull—and now my life has been erased. So, yeah, if fate has such a hard-on for me, then let the motherfucker decide—turn right on West 20th and walk the half block to the 10th Precinct, or keep going straight up Tenth Avenue. Fate's choice, but instead, here we are."

"Yes, here we are, but it's unfinished business that has brought us together, not fate."

"Whatever. Just more of your BS double talk."

David turned away and stared out the window.

- 3 -

As David McBride was being driven uptown, a jacked-up Ford Superduty crew cab smashed through the NuLife gate, dragging a mangled section of hurricane fence behind it as it barreled down the short stretch of road leading to the parking lot. Just before reaching the lot the truck veered left, leaving the road and bashing through dead undergrowth, brush, and small trees. It pulled around the back of the building and stopped, its front end pointed toward the highway, the back end with its four-inch tubular steel wraparound bumper aimed at the side of the red brick structure. The driver gunned the engine, slammed the transmission into reverse and stomped on the gas. About the time it hit 20 mph, the truck rammed the building, reducing the outside wall of Andrew Turnbull's office to rubble. Four men wearing ski masks jumped out. While two of the men dug through busted up bricks and concrete, the other two waved P90s in the air, but the show of force wasn't necessary. Before anyone inside could react, the men found Turnbull's safe and threw it into the bed of the truck. By the time they passed through the gate they had been on the grounds all of two minutes.

- 4 -

After a long, silent drive uptown, Mr. White steered the Mercedes into an underground parking garage below an Upper East Side high-rise. They descended three levels and parked in a dimly lit corner. Mr. White approached an elevator not far from the parking space and held the inner surface of his right wrist up to a detector plate the size of a credit card. He then peered into a scanner, looked up at a camera and said, "Around the rugged rock, the ragged rascal ran." The doors separated. They entered and ascended an unknown number of floors.

The elevator opened into what appeared to be a sprawling penthouse suite. The outer walls were floor-to-ceiling glass, affording views of the East River and beyond. David glanced into the kitchen as he walked by. Granite countertops. Natural wood cabinets. Chrome fixtures. All of the floors were wood, without carpeting or area rugs. The furniture consisted of a black leather couch, a matching chair, and a glass coffee table centered in front of a gas fireplace. A flat-screen TV hung from the wall above the fireplace. A dining table filled an alcove off the kitchen. The place was prime New York City real estate, but it was quite Spartan. The walls were white and bare, and there was no evidence that anyone actually lived there.

Mr. White gestured toward the alcove and the table. "Have a seat. You look like you could use a cup of coffee."

"I'd rather have a beer."

"I'll see what we have." Mr. White reached into the refrigerator, came out with a bottle of Heineken and handed it to David.

David draped his coat over the back of a chair. Early morning sunlight bathed the alcove, and the warmth of the sun felt good as he sat down and popped the cap off the bottle. He took a large swig, held it in his mouth for a moment and savored the cold carbonation.

Mr. White uncoiled his scarf, removed his overcoat and hat, and put them in a closet near the entryway. When he returned to the kitchen he leaned against the counter and folded his arms.

"What is this place?" David asked.

"It's a government safe house."

"Who are you? What's your real name?"

"Richard Whitestone. I'm a senior analyst at the NSA."

"And blackmailing people and forcing them to steal human organs is part of your job?"

"No. None of my activities related to Andrew Turnbull were sanctioned by the United States Government."

"So you're a rogue federal agent."

"Let's just say I'm on sabbatical."

David took another sip of beer. "What's in your arm?" he asked. "You held up your wrist to a detector of some sort."

"It's a rare cesium isotope that has an oscillation frequency of 9.192 billion times per second, about the same frequency as cesium 133, which is used to define one second in a nuclear clock. There is only a small amount in existence, and it's controlled by the US Atomic Energy Commission. The agency thought it would make a nice adjunct to some of the more familiar forms of biometric authentication. Between the biometrics and the cesium isotope, there is no way in or out of this place without a proper escort."

"So I'm your prisoner now. Why else would you completely expose yourself?"

"I just want you off the street."

Mr. White sat down across from David.

"How'd you get involved with Andrew Turnbull?" David asked.

"Our system flagged him as a frequent caller to the Middle East. I started monitoring him and discovered he was offering illegal kidney transplants to wealthy middle-easterners. I contacted him, told him I needed his help, and we came to a mutually beneficial agreement."

"You became his recruiter and fixer."

"Yes."

"And what did you need from him?"

"A kidney," Mr. White said. "My daughter, she's only twenty-six, and she's dying from end-stage renal disease."

"Why hasn't she been transplanted?"

"She has, twice, but she rejected both organs, and she's had innumerable blood transfusions related to years of dialysis. Now her blood is full of antibodies, and she fails the crossmatch every time."

"What about plasmapheresis and immunoglobulins?" David asked.

"Neither has worked, and now we're out of options and out of time, so Turnbull was either going to find her a kidney or grow one for her."

"And now I've killed him."

"Yes."

"You don't seem too upset."

"To the contrary. I'm extremely upset, but it will do neither of us any good if I let my emotions take over. Andrew Turnbull was a sociopathic megalomaniac. Once he kidnapped your wife and she died as a result, his demise became inevitable."

"What do you want with me?" David asked. "When you picked me up, you said this is the beginning. The beginning of what?"

"My daughter's survival is measured in months. I need you to grow a kidney for her."

"Really?" David said, taken aback by the audacity of such a request. "The last time you asked for my help I got shot in the leg, my wife and unborn child were killed, and my father was taken away, and now you're asking again?" He shook his head and chuckled. "You had leverage then. Now you don't. So forget it."

"With Turnbull gone, you're her only hope."

"I'm not interested, so point your arm at the door and I'll be on my way."

"I think after a hot shower, a hot meal, and some sleep, you might have a different outlook on the situation."

"Being clean, full, and well-rested won't change anything."

Mr. White went into the bedroom, returned with a blanket and pillows and set them on the couch. "I have a few things to do, so you'll have this place to yourself."

"Swell," David said.

Mr. White crossed the room, held his wrist up to the detector and repeated the ritual he had performed in the parking garage, then disappeared into the elevator.

David carefully stood, grabbed another beer from the fridge and made his way to the bathroom. The sooner he washed the sewer water out of his wounds, the better. He stripped down, stepped into the shower, and set the water temperature as hot as he could stand it.

The dry scabs that had previously sealed off the entrance and exit wounds were now moist and stringy, which meant the barrier to infection had been violated. Much like he did the night he'd been shot, David drizzled warm, soapy water into the macerated tissue and gently scrubbed with a washcloth. He hoped the heaviest concentration of bacteria was at the surface and not deep in the wound. If that were the case, he'd be able to avoid infection by keeping the area clean and dry. If not...well, he'd deal with that when the time came.

After the shower, David toweled off and checked the cabinets. They were remarkably well stocked. Either Mr. White had known he'd be hosting a guest with a bullet wound to the leg, or the agents that used this place were a bunch of Boy Scouts—Always Be Prepared. He found everything he needed to dress his leg, knees, and elbows, shave, and brush his teeth. There was even a white terrycloth robe and some powder-blue pajamas folded under the sink, and a big bottle of ibuprofen in the cabinet. Percocet would have been his pain reliever of choice, considering the intense throbbing and burning, but a non-steroidal anti-inflammatory agent would have to do.

Back in the front room he downed 800 milligrams of ibuprofen with the last of his beer, piled a couple of cushions on the end of the couch, lay down and propped up his leg. He closed his eyes, and before a single thought of any consequence could form, he was out.

The janitor for the dementia care unit at the Coler Rehabilitation Facility on Roosevelt Island rolled his mop bucket just outside the room where attending physician, Dr. Kenneth Woolsey, and his team of residents and students were conducting morning rounds. The janitor gave a single nod to the cop sitting outside the door, then started mopping the floor as the medical team assembled around the bed of a man who, despite sleeping peacefully, was tied down with leather restraints on his ankles and wrists.

"Dr. Weinberg," Woolsey said to the senior resident, "as we have a new group of interns and students this morning, will you give a brief overview of this patient's history and treatment plan?"

"Yes," Stuart Weinberg replied, turning to face the small group. "This is Mr. Hal McBride. He is a sixty-year-old male with a history of early onset dementia. The patient has a past history of boxing, starting as a young kid and extending through his years in the military. At age fifty-two he showed the first signs of dementia and was later diagnosed with chronic traumatic encephalopathy."

"Also known as CTE," interrupted Dr. Woolsey. He gestured toward a young woman wearing a short white coat over a blouse and skirt. "Student Doctor Ryan, define CTE?"

With an air of authority, she said, "Chronic traumatic encephalopathy is a degenerative disease found primarily in athletes, or anyone who has suffered repetitive brain trauma. The recurrent trauma results in the buildup of abnormal tau proteins, which causes neuronal death and progressive degeneration of brain tissue."

"Symptoms?" Woolsey asked.

"Early on the patient may experience memory loss, confusion, impaired judgment, and difficulty with impulse control. Late symptoms include aggression, depression, and, eventually, full-blown dementia that is indistinguishable from Alzheimer's Disease."

"Is CTE seen only in those who have had clinically diagnosed concussions?"

"No. It has also been seen in athletes with recurring subconcussive hits to the head."

"Treatment?"

"There is no treatment for the underlying disease. Treating the associated symptoms and custodial care are the only options."

Woolsey gave Weinberg a nod.

The senior resident continued. "If you've been watching the news, you are probably aware that Mr. McBride's son has become embroiled in some legal issues and is currently wanted by the NYPD. Mr. McBride has no other living relatives, and is therefore a temporary ward of the state. After spending several days at Bellevue Hospital, where he exhibited what can best be described as a perpetual catastrophic reaction, he was started on a haloperidol drip and transferred to us for long-term management."

Ken Woolsey pointed at a young man in a shirt and tie and short white coat. "Student Doctor Asner, what is a catastrophic reaction?"

With a mild tremor in his voice and a red flush climbing his neck, he said, "Uh, it's a severe overreaction to a…uh…seemingly normal or nonthreatening situation or event."

The attending pointed to another young man, this one wearing a long white coat over a shirt and tie, and a stethoscope draped around his neck. He was one of two new interns. "Dr. Fisher, tell us about haloperidol."

"Haloperidol," the intern said, "is an antipsychotic medication that is used to treat schizophrenia, psychosis, mania, delirium, agitation, aggression, and severe anxiety. It can be administered orally, intramuscularly, or intravenously. Its trade name is Haldol, and it is often referred to as the velvet hammer."

A slight grin creased the attending's lips. "And why is it referred to as the velvet hammer, Doctor?"

"When given intravenously to patients who are in the grip of a major psychotic episode, it rapidly subdues them as effectively as a hammer blow to the head, but in a much gentler fashion, of course."

"Treatment plan for Mr. McBride?" Woolsey asked, directing the question to Weinberg.

"Since his arrival here six days ago we've been loading him with the oral antipsychotics risperidone and olanzapine. We now believe the serum levels of these drugs are maximized, so today we're going to wean the Haldol drip. By keeping the room quiet and dimly lit, and by limiting the number of different nurses and other staff that tend to him, we hope to minimize the severity of his catastrophic reactions, and when he is comfortable with his surroundings, we'll try to assimilate him into the general dementia ward."

"Very good," said the attending. "Next patient."

After the team filed out and moved down the hall, the janitor dragged his mop into the room, took out his phone, and recorded a peacefully sleeping Hal McBride for about thirty seconds.

The Ford Superduty pulled into a cavernous abandoned warehouse somewhere in the bowels of Newark and parked next to a black BMW 760Li. As the four men climbed from the crew cab, Mikhail Petrovsky, Samuel Keating, and Petrovsky's safecracker stepped out of the BMW. Petrovsky motioned toward a steel workbench that had been positioned in the middle of the floor. The men hauled Turnbull's safe from the bed of the truck to the bench, then climbed back in and drove out the far end of the warehouse.

The safecracker went to work, examining the safe, the lock mechanism, the door. Even though he looked like he should be unloading ships on the docks of Murmansk instead of finessing open a safe, he seemed to know what he was doing. The home office had given him their highest recommendation. He turned to Petrovsky. "I can use a robot safe dialer, and with some creative programming, I'll have this open in under an hour."

"I don't care how you get in. Just do it."

While the safecracker went to work, the bigger, taller Petrovsky glared down at the shorter, smaller Keating. "For your sake, the books had better be in there."

Twenty minutes later the robot dialer was ready. The safecracker had mounted a bracket on the door of the safe. Centered within the bracket was a motorized arm—a shaft—with three pincers on the end that grasped the dial. The safecracker entered some information into a laptop, and, accompanied by a soft mechanical hum, the arm started turning the dial, back and forth, back and forth, and then all the way around.

"What's that thing doing?" Petrovsky asked.

"It is programmed to try all possible combinations for this particular lock, but it can do it much faster than a human, and the programming can rule out a large number of possibilities before the robot has to try them."

"Wouldn't it be faster to slap some C4 on the hinges and just blow it open?"

"Yes, but the intense heat would fry whatever's inside."

Thirty-two minutes later, an audible click signaled that the final tumbler had fallen into place. The safecracker pointed at the L-shaped lever on the door. "Turn that forty-five degrees and you are in."

Petrovsky did, and the safe opened. Inside was a stack of black-and-white marbled composition notebooks—the books he'd been trying to get his hands on for eight months. He lifted them out and set them on the table. Each book had a handwritten title corresponding to a specific organ—Lungs, Livers, Kidneys—or a certain aspect of technique—Nutrient Media, Progenitor Cells, Porcine Scaffold.

Keating looked through the stack, then checked the titles a second time.

"Well?" Petrovsky said. "Is this what I need? Can I send these to my employer, and they will be able to grow human organs in the laboratory?"

"Uh, yeah," Keating replied. "I think so."

"What do you mean, you think so?"

Keating spread out the books, reread all the titles, wiped his forehead with his shirtsleeve.

"What do you mean?" Petrovsky said again, yelling this time, his voice echoing throughout the warehouse.

"I think there's one missing."

Petrovsky glared at Keating. "Which one?"

"The one describing the infrared light."

"That's the most important of them all. That is what my employers need most. Check again. Maybe the infrared techniques are written down in one of the other books."

Keating examined each notebook, thumbed through the pages, front to back, back to front, searching for anything related to low-level laser therapy, but he found nothing, and after he'd looked through all of them he turned to Petrovsky. "It's not here."

In one swift move Petrovsky pinned Keating's head to the steel table and shoved his Glock 19 into Keating's mouth. "For eight months," Petrovsky screamed, "I've paid for your gambling and your whores, and still I have nothing."

The safecracker backed away from the table.

Keating gripped the workbench and muttered something unintelligible.

Petrovsky jammed the muzzle of the handgun deeper into Keating's throat. "I want that book, so you better figure out where it is."

Keating gagged and coughed.

Petrovsky removed the gun, wiped the saliva off the barrel with one of the safecracker's lint-free cloths, and slipped it back into his shoulder harness.

Keating rubbed the side of his head, then wiped the spit from the corners of his mouth with his shirtsleeve. After he had composed himself, he said, "I have some ideas."

After five hours of investigating the murder scene at the meatpacking warehouse, Detective Kate D'Angelo caught a ride with a patrol car uptown to the medical examiner's office on the corner of East 30th and First Avenue. Once inside, she found Linda Turnbull waiting on a ratty Naugahyde couch in the hallway outside the body identification room. Mrs. Turnbull seemed reasonably composed and well put together for a woman whose husband had been murdered five hours earlier. She wore a pantsuit under a Burberry trench coat, had taken the time to fix her hair and put on a little makeup. In fact, Kate was surprised by the woman's natural beauty as well as her composure. Based on Andrew Turnbull's history and personality, Kate expected a young piece of arm candy. Linda Turnbull, with her auburn hair, porcelain skin, and lack of artificial enhancements was anything but that. Kate held out her hand as she approached. "Mrs. Turnbull, I'm Kate D'Angelo. I am very sorry."

Mrs. Turnbull stood and offered her hand. "Thank you, and please call me Linda."

"How are you holding up?" Kate asked. "Is there anything you need at the moment?"

"No. I'm okay. I'm just anxious to do this. I want to see him. I need to see him. But at the same time I'm afraid."

"Of course," Kate said. "I will tell you that he's very pale, and his lips and eye sockets are a dark blue, almost purplish color, but otherwise there are no surprises."

As Linda Turnbull thanked Kate for her candor, Kate could see small tears forming in the corners of her eyes, her composure slowly draining away.

She led Mrs. Turnbull into the viewing room. On the other side of the glass, Andrew Turnbull lay supine on a gurney, covered by a white sheet. A technician waited for Kate to nod, then pulled the sheet down to the chest.

Mrs. Turnbull winced, but otherwise stood silently.

Kate said, "That's Dr. Turnbull, yes?"

"Yes." Without taking hers eyes off her husband, she said, "May I go in and touch him?"

"I'm sorry, but until the autopsy has been completed the body can only be handled by the examining doctor and staff."

"I understand," Mrs. Turnbull said vacantly, tears now running down her cheeks.

After a few moments she turned to Kate. "I think I've seen enough."

Kate handed her a tissue, then led her back to the hallway.

"Thank you for coming down," Kate said. "I know you've already had a long morning, and you have a tough day ahead of you. I hate to even bring it up, but the homicide detectives are going to want to talk with you, preferably today."

"Aren't you the detective for this case?"

"Not anymore. It's a matter of jurisdiction. I'm not part of homicide, so they will take over from here."

"So I'll just wait to hear from them?"

"Yes," Kate replied. "They'll be in touch."

- 8 -

The sound of rustling bags, paired with a blast of bright light, startled David awake from a dreamless sleep. With great effort he propped himself into a sitting position, his elbows and knees burning from deep abrasions, his right leg throbbing from the acute disruption of partially healed muscle tissue. Mr. White set a bag of Chinese food and a twelve-pack of beer on the coffee table, dropped a couple of Macy's bags onto the couch, and took a seat in the chair facing the end of the table. David turned and looked out the windows. It was dark outside. "What time is it?" he asked.

"Almost ten," Mr. White replied.

David stretched the dead, tingling arm he'd been lying on for God knows how long, then popped open a beer. He emptied about a third of it, closed his eyes, and rubbed his face with his palms.

Mr. White switched on the flat-screen TV that hung over the fireplace and selected New York 1 from the cable menu. "I think you should watch the news," he said. "The top stories will cycle around in a few minutes."

David already knew, that once again, his mugshot of a photo would be plastered across the screen as the anchor described how organ-snatching ghoul, Dr. David McBride, was now sought in connection with the murder of his former mentor. The thought of it turned his stomach. He'd had enough of being public enemy number one.

He rummaged through the Macy's bags, then placed the containers of Chinese food on the table—kung pao chicken and a pan of dumplings. He turned to Mr. White. "You know my clothing and shoe sizes. You know my favorite Chinese takeout right down to the pan of dumplings, and what kind of beer I like. Doesn't it bother you that you come into the lives of two people, you invade their privacy, manipulate them, and now one of them is dead?"

Mr. White shifted in the chair. "I gathered information. It was the way in which others used that information that resulted in your wife's death."

"I seem to remember *you* sitting in the park with an envelope full of photos, and *you* calling me on the phone multiple times to remind me how vulnerable Cassandra was."

"It was my job to ratchet up the pressure. Under no circumstances would I have actually harmed her."

"You sound like Turnbull with your psycho doubletalk."

"Be that as it may, why don't we put the past behind us and concentrate on moving forward. History cannot be changed."

"Just like that? Keep moving forward? To what? I have no wife. No child. No father. Even my freedom has been taken away. I have nothing. Don't you get it?"

"Of course I get it. I put Cassandra in the car that night. I was trying to save her, and I killed her instead. I think about it every day. And I think about the homeless men we left in the alleys, and the retarded boy who had no understanding of what was happening. I'm haunted by these things, but when you're a parent, and you're watching your vibrant, beautiful child being destroyed by a relentless, insidious disease, you'll do anything to save her."

"A dying child makes all this okay?"

Mr. White lowered his chin to his chest and shook his head. "At the time it did."

David sipped his beer and clicked the sides of the can as he tried to stop the intrusion of unwanted images—the wrecked car, the grotesque deformity of the steering wheel pushing into Cassandra's chest, the glistening tears filling her eyes, the dreamy smile that accompanied her final words. "She had never driven before," he said quietly.

"I know. She told me, but there was no other way to get her out. I thought she'd be okay."

"Was she scared?"

"Yes, but she was also brave, and I came to admire her in the short time I knew her. In fact, Cassandra reminded me of my daughter. They were about the same age."

David stared into his plate, fighting a surge of anguish, and guilt, and pain. He blinked his moistening eyes a couple times, then looked up. "What was the last thing she said to you?"

"I asked her not to go to the police. I told her I was saving her life, and I needed her to help me by remaining silent. She said 'okay.'"

"Was Turnbull really going to harvest her heart?"

"I think so. That's why I helped her escape."

"Then I don't regret killing him."

"No, I don't suppose you do."

David took a bite of kung pao chicken and opened another beer.

Mr. White reached for the remote and turned up the sound on the television.

The weather update was just ending, replaced by an in-studio shot of the evening anchor, and there it was, in the upper right-hand corner of the screen, the same NYU physician ID photo NY1 had broadcast ten days ago when he'd been shot in the leg by a Russian mobster, when he'd left bloody dressings on the bathroom floor of room 1408 at the Hotel Pennsylvania and had landed the top spot on the NYPD's most wanted list. Dr. David McBride, good doctor gone bad, was peering over the left shoulder of the news anchor. And next to David, a photo of the other principal in the story—Andrew, don't call me Andy, Turnbull—the man who would remove the heart of a twenty-eight-year-old pregnant woman. Surprisingly—or not—David was unmoved by seeing the face of the man he had murdered sixteen hours earlier. The anchor began with the day's top story:

> *Former New York University transplant surgeon and stem cell research pioneer, Dr. Andrew Turnbull, was found dead early this morning inside a defunct warehouse in Manhattan's meatpacking district. Officers with NYPD's Emergency Service Unit found*

Turnbull strapped to a hospital gurney in a makeshift operating room, which was hidden inside the warehouse. NYPD detectives are seeking the whereabouts of Dr. David McBride, a former associate of Turnbull's, in connection with what detectives are calling an execution-style murder. Two years ago both Andrew Turnbull and David McBride were dismissed from their positions at NYU Medical Center's Department of Surgery after moving patients up the liver transplant waiting list in exchange for large cash payments. More recently, McBride has been sought in connection with a kidney-snatching scheme that has stolen kidneys from at least two mentally ill homeless men. A $25,000 Crime Stoppers reward remains in effect for any information leading to the apprehension of McBride. And in a related story...

The studio shot cut to what appeared to be cell phone video footage of a smashed-in wall on the side of a single-story brick building out in the woods somewhere.

...within an hour of Andrew Turnbull's death, a large pickup truck rammed the gate of NuLife Corporation, the New Jersey-based biomedical research company of which Turnbull was founder, president, and CEO. The truck then crashed through the exterior wall of Turnbull's office, and while two armed men stood guard, two others retrieved a safe from the wreckage of the office.

David turned toward Mr. White. "What's that all about?"

"Somebody wants whatever is in the safe."

"Yeah, I got that, but what's in there that's worth such a bold show of force?"

"Proprietary information. Andrew Turnbull finally succeeded in growing human organs from stem cells, and all—well, almost all—of his secrets are in that safe."

"He told me he had done it," David said, "but I didn't believe him. Do you know who these people are?"

"Yes."

"And?"

"You needn't concern yourself with this matter."

David grabbed his beer and sank back into the couch. After a few moments, he said, "What makes you think I can grow a kidney for your daughter?"

"You were growing ferret organs during your time in Turnbull's lab at NYU. Using those same techniques, his people at NuLife made the leap to functional human organs."

"Andrew Turnbull had two years, millions of dollars, an army of talented scientists, and a well-equipped laboratory. I have none of that, so to think I can grow a kidney for your daughter is ludicrous."

Mr. White got up and left the room. A few moments later he returned with an iPad and handed it to David. The screen contained a mosaic of book covers—the covers of black-and-white marbled composition notebooks. There were nine in all, and each notebook had a handwritten title on its cover: Hearts, Lungs, Livers, Kidneys, Nutrient Media, Veg-F, Progenitor Cells, Porcine Scaffold, Lab Equipment.

"What are these?" David asked.

"The sum of everything Andrew Turnbull knew about growing human organs."

"In marbled notebooks? Like we used in college?"

"Your former mentor was a strange composite of paranoid sociopathic genius. Tap one and look inside."

David touched the thumbnail labeled "Heart." The cover enlarged to fill the screen.

"Swipe your finger from right to left."

David did so, and the cover flipped open as if it were a print book. He turned the pages with successive swipes of his finger, revealing page after page of meticulous handwritten notes and elegant drawings of the heart, its cellular structure and major blood vessels. The digital pages even crinkled as they turned.

"Andrew Turnbull was convinced that storing the results of his research on computer hard drives left it vulnerable to theft by hackers, so he recorded everything in the physical versions of these notebooks and kept them locked in his safe. It seems counterintuitive, but considering some of our largest retailers, banks, and insurers have been hacked, perhaps there was a method to his madness."

"But I'm looking at digital copies."

"As Turnbull's behavior became increasingly psychopathic, I felt that our mission could collapse at any time, so I cracked his safe, copied his notebooks, and digitized them."

David flipped a few more pages. "Impressive, but it takes more than notes to grow a functioning organ. I'd need a lab, and equipment, and a colony of your daughter's stem cells."

"I can get those things."

"But it could take six months or more just to subculture an undifferentiated line of your daughter's cells. It doesn't sound like she has much time."

"I already have her stem cell line. I took it from NuLife, along with some of the critical pieces of custom-made equipment. As soon as the lab is up and running, we move straight to seeding a porcine scaffold."

"Okay, you have the resources, but for a single person to grow a human organ in some makeshift lab would be a daunting task, a task I'm not up to. I'm tired, too tired to run and hide, too tired to grow a kidney. All I want to do is drink a couple beers, go back to sleep, and in the morning turn myself in to the police."

Mr. White moved to the edge of his chair and planted his elbows on his knees. "You murdered a man this morning. You have committed one of society's greatest transgressions. I would think, given the chance to redeem yourself, you would gladly accept."

David shook his head. "Redemption is a human construct, and I'm no longer human. I feel nothing toward the man I murdered, nor do I feel anything toward your daughter." He placed the iPad on the table. "Why don't you pay someone from NuLife to grow your kidney?"

"Not after everything that has happened today. These people are the best and brightest in their fields. They're not going to involve themselves with something like this."

David stabbed a dumpling with his fork and bit it in half, then something on the television caught his eye. A reporter was standing in front of a nice one-story home that had been roped off with yellow police tape. In the background, the whirling lights of several police cars. The graphic across the bottom of the screen said, "Mrs. Andrew Turnbull brutally attacked in her New Jersey home."

David looked at Mr. White, who was staring at the screen with a stricken look on his face. He grabbed the remote from the coffee table and gave the volume a few clicks. A young female reporter, bundled up in a heavy NY1 parka and knit hat, stood on the sidewalk in front of the house. Frosty puffs of breath filled the air as she reported on the scene behind her:

In a bizarre twist to an already bizarre case, Mrs. Linda Turnbull, the wife of transplant surgeon and research scientist, Dr. Andrew Turnbull, was found brutally beaten earlier tonight following an apparent home invasion robbery at her North Haledon, New Jersey residence. If you have been following the news today, you are aware that Andrew Turnbull was found dead this morning in lower Manhattan, strapped to a surgical gurney in a dilapidated meatpacking warehouse that housed a makeshift operating room. Within an hour of the grisly discovery, a pickup truck smashed through the wall of Turnbull's New Jersey office at NuLife Corporation, where armed men retrieved a safe from the rubble and drove away with it. A few minutes ago, Passaic County Detective Jim Morganson made a brief statement.

The live broadcast cut away to a taped segment of the detective, standing before a small group of reporters and cameras:

In this third, and apparently related incident, armed men posing as detectives from the NYPD were granted access to the home by Mrs. Turnbull after they told her they had news regarding her husband's case. Once inside, they gagged her and duct-taped her to a chair, then proceeded to tear the place apart looking for a notebook containing information vital to her husband's research. After failing to find the book, they turned their attention to a safe that had been discovered in a wall. When Mrs. Turnbull could not provide them with the combination, they savagely beat her, strangled her small dog to death with a piano wire, then ripped the safe out of the wall and left with it.

As the detective was speaking, two paramedics rolled a gurney out the front door behind him. Linda Turnbull. She was packaged in the usual way—on a backboard, wearing a rigid cervical collar, foam blocks on either side of the head, straps across the chest and waist to immobilize the thoracic and lumbar spines. David couldn't assess her injuries based on what he was seeing, but at least she didn't have an endotracheal tube sticking out of her mouth. He turned to Mr. White. "What's going on here? What haven't you told me?"

Mr. White took a deep breath and exhaled slowly. "Not long after joining Turnbull, I discovered that his chief financial officer—a guy by the name of Samuel Keating—was working with a corporate spy. The corporate spy, in turn, is working for a biomedical research company based in Zelenograd, Russia, and they want Turnbull's notebooks. The spy, Mikhail Petrovsky, was able to turn Keating and enlist his help. I didn't tell Andrew about this, but I initiated close surveillance of Keating, Petrovsky, and Turnbull's office safe."

"And now they have the safe. Are the notebooks in it?"

"Yes."

"Then why brutalize Turnbull's wife?"

"One of them is missing, the most important one, the techniques that allowed Turnbull to make the jump from ferret to human organs. It has something to do with infrared light, and it was the final piece of the puzzle, the big breakthrough."

David held up the iPad. "Is it on here?"

"No. When I copied the notebooks, that one was not in his office."

"Did Turnbull keep it at home, in his wall safe?"

"No. I went to see Mrs. Turnbull this afternoon. She knows me as a member of NuLife's scientific advisory board. I stopped by to offer my condolences and see if she needed anything, and while she was making coffee I opened the safe. The missing book was not there."

"Is this how corporate spies conduct business? Beating women and strangling little dogs?"

"Not all of them. Most private intelligence companies recruit ex-CIA, FBI, or MI-6 agents as operatives, and even though the industry is largely unregulated, they follow a set of unwritten rules—no violence, no exploiting children, those sorts of things. But over the last decade there has been an increased presence of East Europeans and Russians, including ex-FSB."

"FSB?"

"Russia's internal security organization—their FBI. It's one of the successor organizations that came from the dismantling of the KGB. Unfortunately, some of these former KGB and FSB agents bring with them a propensity for violence and going beyond established boundaries. In fact, the western companies are concerned that this emerging cadre of thugs is going to bring down the regulatory hammer on the rest of the private intelligence sector."

"And this guy, Petrovsky"—David pointing at the television—"he's one of them?"

"Yes, former FSB who now works for a private firm based in Moscow."

"So, in summary," David said with a heavy dose of sarcasm, "you want me to grow a kidney for your daughter, but the crucial piece of information, which is handwritten in a marbled composition notebook, is missing. In addition, a crazed Russian spy is after the same information."

"I would say that accurately sums up our situation."

David finished his beer and put the can on the table. "I need some sleep."

"And I have an errand to run."

- 9 -

In the same Newark warehouse they'd been in earlier that morning, Petrovsky and Keating watched the robot arm spin the dial on Andrew Turnbull's wall safe. After eighteen minutes, the third tumbler fell into place, and the latch released with a metallic click. Petrovsky turned the lever and opened the door. No lab book, just personal papers. He glared at Keating.

"I have another idea," Keating said, holding up his hands. "The biochemist, Abercrombie. He may or may not have the book, but he'll know what's in it."

"What about the NSA mole, Whitestone? Is there a chance he has it?"

"No. His daughter is too sick. Even if he had all the notebooks, and he found a lab able to do this kind of work, there wouldn't be enough time to grow a kidney."

"You'd better be right," Petrovsky said.

- 10 -

Jeffery Abercrombie sat on his couch, staring at the television in disbelief, fear swelling into terror as he watched Turnbull's wife being wheeled out the front door of her own house and into an ambulance. It was more than he could take. His boss, Andrew Turnbull, strapped to a hospital bed and executed. A truck smashing through the wall of Turnbull's office just down the hall from his own, the bomb-like explosion still reverberating in his head. And now this. He knew what they were looking for, why they had crashed into Turnbull's office, why they had ripped apart Mrs. Turnbull's house, and they'd be coming his way next. The news report hadn't said what time the attack occurred, but the Turnbull home was less than an hour's drive away this time of night. He jumped up, went to the bedroom closet, took the suitcase from the top shelf and stuffed it with socks and underwear, and shirts and pants still on their hangars. In the front room he grabbed his laptop case, flew out the door and thundered down the stairs.

- 11 -

Mr. White parked the Mercedes on W. 31st Street, between Eighth and Ninth Avenues, thankful to find a space only one block over from his destination. He ran around the corner, found the building he was looking for, and hit the button for apartment 427.

No answer.

He tried the button again, held it longer this time, a grating buzz, and he thought of Linda Turnbull and her dog, duct tape and piano wire, then buzzed the superintendent.

"What is it?" an annoyed voice said over the intercom.

"My name is Jim Mulligan, US Department of Immigration and Customs Enforcement. I need to see a tenant of yours, but I don't want to announce my arrival. Will you let me in?"

"Immigration?"

"Yes."

"This late at night?"

"Yes."

Silence. Then, "Come to 214."

The lock buzzed open.

Mr. White bounded up the stairs two at a time and knocked on the super's door.

"Hold your identification next to your face and step in front of peephole," the superintendent said.

Mr. White held up a government ID that carried the name James Mulligan instead of Richard Whitestone. The door opened.

A stumpy little man in a bathrobe stood in the doorway. He scratched thoughtfully at gray stubble. "First NYPD, then Immigration? What is happening?"

Mr. White detected a slight accent—Eastern Europe, Belarus perhaps. "The NYPD were here?" he asked.

"Two detectives. Thirty minutes ago. They just left."

"To see Jeffery Abercrombie? Apartment 427?"

"Yes."

"And they had ID?"

"Of course."

"Do you remember their names?" Mr. White asked.

"Davis, and W something…Wallcott, Wollinsky?"

"Can you recall what they looked like?"

"That is the funny thing. The guy who did the talking, he was Russian, but most Russians I see come here to break the law, not enforce it."

"What made you think he's from Russia?"

"His English was clear, but a couple of times he dropped a word, or transposed them. It's subtle, but noticeable to me. And he just looked Russian."

"Your ear is well-trained," Mr. White said. "You are from eastern Belarus? Vietka perhaps?"

"Your ear is also trained well. Yes, I come from a small town near Vietka. Forty miles from the Russian border. I can tell you who's Estonian, Latvian, Lithuanian, Ukrainian, Polish."

"I'm sure you can," Mr. White said. "And the Russian detective's appearance?"

"He resembled Alexander Litvinenko before the polonium caused him to go bald. Sandy blond hair. Brown eyes. Roundish face. Not as tall as you, but close—maybe five-ten or eleven—a little bigger build, stocky but not fat."

Mikhail Petrovsky.

"What about his partner?" Mr. White asked.

"Caucasian man. Maybe late thirties. Shorter than other guy. Not heavy or thin. Long dark hair—long for police, now that I think about it. Nervous. Very nervous."

Sam Keating.

"I appreciate your detailed descriptions," Mr. White said. "I also have business with Mr. Abercrombie. Is he in?"

"No."

"Did the detectives take him away?"

"He had left a few minutes before they came here."

"You saw him leave?"

"Yes. I hear fast, heavy footsteps—very heavy—coming down the stairs, and huffing and puffing, like someone panicking. I look out the window and see him get into a cab with a suitcase."

"Good. Very good," Mr. White said. "Did the detectives search Mr. Abercrombie's apartment?"

"Yes. They had the warrant."

"I'd like to take a look as well."

"You have a warrant, or whatever Immigration needs for searching a place?"

"I believe Mr. Abercrombie's life is in danger. That gives me probable cause."

"Okay. I get the keys."

They climbed two more flights of stairs. The superintendent unlocked the door to 427, and as it swung open he was aghast. Mr. White, on the other hand, was not surprised. The apartment had been trashed—every drawer emptied, every piece of furniture slashed open and ripped apart. Anything that might hold a marbled composition book was broken or smashed.

"You didn't hear this?" Mr. White waving his hand in an arc over the wreckage.

The Belarusian shrugged. "My wife, she snores, and the TV was on loud."

The super stepped through the door. "Those guys are not police, are they?" He turned around. "And I don't think you are who you say you are. Why would Mr. Abercrombie be in trouble with Customs? He is from Connecticut."

Mr. White held the Belarusian man by the shoulders, firmly but not forcefully. "You're right, I'm not with Immigration. I'm with Immigration's nasty cousin, and I can manufacture evidence that ties you to Russian mobsters, Islamic terrorists, or even Chechen separatists—my choice—and at the very least you'll be facing deportation. At the very worst?" Mr. White shook his head in a disapproving manner. "You don't want to think about that. So, I'm going to go in and look around. When I'm done you will lock the door, forget what you saw, and should Jeffery Abercrombie or the Russian return, I want you to call me." Mr. White handed the man a business card with nothing more than a phone number printed on one side. "Understood?"

"Yes, understood," said the stumpy man from Belarus.

- 12 -

The voice on the Mercedes' navigation system said, *"You have reached your destination. Your destination is on the right."* The destination was 4314 N. Visscher Street, West Hartford, Connecticut. The occupant of that address, Mrs. Ruby Abercrombie, the widowed mother of Dr. Jeffery Abercrombie, PhD in biochemistry.

Mr. White silenced the navigation system and continued past the house at a slowed but unsuspicious pace. It was now 1:30 a.m. The houses were small and close together, the narrow street unevenly illuminated by the occasional streetlight. A dark Mercedes moving too slowly through the modest neighborhood might be enough to garner attention.

As he circled around the block, he came upon a black BMW 760Li parked at the curb. He recognized the car and the license plate—Mikhail Petrovsky. Mr. White drove a hundred yards up the street, parallel parked between two sedans and climbed from the car, grabbing his agency-issued Glock 23 from the glovebox on the way out. He walked the block and a half over to the Abercrombie home with a controlled but determined stride, the tension rising with every step. He was competent with certain components of the spy's toolbox—or tradecraft, as agents referred to it—but he was not a field agent. When it came to surveillance, he was top tier. When it came to physical confrontation, this was not exactly his area of expertise, and even though he'd been trained in firearm basics, it had been years since he'd visited the practice range.

At the Abercrombie house, Mr. White ducked down the thin strip of driveway leading to a detached single-car garage. Around the back, he quietly approached the only window with a light on. Through a gauzy curtain he could see Mrs. Abercrombie. Her ankles and right wrist were duct-taped to a kitchen chair. Her mouth had been stuffed with a cloth. A large, thuggish man in an overcoat was holding her left hand palm down on the table. Another overcoated thug raised a cast iron frying pan over his head. The kitchen had been trashed, everything in the drawers and cupboards scattered all over the floor.

"Wait," Petrovsky said, his voice carrying through the single pane glass. "Don't hit her with the flat part. Turn it sideways so it comes down like a hammer."

Mrs. Abercrombie struggled to pull her hand loose. The rag in her mouth muted her screams of terror.

"This is your last chance," Petrovsky said to the woman. "Where is your son?"

Her words were garbled, but it was clear that she said she didn't know.

"Very well." Petrovsky gave the thug with the pan a nod.

Mr. White crashed through the door shoulder first, gun pointed at Petrovsky's chest, which was no more than three feet away. "Stop! And everyone keep your hands where I can see them, or your boss hits the floor first."

The man holding the frying pan slowly lowered it to the table.

Petrovsky sized up Mr. White. "Quite bold for someone who taps a keyboard all day."

"At this distance, a three-year-old could put a slug through your heart."

"Now, now. Such threats are unnecessary. There's nothing here worth dying for."

"But a crushed hand is acceptable?"

"A scare tactic. We wouldn't actually hurt such a lovely lady."

"You savagely beat Mrs. Turnbull and killed her dog."

"We are looking for something of great importance. What are you looking for, Mr. White?" Petrovsky inserting air quotes around *White*. "What brings you to West Hartford?"

"I have a personal interest in this woman's safety."

"Of course you do, because you need to find her son so you can save your daughter. I thought maybe you had the missing notebook. Now I know you don't. It seems the race is on, and having said that, perhaps my friends and I should be going."

"A good idea, Mikhail, but first I have a proposal. As you know, time is of the essence, so why don't we work together. If you find the book first, I would ask that you share its contents with me before you send it off to your employer. If I find it, I copy what I need and give you the original. Either way, everybody wins."

"Sorry," Petrovsky countered. "My clients want full ownership of the technology. They want to be first to market with off-the-shelf organs, and they don't want any competitors."

"I have no reason to pass this information to anyone else. I just want to save my daughter."

"It doesn't matter. I have been given a very clear directive."

Petrovsky looked at the other men and nodded toward the back door. "I'm sorry, Richard, but this is the way it must be. And by the way," Petrovsky said, moving closer to and glaring at Mr. White, "nobody has ever pointed a gun at me and lived to tell about it, three-year-olds included."

After the men disappeared out the back, Mr. White removed the rag from Mrs. Abercrombie's mouth.

"What the hell's going on here?" she said. "Are those the men that ran into Jeffery's building?"

"Yes."

"And who are you?"

"I'm a friend of Jeffery's." Mr. White picked up a steak knife from the floor and sawed through the duct tape wrapped around her wrist and ankles. Mrs. Abercrombie grimaced as he gently peeled the tape from her fragile skin. "This book you heard us talking about, it's very valuable to the other man that was here and extremely important to me. As you already know, he will resort to violence to get it, and now he's going after Jeffery. Does Jeffrey have it, Mrs. Abercrombie?"

"No," she said as she gently massaged her wrists, her hands trembling. "He's never mentioned anything about a book."

Mr. White pulled a chair in front of her, sat down and leaned in close. "Do you have it, Mrs. Abercrombie."

"No, I don't."

Mr. White leaned back. "Even if Jeffery doesn't have the book, he knows what's in it, and that puts him in grave danger. If you've been watching the news, you're aware of what these men are capable of."

"Can you help him?" Mrs. Abercrombie asked.

"I can, but I need to know where he is."

"He won't tell me. He's scared, and he says he needs to hide for a while."

Mr. White placed one of his number-only business cards on the table. "If you talk to him, tell him not to come here. They'll be watching the house. But make sure you give him my number. He knows me as Mr. White from NuLife, and he can trust me." Mr. White leaned closer, took the woman's hands in his and looked her in the eyes. "Now, I'm going to ask that you don't call the police. If they get involved, it will hinder my efforts to help Jeffery. I'll send someone to fix your door and check on you, but please, no cops."

She looked down at his hands holding hers. "You promise you're going to help him?"

"I promise," Mr. White said. "Do I have your word? No police?"

"Yes."

Mr. White wasn't sure he believed her, but what could he do? His bag of threats was running low. He thanked her and slipped out the back.

Once he had returned to his car, Mr. White dialed a phone number, verbalized a code when prompted, then stated Jeffery Abercrombie's home phone number, cell phone number, and his mother's cell and home numbers.

- 13 -

About thirty miles west of Hartford, Mr. White pulled off the interstate and stopped in a rest area. From the trunk he retrieved a three-foot-long wooden dowel with a radio frequency detector zip tied to the end. He extended the antenna, and using the full length of the dowel, he proceeded to sweep the undercarriage of the Mercedes with the RF detector. He started with the rear and front bumpers and wheel wells, which were clean, but when he reached farther underneath, closer to the gas tank, the red indicator light started blinking. He lay on his back, slid himself under the chassis and felt along the edges of the tank until he found what he was looking for—a GPS tracking device. He slipped it into his pocket, swept the remainder of the car inside and out, then placed the GPS transmitter in the wheel well of a car with Florida license plates and got back on the interstate.

- 14 -

For the second time in twelve hours David was awakened by the sounds of Mr. White entering the apartment, but this time the room was full of early morning light, which his tired eyes did not appreciate. In a repeat of last night's laborious effort, David raised himself to a sitting position on the couch and carefully lowered his leg to the floor. It had been about twenty-four hours since he'd crawled through the drainpipe, waded through the sewer, and climbed a ladder to the street, and now his leg was paying the price, the swelling about twice what it was last night. His skinless knees and elbows were also worse for the wear. The abrasions had contracted and tightened, making it difficult to bend any extremity without it feeling like the skin was going to split open. And, for the second time in twelve hours, Mr. White handed David a couple of bags and told him he needed to watch the news.

"What now?" David asked.

"The NYPD is about to hold a live press conference."

"Marvelous," David said.

Mr. White turned on the television as David examined the bags—plastic and paper, the former from a Duane Reade drugstore, the latter stained with grease.

"Sausage-egg-and-cheese bagels, I presume," David peering into the greasy bag. The other contained a box of Just For Men hair color—obsidian black.

"Hair dye?" David asked.

"It's only a matter of time before the NYPD releases a composite sketch of you with your bleached, close-cropped hair and matching beard. I suggest you dye everything black, turn your beard into a goatee, and let it all grow out."

David tossed the box onto the couch cushion beside him and turned his attention to the greasy bag. As he unwrapped one of the bagels and took a bite, the television flickered. He looked up, and once again the twin photos of himself and Andrew Turnbull were staring down at him. The morning anchor:

> *In just a few minutes, we'll be taking you to One Police Plaza for a live press conference addressing what can only be described as a series of bizarre events that have unfolded over the past twenty-four hours. They began yesterday morning with the execution-style murder of former NYU transplant surgeon and biomedical researcher, Dr. Andrew Turnbull. Within an hour of the discovery of Turnbull's body, his New Jersey office was attacked, and the crime spree culminated last night with the brutal assault on Mrs. Linda Turnbull in her New Jersey home. These events are believed to be connected to a former surgeon and student of Turnbull's, Dr. David McBride. McBride has recently been linked to a kidney-snatching scheme that has stolen kidneys from at least two mentally ill homeless men, and it's believed all of these events are related.*

"I'm being blamed for all of this?" David said, turning to Mr. White.

"Apparently so."

The broadcast went live, and David immediately recognized the two cops standing on the steps of One Police Plaza—Lieutenant Joseph Hernandez from the 13th Precinct and his grim-faced female detective, Kate D'Angelo. The lieutenant spoke into a bank of microphones representing every news organization in the tristate area:

> *These attacks have been violent. These attacks have been brazen. The perpetrators have impersonated law enforcement personnel, and a woman has been savagely beaten not more than twelve*

hours after she learned her husband had been murdered. We
believe we now have four deaths related to this case, along with
at least two homeless men who have been forced to undergo sur-
gery for the removal of an organ. These crimes span states, juris-
dictions and departments, and will, therefore, involve the efforts
of many. In order to coordinate these efforts so man-hours are not
wasted and significant leads are shared, I have named Detective
Kate D'Angelo as the liaison officer for this case. She will head
the robbery and assault-and-battery investigations, and will,
through the formation of a task force, coordinate with the Passaic
County Sheriff's Department, detectives from the Passaic
County Prosecutor's Office, and Manhattan South Homicide.
As a department, we find this series of crimes to be particularly
heinous and will devote all available resources and manpower to
the apprehension of the perpetrators. As an incentive to engage
the public's help in this complex investigation, the Crime Stoppers
reward for any information leading to the whereabouts of David
McBride, or anyone else involved in these cases, has been raised to
$75,000.

David sat back, stunned into silence.

"Do you still want to turn yourself in?" Mr. White asked.

David leaned forward and rubbed his face with his hands. "I
have no idea what to do, but I can say this: I can't spend the rest of
my life running. I'm just not cut out to be a fugitive."

"There are fugitives," Mr. White said, "and there are people who
fall off the grid and reemerge with new identities and lives. The
federal government helps people disappear all the time. You say the
word, I can make it happen."

"Yeah, I know, if I grow a kidney for you, but I said it yesterday,
and I'll say it again today—the whole idea is preposterous. I mean, a
missing book? A Russian spy? And then you'll make me disappear?
Come on, Mr. White. I, of all people, understand how dire your
daughter's circumstances are, but you're grasping at straws."

Mr. White finger-scrolled his iPhone. "Maybe if you met her.
Let me show you a—"

David held up a hand. "I'm not interested. Appealing to my softer side isn't going to work. My compassion is gone, calcified and pissed away like a kidney stone."

"Then you should have a look at this." Mr. White tapped his phone. "This is video from the long-term dementia care unit at the Coler rehab hospital on Roosevelt Island. It was taken yesterday morning at about nine a.m." He gave the phone to David.

David took it in his hand and stared at it, knowing it held something he did not want to see. "So we're back where we started five weeks ago? You're going to blackmail me again, except this time you're using my father instead of Cassandra?"

"He needs your help, and so do I."

David closed his eyes tight, took a deep breath and slowly shook his head.

"Tap the screen, David."

He did and set into motion a grainy but unmistakable recording of his father, bound to a hospital bed with four-point leather restraints, resting quietly. David watched for a few moments, then said, "He's tied down like an animal, but at least he's sleeping." David looked up at Mr. White. "How'd you get this? Did you see him?"

"No. I wasn't there. These videos were emailed to me."

"Videos? There's another one?"

"Yes. Taken about six hours later. Scroll to the next file, but brace yourself. It's quite unsettling."

David touched the screen. In this video his father was completely out of control, trying to sit up, pulling against the restraints and thrashing back and forth while screaming, "They're killing me. They're killing me. Somebody help. Somebody help me, please."

"What is this?" David tossing the phone at Mr. White.

"The physicians are trying to wean your father off a haloperidol infusion so he doesn't have to be drugged and tied to a bed twenty-four hours a day. In the first video he's sedated. When he's off the drip this is his baseline behavior."

David's eyes filled with tears. His father was alone, afraid, and confused. He had no idea where he was, or what these people were doing to him, and because of this, he had slipped into a perpetual catastrophic reaction.

"If they can't control him," Mr. White continued, "they'll have to keep him permanently sedated and tucked away on some isolated ward."

"All right, enough!" David said. "I'll do whatever you want. Just tell me you can get him out of there."

"I can get him out of there."

- 15 -

After twenty minutes of massaging obsidian black hair dye into his scalp and new goatee, David showered, threw on a pair of jeans and a polo shirt, and sat down at the kitchen table with Mr. White. They needed to formulate plans—for finding the missing book, and for getting David's father out of Coler. Mr. White gestured toward the refrigerator. "Too early for a beer?"

"It's never too early," David said.

Mr. White handed David a beer, fixed himself a cup of coffee, and sat down.

David took a drink, savoring both the cold carbonation and the warmth of the sunbathed kitchen alcove. "Okay," he said. "What about last night. You said you had an errand to run, and this morning you show up looking less than well rested. None of my business? Or were you out searching for marbled composition books?"

"The latter, more or less."

Mr. White recounted the series of events, beginning with Jeffery Abercrombie's apartment and culminating with the confrontation at Mrs. Abercrombie's home in West Hartford.

"You think Petrovsky was really going to smash her hand?" David asked.

"Yes."

"And Linda Turnbull. Have you heard anything?"

"Two swollen, blackened eyes, and obviously shaken up, but she's otherwise okay."

"Jesus, this guy's an animal."

"Of the worst kind. We'll need to be careful."

"The biochemist," David said, "you think he knows anything about the missing book?"

"I think he has it, but if he doesn't, he at least knows what's in it. One day we have a meeting and he mentions infrared laser therapy, and a month later we have fully functional human organs growing in the laboratory."

"One month," David said, shaking his head. "Labs around the world have spent years trying to make the leap from ferret to human organs, and Turnbull does it in a month?"

"The man was a genius. Unfortunately, he was also a sociopath."

"Now that the biochemist is hiding from the crazy Russian, how will we find him?"

"We're watching for credit-card use, ATM and bank withdrawals, any sort of financial transaction by him or his mother. I've tapped their cell phones and landlines. Jeffery has an iPhone. If his geo-locater function is turned on, I'll get a call giving me his location"—Mr. White checked his watch—"hopefully within the hour."

"The location of his phone, anyway," David added. "And if the locator is not turned on?"

"It can still be tracked, but it will take longer."

"Who is 'we'? You said 'we are watching.'"

"I have some trusted friends in the agency with whom I exchange favors."

"And you and your friends don't have a problem with this?" David said. "Watching bank accounts and ATMs? Tapping phones? All without a court order, or a warrant, or whatever it is you need?"

"Let me worry about how we find Jeff Abercrombie. We passed over the gray line that separates legal and illegal a long time ago."

"There's an understatement." David leaned back in his chair and sipped his beer.

Mr. White sipped his coffee.

"How much does Petrovsky know about you?" David asked.

"Everything. He had already turned Keating before I came to NuLife, so as soon as I joined the scientific advisory board he started digging into my background. He's an accomplished agent with vast resources. I anticipate he will be a formidable adversary."

"Why don't we just turn him in for the attacks on NuLife, Linda Turnbull, and Mrs. Abercrombie?"

"If we send him down, he'll take us with him."

"And what keeps him from turning you in to get you out of the way?" David asked. "He probably knows about the homeless men and the illegal transplants."

"I'm of more use to him on the outside. He'll watch and wait, and if we find the book or the biochemist first, he'll move on us."

David shook his head. "Sounds like it could get ugly—well, more ugly than it already is."

"It will, but I'd like you to focus on getting the lab up and running, so as soon as we get the notebook—or learn what's in it—you're ready to go. Heather doesn't have much time."

"What do the doctors say?"

"She has a month, maybe six weeks. She's developed neurologic symptoms, and her mental status is declining. She sleeps most of the day. She's not eating. They say she'll slip into a coma and die shortly thereafter."

Mr. White was describing uremic encephalopathy compounded by failure to thrive. The dialysis machine did a good job of balancing electrolytes and removing nitrogenous wastes and excess fluid, but other metabolic waste products were less dialyzable. Add to that the hormonal changes and neurotransmitter disturbances associated with long-term dialysis, and eventually the patient deteriorates to a state from which it is difficult to recover. Time was not on Heather Whitestone's side.

"Four to six weeks doesn't give us any margin for error," David said.

"No, it doesn't."

Mr. White got up, poured himself another cup of coffee and grabbed David another beer.

"About my father," David continued. "How are you going to get him out of Coler? You can't exactly wheel him out the front door. I'm sure the NYPD is watching his room 24/7."

"I plan to use the back door, and the NYPD does, in fact, have an officer assigned to his room, but we can work around that."

"What about the nurses and ward clerks? Whenever a patient leaves the floor they have to be signed out, and someone strapped to a bed with an IV pole in tow is going to draw attention."

"Every detail and contingency is being taken into consideration. The stakes are high, so I will make this happen, and it will happen seamlessly."

"When?"

"Days—three, maybe four."

"Once he's out, what are we going to do with him?"

"I'm making arrangements with a doctor who has a novel approach to caring for Alzheimer patients."

"It will help if I'm sitting at his bedside, comforting him as the Haldol is weaned and he emerges from the fog."

"Not a problem," Mr. White replied.

"Even though I'm the most wanted fugitive in the tristate area?"

"Not a problem."

David sipped his beer and regarded Mr. White with a big dose of skepticism. On the other hand, his daughter's life depended on David's ability to remain at large, so if Mr. White had figured out a way to pull this off, David would just have to go with it.

"Okay. So where exactly is this lab of yours?"

"Down the hall."

David cocked his head back in disbelief.

Mr. White led David down a long hallway that, prior to now, he had not felt compelled to explore. He'd been content to confine himself to the kitchen, living room, and bathroom—the front half of the apartment—and hadn't really given the rest of the place much thought. They passed a couple of closed doors on the right before coming to a door at the end of the hall.

"The lab is in there," Mr. White pointing straight ahead, "but let me show you the master suite first." He led David to a set of double doors further down the L-shaped hallway. David followed him into the room. "Why don't you start sleeping here?" Mr. White said.

Master suite was a misnomer—nothing more than a king-size bed and two nightstands—but the room was spacious, and the bed looked enticing. David had been sleeping on either a pullout sofa or somebody's couch for longer than he wanted to admit. "You haven't staked this out for yourself?" he asked.

"I have a small apartment in Midtown."

"Does it have a view like this?" David nodding toward the floor-to-ceiling windows.

"No. It's close to street level and quite unremarkable."

"How come you don't stay here?"

"This is a recent acquisition. As soon as Turnbull went socio-pathic, I knew I was going to need the equipment and space to build a lab," Mr. White said.

"But it's a government safe house. What if someone needs the place, and we're growing organs in the back room?"

"I took it off the books."

"What does that mean?"

"After 9/11 we thought we were going to snare large numbers of domestic-based Islamic terrorists, so Homeland Security started buying up properties to be used as black interrogation sites. As you know, our nets have come up empty, so now these places are going back on the market. I simply went into the system and marked this one as sold." Mr. White gestured toward the lab. "Let's have a look."

The door opened into a moderate-size room, the center of which was dominated by a waist-high bench top. A glass cylinder, about eighteen inches in diameter, sat in the center and was flanked by a roller pump, Silastic tubing, and a variety of glassware. Floor cabinets lined two of the walls, and their countertops held other pieces of equipment, including a blood gas machine, a serum chemistry analyzer, and a warm-water bath. A stainless-steel canister, about the size of a travel trailer propane tank, occupied a corner of the countertop. The equipment and supplies had not yet been fully set up and organized, but he could tell that Mr. White had acquired most of what was needed.

David motioned toward the canister. "Heather's stem cells?"

"Yes."

"What's the storage temperature?"

"Minus 150 degrees Celsius."

"Liquid nitrogen?"

"Liquid nitrogen vapor."

A screen the size of an iPad sat next to the canister. The two were connected by a USB cable. "Continuous monitoring?" David asked.

"Yes. If the temperature rises or falls more than five degrees an alarm will sound, plus I'll get a text and a phone call."

David tapped the screen. A graph depicting the core temperature of the canister came up. It had fluctuated no more than one or two degrees.

"Mind if I take a look at her cells?"

"Not at all. Let me deactivate the alarm."

David slipped into a pair of Kevlar gloves and released a series of clasps. The lid opened with a hiss. Nitrogen vapor poured over the rim and spread along the countertop. David reached inside and removed an aluminum rack that held three vinyl bags. Each was about the size of a unit of blood, but the contents were darker than blood, more of an iodine color.

"How many cells per bag?" David asked.

"Two of the units contain two hundred and fifty million progenitor cells each. The third contains three hundred million endothelial cells. Turnbull's people grew a liver using those numbers."

"And these are induced pluripotent stem cells?"

"All I know is they harvested some of Heather's skin, did something to the DNA, and they reverted into embryonic stem cells."

David held up the rack and admired the frozen bags. "Stem cells that now have the capacity to differentiate into any kind of cell found in the human body. All we have to do is provide the proper signals." He paused for a moment, wishing he had tempered his enthusiasm. "As you can tell," David said, "I get excited by this stuff, but I need you to understand that each step of the process is fraught with complications. During the freezing process, ice crystals can form within the cells and cause them to rupture. These bags may contain nothing more than cellular debris."

"I know," Mr. White said. "I spent enough time with Andrew Turnbull to understand the extreme complexity of all this."

"Okay." David lowered the bags back into the canister and sealed the lid. "Consider the process underway. I'll start organizing the equipment today." He peered into a box containing a variety of glassware. "So you just went through the lab books and collected everything we'd need?"

"Yes," Mr. White said. "Courtesy of NuLife Corporation."

"And nobody noticed."

"You know, a piece here, a piece there over the course of a couple weeks."

"And the three-foot-tall glass cylinder? You just carried it out to the trunk of your car?"

"More or less."

"Wait a minute," David said. "Two weeks ago you couldn't have known I was going to send Andrew Turnbull into the white light and bring your kidney-growing mission to an end."

"No, but following Cassandra's death and your disappearance, I had a feeling trouble was on the way, be it you or law enforcement, so I developed contingency plans and started making preparations."

"And here we are."

"Yes. Here we are."

17

Kate was happy to be back at her desk at the 13th Precinct. Live press conferences from One Police Plaza were a pain in the ass for any detective, unless you were a climber like Kate's boss, Lieutenant Hernandez. That said, she was pleased Hernandez had named her lead detective of the McBride Task Force. Making sure everyone in the sandbox played nice while solving a complex set of crimes would move her closer to homicide and the coveted gold shield that came with it. Not that *she* was a climber. Homicide was as high as she wanted to go.

As for the case itself, there was no doubt in her mind that the murder of Andrew Turnbull by David McBride was a revenge killing. Turnbull ruins McBride's career and two years later destroys his life. McBride loses everything, so he ends Turnbull. But then the attack on NuLife and the savage beating of Mrs. Turnbull? Somebody is looking for something very important—a notebook, according to Linda Turnbull—probably containing valuable trade secrets. If David McBride wanted the book, he could have tortured Turnbull to get it, used a scalpel to cut off a finger every five minutes or something like that. There would be no need to stage an elaborate surgical procedure that only pretended to remove life-sustaining organs. Such methodical planning, culminating in an actual execution, said one thing to her—revenge.

Kate believed this case now had two parts—everything that had happened prior to Turnbull's murder, and the events that occurred in quick succession after. Andrew Turnbull and a coerced David McBride were the principle players in part one. Then, Turnbull's death unleashes a second set of players who want his secrets. They drive a truck through a wall and savagely beat a woman while stealing two safes. Did they get the book? Were the various players now going to recede into the shadows and disappear? An hour later her question would be answered.

Desk Sergeant Morales called into the squad room. "Kate... Morales. I got a Detective Chuck Foley from the West Hartford PD on the line."

"As in Connecticut?" Kate asked.

"Yeah. Says he has something that might be relatable to the McBride case."

She told Morales to put the call through. "Detective D'Angelo," Kate said, flipping open her notebook and grabbing a pen.

"Chuck Foley," replied the detective. "We had a home B and E with assault this morning at about 1:30 a.m., and it might have something to do with your kidney-snatcher case." The detective described how a neighbor had called in a disturbance, and when the patrol officers arrived they found a smashed-in kitchen door and a frail elderly woman trying to figure out how to get it closed so she could lock it. She was scared and had been manhandled a bit but was otherwise uninjured.

"When I questioned her," Foley said, "she started in with the same story she told the patrol officers—that two men had broken in demanding money—but then she breaks down and gives me a completely different story about three men who are looking for her son. They come in through a window, tape her to a kitchen chair, and they're about to smash her hand with a cast iron skillet when a fourth man crashes through the back door and runs off the other three. Turns out the fourth man knows the son, and they both worked for the CEO who was found dead in the meatpacking warehouse yesterday morning."

Kate's process-of-discovery buzz kicked in. "Does she know why they want her son?"

"She said she has no idea, but I think she's lying."

"Does she know where her son is?"

"Again, no, but I don't buy it."

"Did she tell you why she didn't call the police herself after being threatened with bodily harm?"

"She was scared and confused and trying to get the door locked before the men came back."

"Did she sell you on that one?"

"No. She was frightened and upset, but she also seems like a tough old bird. I think she would have had the presence of mind to call 911 and then go to a neighbor's house or sit in the corner with a carving knife until we got there."

"Okay. Good," Kate said. "You mind if I drive up there and have a chat with her?"

18

David stood, stretched, and took a deep breath, trying to shake his anger. Following the tour of the penthouse, he had spent the remainder of the morning in the lab, in a comfortable desk chair with his feet up, reviewing the digitized composition books on the iPad and trying to get some relief from the swelling in his leg.

At first, reading through the lab books was interesting from a scientific standpoint, but it didn't take long to go from intellectual stimulation, to depression, to agitation, and now anger. Much of the early ferret work originated during David's surgery residency and his two-year tenure in Turnbull's lab at NYU. Some of those books, now digitized and on the iPad, were in David's handwriting. It was difficult to read them, reminding him of a time when he had complete control over his destiny. If he showed up and did the work—in the OR, on the wards, in the lab—he'd be rewarded with a transplant fellowship, which would open doors to the high-powered academic career he wanted. He had done all that, had landed the fellowship, and had been standing on the threshold of a brilliant career when it all blew up. And now this—wifeless, fatherless, homeless, nursing a shredded gunshot wound in his leg and hiding from the law in some kind of spy lair, while trying to figure out how to grow a human kidney. Was this absurd? Insane? Idiotic? He had long ago run out of superlatives to characterize such an unfathomable turn of events. And as if to rub salt into a gaping, festering wound, the window over the desk at which he now sat faced due east, giving him an unobstructed view of Roosevelt Island and the Coler rehab hospital sitting on its northern tip.

Mr. White walked into the room. He seemed almost animated. "We've located Jeff Abercrombie. He's in northwest Connecticut, about two hours from here. Let's get there before Petrovsky finds him."

"Let's, as in let *us* get there? You want me to go?"

"Why not?"

"Uh, because I'm the most wanted person in the Northeast United States?"

"Dyeing your hair has dramatically altered your appearance. Put on a hoodie and glasses, don't call attention to yourself, and you'll be fine."

"But why even risk it?" David asked.

"If we actually find Jeffery, and he's willing to tell us what he knows, I want you to be there to interpret."

"How do you know where he is?"

"Earlier this morning he turned on his phone just long enough to make a short call to his mother. The geo locater was off, but we were able to pinpoint his location anyway."

- 19 -

By midday Kate was rolling into West Hartford, Connecticut in a departmental Ford sedan. She stopped at the main office of the WHPD, picked up Detective Chuck Foley, and together they went to see Mrs. Ruby Abercrombie. After introductions were made and the detectives declined offers of coffee or tea, they moved into the kitchen, taking care not to step on the debris—Mrs. Abercrombie's busted up personal belongings—that the intruders had left behind. As Kate slipped out of her overcoat, she noticed the repairs of the back door. The jam, latch, and molding had been replaced, and the nail holes filled with putty and sanded over. All it needed was a coat of paint. Kate glanced at Chuck Foley. He shrugged and turned toward Mrs. Abercrombie, who was putting a kettle of water on the stovetop. "Pretty quick repair job on that door," he said.

"There was a man here by eight a.m."

"You must have friends in high places," Kate added.

"I don't know. I suppose I do." Mrs. Abercrombie gestured toward the table. "Please sit."

Kate sat across from Mrs. Abercrombie. In the bright light, the effects of the early-morning ordeal were apparent. The woman's face was gaunt and pale with dark bags under her eyes, her hands were trembling, and despite the long-sleeved sweater, the injuries to her wrists were obvious.

Kate reached for her hands. "May I take a look?"

"Uh, sure, if you'd like."

Kate gently rotated each hand. The right wrist was raw with abrasions where the tape had torn off the superficial layers of skin.

The left wrist was black and blue with circumferential bruises. Both hands were cold and clammy. "And your ankles?"

"More missing skin and bruises. That duct tape is rough stuff."

Kate asked if the intruders had hit her or knocked her around. Did she have any other injuries that might need a doctor's attention? The answer was no. Kate took out her notebook and voice recorder and suggested they get started.

"On our way here," Kate began, "Detective Foley filled me in on the details of the attack as you reported them earlier this morning. Basically, three men wearing overcoats break in and threaten to hurt you unless you can tell them where they can find your son, Jeffery?"

"Yes."

"And you couldn't—or wouldn't—tell them where he is?"

"Couldn't. After he saw the news about Mrs. Turnbull last night, he called me and said he was scared and was going to disappear for a while."

"Did he tell you why he was scared? Why the same men might be coming for him?"

"No."

"Do *you* have any idea why these men are pursuing your son?"

"No."

"Were they looking for something?"

Mrs. Abercrombie shook her head and said no.

"Yet they ransacked your house."

"I guess. I don't know. I don't know how these people think."

"Fair enough," Kate said. "Could Jeffery be in some kind of trouble? Gambling, drugs, betting on fantasy sports teams—anything that might expose him to a criminal element?"

"Did you ask Mrs. Turnbull the same questions after she was beaten? Don't you see that this is related to Andrew Turnbull and NuLife, and not gambling or drugs?"

"Of course, Mrs. Abercrombie. This is almost certainly related to the events of yesterday morning, but these are routine questions we always ask when someone is in danger."

"The answer is no. Jeffery has never been in trouble."

"Okay," Kate said, jotting a few notes. "And then a fourth man wearing an overcoat and a fedora type hat crashes through the door right over there, points a gun at the men and tells them to get out?"

"Yes."

"He doesn't want to call the police?"

"Uh, I guess not."

"Isn't that strange?"

"The whole exchange was bizarre."

"In what way?"

"They seemed to know each other, and they bickered back and forth, and then the thugs left. I kinda had the feeling that whoever these guys are, they operate above the law."

"Interesting," Kate said, adding this to her notes. Then, "Did these guys use one another's names while they were bickering?"

"First names, sort of."

"What do you mean?"

"The leader of the thugs, he called the other man Mr. White, but he used his fingers to make air quotes around White and said it sarcastically. Mr. White called the other guy Mikhail."

"No air quotes or sarcasm?"

"No."

"Was there a last name for Mikhail, or a first name for Mr. White?"

"I think Mikhail referred to Mr. White as Richard at one point."

"Were the other two men called by name?"

"No."

"What did Mr. White and Mikhail say to each other?"

"They talked about how they were both looking for Jeffery."

"But not *why* they were looking for Jeffery?"

"No."

"And this man, Mr. White, he works with your son?"

"That's what he told me later. He said Jeffery would know him as Mr. White from NuLife and for me to tell Jeffery he wanted to help."

Kate wrote down and underlined "Richard White, NuLife" in her notebook, then flipped to another page and scanned it. "You gave Detective Foley physical descriptions of all four men."

"That's right."

"Did Mikhail or Mr. White speak with an accent?"

"No."

"What about the other two men?"

"They didn't really say anything."

The teapot whistled. Mrs. Abercrombie jumped up to silence it. As she made herself a cup of tea, she turned toward the detectives. "Anybody change their minds?"

They both said no.

"What happened after the thugs left?" Kate asked as Mrs. Abercrombie returned to the table.

"He cut the tape, made sure I wasn't hurt, then he left."

"Just like that? He just took off?"

"He asked me again if I knew where Jeffery was, kinda like he didn't believe me the first time, but I told him I didn't know."

"So he leaves through the back door, and that's when you called 911?"

"No. I didn't call the police. A neighbor did."

"Oh, that's right." Kate paused as though pondering something. Then, "How come you didn't make the call?"

"I was scared and confused. I wanted to get the door closed and locked."

"I see," Kate said, pausing again for a moment. "How did you get your door fixed so fast, Mrs. Abercrombie? The attack happened at approximately one-thirty a.m., and you had a repairman here by eight? Did you call a twenty-four-hour emergency service? Like the locksmiths have?"

Mrs. Abercrombie fiddled with her teacup. "Mr. White said he would get it fixed. I was really scared, and he said he would get it taken care of as soon as possible."

Kate nodded. "It's interesting that this man, a gun-wielding employee of a biomedical company, is so concerned with the welfare of both you and your son."

"I don't understand it, either. I'm sure if you could talk to Jeffery, he'd be able to explain what's going on."

"Yes, I'm sure he could. Have you heard from him, Mrs. Abercrombie? Is he okay?"

"Actually, he called earlier this morning. He's still scared, but he's in a safe place."

"Did he tell you where?"

"No. He doesn't want to say over the phone."

Kate put her pen down and leaned back in her chair. "Detective Foley, do you have any additional questions for Mrs. Abercrombie?"

"No," Chuck Foley replied. "I think between the two of us, we have it covered."

Kate handed one of her cards to Mrs. Abercrombie and thanked her for her time. "Of course, we'll be in touch if we learn anything. And we would very much like to speak with Jeffery. I think that would unlock this whole case—the attacks on NuLife and Mrs. Turnbull, and what happened here earlier this morning."

"I'll tell him as soon as I hear from him again," Mrs. Abercrombie said.

- 20 -

Two hours and five minutes after leaving the safe house, the black Mercedes was driving north on Connecticut State Route 272 about ten miles outside of Torrington. Mr. White cross-checked the latitude and longitude obtained from Abercrombie's phone with the coordinates on the car's navigation system. They were close, he said to David.

The road was an old, but well-maintained two-lane highway with thin strips of shoulder. The dense trees and undergrowth crowding the roadside were more-or-less continuous, interrupted only by the occasional home. David imagined Jeffery Abercrombie hunkered down in a clearing in the woods, camping out of the back of his car, all paranoid and jumping at every noise emanating from the forest around him.

"Google Earth shows a small resort on a lake, like a group of cottages, that match the coordinates. I believe we'll find Jeff Abercrombie there," Mr. White said, as if reading David's thoughts and correcting him.

A few minutes later they came to a sign indicating the turnoff to Deception Lake State Park. They followed the road a couple of miles to a collection of rental cottages situated along a large circular drive. Mr. White turned the Mercedes into the driveway, a layer of gravel crunching under the tires.

- 21 -

Mikhail Petrovsky put his mouth inches from Jeffery Abercrombie's ear. "Listen fat boy," Petrovsky said in a strained tone, "I'm losing my patience, and my guy here, his arms are getting tired from swinging the bat. So tell me, where is the book? You will help us learn how to grow kidneys, or we will smash yours."

Inside a small rental cottage in rural northwest Connecticut, Petrovsky and his two goons—Anatoly and Viktor—stood over Jeff Abercrombie. He had been forced to sit backward in a wooden chair. His legs straddled the seat. His ample belly was squeezed up against the back. His arms hung down behind the chair, and tight straps of duct tape around his wrists and ankles served as restraints. His shirt had been torn off and stuffed in his mouth. He groaned in pain and was struggling to breathe. He'd been hit with a baseball bat high on the back and below the angle of the ribs on both the left and right sides. Large purple bruises had already formed.

Petrovsky removed the shirt from Abercrombie's mouth. "Last chance, big boy."

Abercrombie struggled to lift his head. "I don't know—"

Petrovsky shoved the shirt back in his mouth. "Hit him again," he said to Viktor, the goon with the bat, "but get the kidney this time."

"I got it last time," Viktor said.

"No, you got his ribs."

"The kidneys are up under ribs."

"They're below the ribs, down here," Petrovsky said, pointing low on the back.

"I think Viktor is right," Anatoly said. "Up higher, under ribs."

Abercrombie groaned and violently shook his head back and forth.

"Okay," Petrovsky said. "Hit him in both places."

Viktor swung hard, driving the bat into Abercrombie's flank. Then he swung again, drilling the mid back. A loud snap filled the room. Abercrombie screamed, his body shuddering.

"Did you hear that?" Petrovsky said to Abercrombie. "That was the sound of a rib breaking. I know it well."

Abercrombie's head fell forward.

Petrovsky lifted it and pulled the shirt from his mouth. "Come on big fella. The book."

Abercrombie tried to speak, but he was gasping for air, unable to form words. Then his eyes widened, full of panic, his arms and legs pulling and thrashing against the tape.

"I don't think he breathes so well," Anatoly said.

From outside the cottage, the sound of crunching gravel as a car pulled into the circle drive. Petrovsky quickly walked over and peered out the window. "For Christ's sake. What are the odds?"

The three men rushed out the back door toward the lake and the car.

- 22 -

"There's Abercrombie's car," Mr. White said, pointing toward a blue Tesla. They parked next to it, jumped out and knocked on the cottage door. No answer.

David peeked through the window. The blackout curtains were drawn.

Mr. White tried the knob. The door opened, and he entered, followed closely by David.

David's eyes took a moment to focus in the dim light but quickly registered the horrific scene that lay before him. An obese man—Jeffery Abercrombie—had been duct-taped backward to a chair. His shirtless back and flanks were covered with massive bruises. His head hung over the back of the chair like that of an unconscious person. Judging by the angle of the neck, there was no way he was moving air.

"Fucking animals," David blurted as he rushed over.

He lifted Abercrombie's head and looked into his face, then pried open his mouth. "His lips and tongue are blue. He's not breathing. Call 911."

Mr. White pulled his phone from his pocket, dialed, and began speaking to the operator.

David slapped Abercrombie across the face as hard as he could. No response. He hyperextended Abercrombie's neck and felt his trachea—deviated way to the left—then grabbed his wrist and held it for a moment. He found a pulse, but it was weak. David tried to rip through the restraints, but the Russians had made multiple passes with the duct tape, making it too thick to tear. He turned to

Mr. White. "Do you have anything sharp in the car? A knife or box cutter?"

"No," Mr. White replied. "The operator wants to know what we're dealing with."

"Tension pneumothorax in a thirty-year-old obese male."

David slapped Abercrombie again and yelled at him, told him to keep breathing. If David could stimulate the adrenal glands they might secrete enough epinephrine to keep the guy's heart beating. And as he slapped, yelled at, and shook Abercrombie, he looked around the room—at the mirror on the wall, a roll of duct tape left behind by Petrovsky, a floor lamp in the corner.

"Get that tape," David pointing toward the desk, "and tear off a long strip, about eighteen inches, then stand back."

David grabbed the floor lamp mid shaft and swung it like a bat, ripping the cord out of the wall, slamming the heavy base into the center of the mirror, the crash of shattering glass ringing out as daggerlike shards rained down on the floor. He found one the size and shape of a carving knife and carefully picked it up.

"The tape," he called out to Mr. White, who stood dumbfounded in the corner.

David wrapped the thick end of the shard, effectively adding a handle to his knife, then used it to slice through the layers of tape encircling Abercrombie's wrists and ankles. His arms and legs now free, David and Mr. White turned the chair so Abercrombie was lined up with the bed, then wrestled him onto it.

"Hollow out that ink pen over there and screw the two pieces back together," David again pointing at the desk. He then pushed the fingertips of his left hand deep into Abercrombie's chest wall about an inch below the right clavicle. When he felt the top of the second rib—no easy feat with all the extra adipose tissue—he stabbed the tip of glass shard through the skin, over the top of the rib, and into the chest cavity.

David took the gutted ink pen from Mr. White and slipped it into the stab wound until he heard a rush of air. With his free hand, he pinched one of Abercrombie's nipples and twisted it as hard as he could.

Abercrombie did not react to the deep stimulation.

David twisted again, harder this time. As a resident, the nipple twist was one of the most effective ways to bring a patient out of the depths of a depressed mental state.

He asked Mr. White to hold the ink pen and then he grabbed both nipples, twisting and pulling, and yelling and slapping Abercrombie's face. It was like delivering a baby. He needed Abercrombie to wake up and take a big breath, which would get the right lung to expand and expel more air out of the pleural space, thus relieving the pressure on the heart.

David grabbed Abercrombie's wrist. The pulse felt stronger. He twisted nipples and slapped cheeks and yelled, and finally Abercrombie opened his eyes, groaned, and took a swing at David. Always a good sign. And as Abercrombie's breaths deepened, air continued to hiss through the hollow ink pen.

"Jeffery, can you hear me?" David yelled into the big guy's ear.

Abercrombie mumbled, thrashed his head back and forth and swatted at the air.

"Deep breaths, buddy. Take some deep breaths for me."

David checked the radial pulse. Nice and strong, and fast. The heart was pounding away, trying to get blood to all the tissues of the body, tissues that had been starved for oxygen for at least ten minutes.

Sirens in the distance.

"We need to get out of here," Mr. White said. "Will he be okay?"

David advanced the ink pen another inch into the chest and secured it to the skin with scraps of duct tape. "Not sure, but there's nothing more we can do."

- 23 -

The ambulance spewed gravel and dust as it left the circular drive and hit the blacktop with lights flashing and siren blaring. The Mercedes fell in behind but made no attempt to follow too closely. The final destination—Litchfield County Medical Center, Torrington, Connecticut—had been made obvious by the billboard-like signage on the side of the boxlike vehicle.

After eight or ten miles, Mr. White turned toward David, who was staring straight ahead without any discernable emotion on his face. "What happened back there?" Mr. White asked.

"He had a tension pneumothorax," David said blankly, as if lecturing medical students. "One or more broken ribs punctured his right lung. With each breath, air escapes the lung and fills the thoracic cavity on that side. As the air accumulates, so does the pressure. When the pressure gets high enough, the lung completely collapses and compresses the heart to the extent that it can no longer pump blood, and the patient has a cardiac arrest."

"You knew this from feeling his throat?"

"With the bruises on his back, I figured he had some broken ribs. When the trachea is shifted away from the midline, that's the hallmark sign of tension pneumothorax."

"And the makeshift knife and ballpoint pen?"

"I made a small opening in the thoracic cavity with the piece of broken glass, and the hollowed-out pen acted as a conduit to let the air escape and take the pressure off the heart."

"Remarkable," said Mr. White. "You walk into a room, quickly make an assessment, and save a man's life with a shattered mirror and an ink pen."

"He's not out of the woods yet. He probably has multiple rib fractures, he could be bleeding into both thoracic cavities, and I wouldn't be surprised if he has bilateral pulmonary contusions. In a big guy like him, any of those complications can be fatal."

"Nonetheless, if you hadn't done what you did, he'd be dead."

David turned toward Mr. White. "And if those psycho mother-fuckers hadn't beaten him with a bat, or a pipe, or whatever they used, he'd probably be eating lunch right now."

David looked away, staring out the window at the trees rushing by like toothpicks. Under his breath he mumbled, "For as smart as we are, we're really stupid."

"I'm sorry?" replied Mr. White.

"The human race," David said, turning squarely toward Mr. White. "We have the capacity to do great things—science, medicine, art, architecture. But we also have the capacity to do really bad things. We rape and murder our children. We wage war against one another, often over religious differences. We beat, maim, and bludgeon each other, and we kill for pride, envy, greed, lust, and revenge—and sometimes just for sport. We are smarter than the rest of the animal kingdom, yet animals don't treat each other with such barbarism. You have no idea the crazy shit I saw in the Bellevue ER night after night. Gunshot wounds, stab wounds, ax wounds, and hatchet wounds. Beatings, clubbings, cars used as weapons, people thrown from cars, and more than one crazy bitch who dumped scalding hot water or boiling oil on her sleeping husband, who probably deserved it."

"That's a pretty dark view of humankind."

"Yeah? Well, you and Andrew Turnbull have certainly done your part to enhance my disdain for the human race, and now that I can add revenge killer to my resume, I'm no better than the rest of you."

After ten more minutes of watching the trees and shrubs rush by, David turned toward Mr. White. "I'm not sure following this guy to the hospital is worth the risk. It's going to take them a couple of hours to place chest tubes, get before-and-after X-rays, a CT of his abdomen to make sure his liver, kidneys, and spleen aren't pulverized, and in all likelihood, he's going to be on a ventilator. The only way to mechanically ventilate a man this large is to paralyze him and snow him with narcotics. He's not going to be propped up in bed eating Jell-O."

"We have to try," Mr. White said. "He's our only lead."

- 24 -

David put on his drugstore reading glasses and pulled his hoodie low over his face as he and Mr. White entered Litchfield County Medical Center. David sat down in the ER waiting area, while Mr. White went over and asked if they could visit Jeffery Abercrombie, the trauma patient who had just been brought in. The admissions clerk—a young tattooed woman with so many piercings she'd lose most of her face if she went near an MRI machine—said only immediate family would be allowed into the room, and only after the patient was stabilized and the doctors gave the okay. Mr. White pulled out his ID—his NSA identification, David presumed—and leaned in close to the clerk. After a few moments of back-and-forth discussion, with the clerk's face becoming increasingly distorted with anger, Mr. White waved David over, and they were buzzed through the ER doors and ushered to a spot in the hallway outside of trauma room one.

As David had predicted, Jeffery Abercrombie was not eating Jell-O. Instead, he lay unresponsive on a gurney. A white-coated ER physician—forties, salt-and-pepper hair, Dr. Mason according to his nameplate—was setting up for intubation while one of the nurses opened a chest tube tray. Other nurses and techs were busy cutting off clothes, placing IVs, and drawing blood. A male nurse slipped a urinary catheter through the penis.

"Don't wait for the type and cross. Get six units of O-neg up here STAT," Dr. Mason said. "We'll need a portable chest X-ray and a KUB, and have CT on standby."

David glanced at the array of monitors. Blood pressure was ninety over forty-five. The cardiac rhythm was regular but fast, 155 beats per minute, sinus tachycardia. The oxygen saturation had dropped into the low eighties. If it fell much lower, cardiac arrest would follow. Intubation and mechanical ventilation would quickly improve the O2 saturation and blood pressure, and slow the heart rate, but intubating a 350-pound man was no chip shot.

As soon as Mason slipped the laryngoscope into Jeff Abercrombie's trachea, the first step of intubation, Abercrombie bucked and flailed, reaching for the doctor's hands. With the burst of activity, Abercrombie's oxygen saturation dropped to 79 percent, and his heart rate jumped into the 170s. Alarms sounded. Mason shed his white coat and wiped his forehead with his shirt sleeve. "I can't see his cords. Paralyze him with succinylcholine, and open a tracheostomy tray."

Not good. David had been in this position numerous times. The morbidly obese had a lot of redundant tissue in the pharynx making it difficult to visualize the vocal cords. Plus, Abercrombie possessed just enough mental awareness to fight the gag reflex stimulated by sticking a plastic tube down his throat. Succinylcholine would paralyze him and stop him from fighting and gagging, but it would also render him unable to breath. If Dr. Mason could not get the tube into the trachea quickly, he would have to resort to emergency tracheostomy, and performing a surgical procedure on a neck encased in inches of fat, in a hypoxic hypotensive patient, was exceptionally difficult.

The respiratory therapist hyperventilated Abercrombie with a face mask and ambu bag. The O2 sat remained in the high 70s despite the bagging. The alarms continued to ping.

"One-fifty of succinylcholine is in," said the male nurse as he slipped the needle out of the injection port on the IV tubing.

Abercrombie began to twitch, the facial muscles first, followed by the extremities and the whole body.

"Coming through," called out a voice down the hall.

David and Mr. White stepped out of the way as paramedics rolled a stretcher past them. A scrawny young male wearing shabby clothes lay on his side, vomit oozing from his mouth, the crotch of his pants wet. His eyes were open, but the pupils were constricted to pinpoints. He was unresponsive, and his oxygen saturation wasn't much higher than Abercrombie's. An opioid overdose. David had seen it countless times.

Jeff Abercrombie stopped twitching, total paralysis now complete. Mason suctioned out the pharynx and inserted the laryngoscope. "Somebody give me some cricoid pressure. Quickly."

One of the nurses pushed on the neck at the level of the larynx.

"Harder," Mason said. "I can't see his cords."

The nurse doubled her effort.

Mason suctioned and looked again, then held out his right hand. "Tube."

He slipped the tube past the laryngoscope, looking confident as he withdrew the scope and inflated the balloon with a 10cc syringe.

The respiratory therapist connected the ambu bag to the endotracheal tube and bagged Abercrombie while Mason listened to his lungs. "Breath sounds are good. Hyperventilate him until his O2 sat is up. Run in a liter of lactated ringers while we're waiting on the blood."

"Impressive," David said to Mr. White. "If he doesn't get that tube in on the first or second try, Abercrombie is probably dead."

Once the oxygen saturation and blood pressure had stabilized, and the heart rate had dropped below 110, Dr. Mason proceeded with placement of a chest tube. He made a two-inch incision high up on Abercrombie's right flank, almost in his armpit, and bluntly dissected through the adipose layer with his index finger. He opened the pleural space by driving a Kocher clamp over the top of the rib and punching through the intercostal muscles. Mason then slipped a 40 French chest tube through the hole he had created in the chest wall and advanced it into the right pleural space.

As soon as the tube was connected to a Pleur-Evac, the collection chamber quickly filled with a liter of dark venous blood, but then slowed to a trickle, which was a very good sign. If the blood had been arterial—bright red instead of dark—or if the drainage continued at a brisk rate, Abercrombie would need emergency surgery.

The chest X-ray showed good placement of Dr. Mason's chest and endotracheal tubes, total evacuation of the hemothorax, and complete expansion of the right lung. Blood pressure, heart rate, and oxygen saturation had all quickly normalized now that Abercrombie was sedated and the ventilator was breathing for him. But, both lung fields on the chest X-ray were white with patchy infiltrates, as opposed to dark with normal air-flow patterns. The blunt trauma to the chest had resulted in bilateral pulmonary contusions, and this was what David feared most. As the injured lungs filled with fluid—the patchy infiltrates seen on the chest film—gas exchange would become increasingly difficult, and Jeffery Abercrombie would suffocate despite being on a mechanical ventilator. And pulmonary contusions generally worsened over the first forty-eight hours.

"We might as well go," David said to Mr. White. "He won't be alert and talking anytime soon. If he survives the next forty-eight hours, it will be a number of days before he is weaned off the ventilator, and that's a very optimistic scenario."

David followed Mr. White through the automatic doors and into the ER waiting room. Over at the clerk's desk stood a petite, elderly, teary-eyed woman begging to be allowed into the back to see her son.

"I'm sorry, ma'am," the clerk said. "I cannot let you go back until he is stabilized, and the doctor says it's okay."

"Please," cried the woman. "I just need to see him."

Mrs. Abercrombie, David surmised as Mr. White walked over to her.

"I'll handle this," Mr. White said to the clerk.

"All yours," she replied with a whatever-asshole tone.

Mrs. Abercrombie's eyes widened. "It's you. You know who did this. I'm calling the police right now." She pulled a cell phone from her purse. "I should have called them last night when they broke into my house."

"Please, Mrs. Abercrombie, just hear me out."

Mr. White turned to the clerk. "Is there a place where I can speak to this lady in private?"

"Down the hall to the left. It's called the quiet room. No one is using it right now."

The small room was softly lit and furnished with two opposing couches, a place to shuttle the families whose loved ones were unlikely to survive their visit to the ER.

Mr. White gestured toward one of the couches. "Please, Mrs. Abercrombie. Take a seat."

She did, and Mr. White sat next to her. David sat down across from them. "First, you need to know that the man sitting here"—Mr. White pointed at David—"is a doctor, a surgeon, and he saved Jeffery's life. We found him bound to a chair in a lakeside cottage, and he wasn't breathing. This man made a small incision and inserted an ink pen into his chest and saved his life." Mr. White looked at David, then back to Mrs. Abercrombie. "I have never seen anything quite so dramatic. Your son was blue. He was going to die, and"—Mr. White again looking over at David—"he acted by instinct and saved your son's life."

Mrs. Abercrombie crumpled, burying her face in her hands.

She then looked up, tears streaming. "I have what they want."

"You have the book?" Mr. White and David exchanged glances.

"Jeffery had me put it in a safe deposit box. He said it was worth millions of dollars, and it would change the world. He told me not to give it up, no matter what." Mrs. Abercrombie rocked forward, elbows on knees. "But I can't take this anymore. I was assaulted, Jeffery was beaten, and now he could die because of the goddamned thing." She sat up and looked at Mr. White, then at David. "You were back there. Can you tell me how he's doing?"

David moved to the edge of the couch and leaned closer to Mrs. Abercrombie. He had to tread lightly. She needed to know the truth, but he had to give her a shred of hope to hang on to.

"Jeffery was repeatedly hit on both sides of his back with something like a pipe or a bat," David said, and he went on to explain the fractured ribs, punctured lung, and bleeding in the chest. "His biggest problem now is what we call pulmonary contusions, or bruising of the lungs. Just as blood collects under your skin to form a bruise, fluid fills the air sacks of the lungs, making it difficult to move oxygen into the bloodstream, and this condition usually gets worse before it gets better. He is stable right now, but the first forty-eight hours will be critical."

"He could die from this?"

"I'm afraid so."

Mrs. Abercrombie buried her face again and sobbed. Mr. White offered her a box of tissues he found on an end table. She blew her nose and wiped her eyes, then said, "We need to call the police. I want those men arrested."

"Actually, Mrs. Abercrombie, I am the police." Mr. White removed his ID from the inside of his lapel and showed it to the her. "I'm a federal agent with the Justice Department, and we've been trying to gather enough evidence to arrest this man for a while now. Unfortunately, we didn't actually see him in that room today. We can only surmise he is responsible."

"But you saw him at my house last night. You saw what they did to me."

"I did, but that was simple assault. This man is responsible for a series of heinous crimes, including the attacks on NuLife and Linda Turnbull, but we need to gather the appropriate evidence before we arrest him. I can assure you that the United States government is very interested in putting him behind bars."

Mrs. Abercrombie shook her head, tears running down her cheeks. "It doesn't make any sense."

"I know," Mr. White said. "It's confusing, but this is a complicated case, and those of us in law enforcement have to be patient and wait for the right time to make an arrest. I'm going to ask you to do the same." Mr. White gently took her hand in his and looked her in the eyes. "Be patient while we build our case. He will be arrested, and you will get your day in court. I promise. In the meantime, you'll need to hand over the book. It is now evidence and must be returned. More importantly, once it's no longer in your possession, this man has no reason to bother you or your son."

"But…I can't leave," Mrs. Abercrombie said, "not before I see Jeffery."

"How long will it take you to get the book and come back?" David asked.

"About an hour, I suppose."

"By then your son will be transferred to the ICU, and you'll be able to spend all the time you want with him. We'll see to it." David paused for a moment, then said, "Why don't I stay here and get updates on Jeffery. Mr. White will go with you, and when you get back we'll get you in to see your son."

"Okay," Ruby Abercrombie said meekly.

- 25 -

By the time Kate was back in the city, she'd received a text with Jeffery Abercrombie's address. Thanks, Wayne DeSilva. Both Kate and Chuck Foley were convinced Mrs. Abercrombie was hiding something. Unless a person is dead or dying or has been beaten in the head, they will get to a phone and call 911 after a violent attack. She did not beg them to find her son and protect him, nor did she seek police protection for herself. In addition, Kate found it hard to believe that these men, who have waged a three-state crime spree searching for a book, didn't ask her if she had it or knew where it was, yet tore apart her house looking for it. Both Kate and Detective Foley believed that one of the Abercrombies—probably Jeff—did in fact have the highly sought-after book. Jeffery was on the run, and Ruby was covering for him, so Kate thought it best not to alert the woman that her son's apartment was Kate's next stop.

After turning left off Ninth Avenue onto West 30th, Kate found a parking space, locked up, and walked a hundred feet down the sidewalk to Jeffery Abercrombie's building. She buzzed his number, not expecting an answer and not getting one, then buzzed the superintendent.

"What is it?" an annoyed, gravelly voice said.

"I'm Detective Kate D'Angelo, NY—"

"I didn't call you."

"What?" Kate said.

"I didn't call the NYPD. I want it on the record."

"Sir, I'm not sure what that means. May I come in and talk to you about—"

"Jeff Abercrombie?"

"Uh, yes, and how did you—"

"Apartment 214." The door buzzed open.

Kate climbed the two flights of stairs and knocked on 214.

"Please hold your ID next to your face and step in front of the peephole."

Kate did, and the door opened.

A short, chunky man stood in the doorway, scratching at gray stubble. "Can I see your identification again?" he asked, holding out his hand.

Kate handed the man her badge and ID.

"It is real this time? You are a cop for sure?"

"I'm sorry, Mr.—?"

"Kovalenko."

"I'm sorry, Mr. Kovalenko, but I'm not following you."

The man handed Kate her ID. "This is the third time someone comes looking for Jeffery Abercrombie. Late last night, two fake detectives from NYPD, then not long after that, a man who says he is from Immigration, but then says he is not."

"Why don't you start from the beginning," Kate said.

"Last night I am watching the news about the murdered man in the warehouse, and the truck, and the attack on the dead man's wife in New Jersey, and then I hear really heavy footsteps coming down the stairs. It is Mr. Abercrombie, with a suitcase, and he gets into his car." Mr. Kovalenko went on to describe the visit by the supposed NYPD detectives shortly after Jeff Abercrombie left, and the subsequent appearance of a tall man who, at first, claimed to be from Immigration and Customs. Based on the physical descriptions, Kate was certain the fake cops were Mikhail and a new player, and the bogus immigration man was Richard White.

After the superintendent had given Kate the full story, they went up to the fourth floor. The son's apartment looked much like the mother's house—anything and everything that might conceal a notebook had been broken, ripped apart, upended. Kate did a quick walkthrough of the wreckage to make sure there were no dead or injured bodies, then called out the CSU, Tommy Li, and Wayne DeSilva. And as she ended the call, her phone rang. "D'Angelo," she said.

It was Chuck Foley, and he dropped a bomb. "I just heard from Ruby Abercrombie. She had the book all along, in a safe deposit box, and about an hour ago she handed it over to Richard White and a young surgeon who stuck an ink pen in her son's chest and saved his life."

"Wow," Kate said, dumbfounded by the thought of sticking an ink pen into someone's chest, and excited to know that David McBride had come out of the woodwork. "McBride," she said, "he's the surgeon."

"I'm going to the hospital now to see if they have security cam footage of him and White. I'll let you know what I find."

"Thanks," Kate said. "The son, Jeffery—is he gonna be okay?"

"The doctors aren't too optimistic."

"I'm sorry to hear that. Mind if I pay you another visit?"

"You know where to find me."

- 26 -

Kate had spent the second day of the McBride investigation in Connecticut questioning a skittish elderly woman, then sifting through the wreckage of her son's apartment in midtown, then back to Connecticut for a second round of questions with the same skittish elderly woman who had just come face to face with David McBride and Richard White. Detectives from the Passaic County Prosecutor's Office, along with Manhattan South Homicide, went to see Linda Turnbull—who was doing okay—then questioned the bartender from the Elbow Room and everyone from NuLife, with one notable exception—the CFO Samuel Keating, whom they couldn't find. Chuck Foley and his men canvassed Ruby Abercrombie's neighborhood and reviewed the security camera footage from the Litchfield County Medical Center ER, which showed nothing more than the top of a fedora and the hood of a hoodie. Tommy Li, Wayne DeSilva, and a handful of uniformed cops canvassed the area around the meatpacking warehouse, reviewed surveillance cam footage of McBride climbing from a manhole on Gansevoort, interviewed a couple of witnesses who saw the same, and reviewed additional footage of McBride climbing into a black Mercedes S500 on Tenth Avenue near West 16th. And as the sun set over the tristate area, all of these detectives came together in a shiny white conference room at Manhattan South to share their findings.

Now the sunset was a distant memory, replaced by the cold of a February night, and Kate was back at her desk in the cramped, dingy squad room of the 13th Precinct. She added a Splenda to her third cup of coffee of the evening and gave it a stir. Turnbull's murder investigation was just over thirty-six hours old, and it was a statistical fact that the probability of solving a murder decreased by half after the first forty-eight. The task force had suspects, descriptions, witnesses, theories, and some solid leads, but the leads were taking her nowhere. She believed she was dealing with a spy vs. spy scenario, and when spies did not want to be found, they disappeared into the cold.

Kate took a legal pad from a desk drawer and started jotting notes. Spy number one, Richard White, she wrote. About six months ago, insinuates himself into NuLife as a bogus member of the scientific advisory board. Gets close to Turnbull. Wants to steal Turnbull's trade secrets. A corporate spy stealing information. For whom? For sale? What was McBride's role in this, if any?

Spy number two, Mikhail. He turns the CFO Sam Keating and works through him to steal Turnbull's secrets. A Russian corporate spy. Working for a private firm? Working for the mother country?

Neither man gets what he needs—the book—and when Turnbull is murdered, the race is on to find it. And now Richard White has it, but what is he going to do with it?

On a new line, Kate wrote "Who is Richard White?" and underlined it.

All of those who had described him had provided a similar physical description—a tall but otherwise generic-looking Caucasian male with no distinguishing features or mannerisms. The sketch artist would soon have a likeness to work with.

Kovalenko, on the other hand, had said a couple of things about Richard White that had intrigued Kate. He'd said White possessed a highly tuned ear for language and dialects. Based on a brief exchange, Richard White had been able to determine that Kovalenko was from Belarus, and not just the country, but a region of the country near the Russian border. And then there was the threat made by White that he was not from Immigration, but—Kate checked her notes—Immigration's nasty cousin, and he, White, could manufacture evidence linking Kovalenko to Russian mobsters, Islamic terrorists, or even Chechen separatists. If he called the police, White had told Kovalenko, he would face deportation, or worse. And then he tells Mrs. Abercrombie he's with the Justice Department and shows her an ID.

So, if Richard White was a government entity, to which agency did he belong? Who was Immigration's nasty cousin? Who had the ability to create credible evidence that Immigration, or the courts, would act upon and deport or prosecute an individual? Of course, the CIA and NSA were built around identifying threats to homeland security, but the FBI also had its own robust counterterrorism department. An individual in any one of these agencies could manufacture evidence that would stand up to careful scrutiny. It was time to make some phone calls and rattle the cages.

- 27 -

It was now dark. David reached up and turned on the passenger-side reading light as Mr. White drove the Mercedes south on State Route 63—an unlit, remote, two-lane highway. They needed to link up with I-95, which would take them back to Manhattan.

David opened the marbled composition notebook titled Low Level Laser Therapy. He thumbed through the pages for about ten minutes then looked up at Mr. White. "This is pure genius," David said. "Andrew Turnbull figured out that if you add microscopic gallium arsenide crystals to the organ-growing broth and the perfusate, and then expose the crystals to an electric current, they'll emit photons of light in the near infrared spectrum. These photons can then be used by the cells of the developing organ to generate ATP."

"That's how they made the jump from ferret organs to the pig scaffold," Mr. White added.

David waggled the book in front of Mr. White. "We now have everything we need to grow a human kidney in the laboratory. And when we're done? When we have a new kidney for Heather? I'm going to copy all the books and send them to every university-affiliated organ fabrication lab in the country. No way is Petrovsky getting his hands on this stuff. If a privately-held company patents this technique and takes it to market, there won't be any competition—"

Bright light flooded the interior of the Mercedes.

David turned and looked out the rear window.

Headlights, gaining quickly.

"Hang on!" David said as the car rammed them from behind, sending a shockwave through the Mercedes. Mr. White fought the steering wheel, keeping them on the road. The other car fell back about twenty yards, sped up and rammed them again, this time sending the Mercedes into a spin, tires screeching, and off the side of the road. They careened down a steep embankment, mowing down small trees and undergrowth, slamming into the trunk of a large tree, bouncing off and slamming into another. The air bags exploded out of the steering column, dashboard, and door panels, a haze of white powder filling the air. They hit another tree, hard on the driver's side. The sound of shearing metal and breaking glass formed a sickening noise. Then they came to rest at the bottom of a deep ravine. The engine had died, but the headlights and tail lights remained illuminated, giving the surrounding trees and undergrowth an eerie glow.

"What the fuck!" David said, rubbing his leg. The thigh with the gunshot wound had erupted in pain. He looked over at Mr. White, who was covered in shattered glass. "You okay?"

"My legs are pinned."

Mr. White tried the door. It didn't budge. "Help me get out. Petrovsky's gonna come down here and kill us for that book." He then tapped the base of his skull, just behind his right ear—three quick taps, followed by three slow taps, followed by three quick ones.

"What are you doing?" David asked.

"Later. Just get me out of here."

David pushed the deflated airbag out of his face, undid his seatbelt and climbed out of the car, book in hand, which he slipped inside his coat, then limped around to the driver's side. The left front quarter panel and driver-side door were caved in, the window gone. David pulled on the handle as Mr. White hit the inside of the door with his shoulder. Nothing.

"Can you climb over the console and go out the passenger side?" David asked.

"I don't know."

David started for the other side of the car when he heard leaves rustling and twigs snapping. Two, maybe three, people were coming down the embankment. He hurried around and leaned into the car. "They're here. Do you have any weapons?"

"There's a handgun in the glove box."

David looked for the glove compartment, but the airbag had blown apart that side of the dashboard.

The sound of snapping twigs and crunching leaves grew closer.

David climbed from the car and turned an ear toward the embankment. Now it sounded like three men had spread out and were coming down the hill. They made no effort to conceal their presence.

"I can't find the gun," David whispered loudly. "Is there anything else? Something in the trunk, maybe?"

"I'm not sure. Take a look."

Mr. White popped the trunk, then continued trying to free himself.

David pulled the liner from the floor and searched the spare tire compartment. There was nothing that could be used as a weapon, but he did find a couple of road flares and an aerosol can. He held it up to the light. Fix-Your-Flat. The same stuff he had used to fix his bicycle tires when he was a kid. It had a nozzle like a can of whipped cream, and it sprayed a pressurized foam that sealed the leak and inflated the tire at the same time. He checked the label, and there it was, what he had hoped to see: flammable.

David stepped outside the halo of light given off by the Mercedes and moved behind a tree, the footsteps now very close. He peered into the darkness, toward the crunching and snapping, but saw nothing. He shoved the Fix-Your-Flat into his coat pocket, took the cap off the flare and struck it against the igniter. The flare hissed to life. It glowed brilliantly, sending a plume of sulfur-laden smoke into the night air while lighting up the hillside and the canopy of leafless trees overhead. He held it at arm's length like a flashlight and turned in a semicircle. Straight ahead of him, maybe fifteen feet away, stood Mikhail Petrovsky. To either side of Petrovsky, spaced about twenty feet apart, two other men.

Petrovsky shielded his eyes from the red glow of the flare. "Is that the famous Dr. McBride?" he said as he raised his gun and pointed it at David.

"Does it bother you that you and your goons almost killed Jeffery Abercrombie?"

"He had numerous opportunities to give us we wanted, and he failed. I hope you don't fail us, Doctor."

"We don't have the book, so why don't you turn around and climb back up to your car."

"But you do have it. I followed the big guy's mother and your friend"—Petrovsky waving his gun at the Mercedes—"to a bank not too far from her home. I'm fairly certain they were not there to make a deposit."

Petrovsky moved toward the wrecked Mercedes, his gun alternating between David and Mr. White, who, in the dim light of the car interior, could be seen struggling to free his legs. David took the aerosol can from his pocket, held the nozzle close to the flare and sprayed a cloud of flaming foam. He focused the spray on Mikhail Petrovsky for a few seconds, aimed at the other men, then sprayed Petrovsky again until the can was empty. They dropped their guns as burning clumps of foam adhered to hands, arms, and faces. And as their clothing caught fire, they fell to the ground and frantically rolled in the dirt, screaming in horror.

David dropped the can and the flare and ran over to the Mercedes. He reached in, hooked his arms under Mr. White's and pulled him out of the car. Mr. White tried to stand, but his left leg buckled under him. "My ankle, I think it's broken."

"Put your left arm over my shoulders. Use me as a crutch."

"We'll never get back up the hill."

"Then let's follow the ravine downhill. It's our only choice."

As they hobbled away from the carnage of a wrecked car and three burning men crumpled on the ground, Mikhail Petrovsky called out. "Both of you are dead," he screamed, "but you, McBride, you will suffer in unimaginable ways."

"How are we gonna get out of this clusterfuck?" David asked.

"All we need to do is find a road," Mr. White said. "Any road."

- 28 -

Petrovsky worked his way onto his elbows and knees, then struggled to get to his feet without using his hands. His face, scalp, and
palms were burning as if covered by thousands of stinging wasps.
He checked on the other two men, who were now standing. "Can
you walk?" he said, his voice raspy with secretions. He launched into
a violent coughing fit.

"Yes," their voices also raspy and wet.

They started up the steep hillside, their feet slipping in the
dense layers of moldering leaves, their hands in too much pain to
grasp the small trees and saplings that would've otherwise provided
help. They fell to their elbows and knees, crawling like infants,
but the leaves—dry and crunchy layered on top of wet and rot-
ting—made traction impossible. For every foot of upward progress,
they slid downhill two feet, wheezing and coughing and groaning
in pain.

- 29 -

The farther David and Mr. White moved down the ravine and away from the lights of the car, the more their eyes adjusted to the darkness. It was a clear night with a three-quarter moon, and before long they were able to see the larger obstacles on the ground. That's not to say it was easy going. A thick layer of leaves covered smaller rocks and tree branches, and dense clumps of undergrowth forced them to veer from the dry streambed they were following. Each time they would stumble and put full weight on their banged-up limbs—David's twelve-day-old gunshot wound in his right thigh, and Mr. White's possibly broken left ankle—they would mutter and curse and drop f-bombs through clenched teeth. Well, David did, anyway. Mr. White was more stoic, suffering in silence. And after twenty minutes of stumbling, near falls, and pain radiating from his thigh to the rest of his body, and after twenty minutes of agonizing over his dead wife and unborn child, his medically comatized father, the vicious murder of his former mentor thirty-six hours ago, and the intentional, even wanton destruction of human flesh using an incendiary device—after all of this, David McBride—Doctor David McBride—who had taken the Hippocratic oath and had sworn to first do no harm, sat down on a rock and vomited.

"Jesus," Mr. White said. "Are you okay?"

"No, I'm not," David replied. "I just inflicted severe burns on three men—burns that may be fatal. The lining of their tracheas could be swelling shut and cutting off air flow as we speak. And if they live long enough to get to the hospital, the skin on their hands and faces will be sloughing off in sheets, and their scalps will be charred, and their hair singed down to the follicles. I've seen this many times, and it's gruesome, and the smell is sickening, and if they survive the initial trauma, and then survive months of wound care and skin grafts, and they don't die from infection and sepsis, they'll be hideously deformed monsters for the rest of their lives."

"It was us or them," Mr. White said. "Petrovsky was going to kill me *and* you."

"What if we had just given him the book? I know what's in it. I should've just handed it over instead of torching them."

"He would have killed us anyway. Last night at Mrs. Abercrombie's house, I tried to reason with him. I told him if we found the book first, we would copy it and then give it to him, but only if he agreed to do the same if he found it. He said no. His client does not want anyone else to have this technology. There is no doubt in my mind that once he had the book in his hands, he would have murdered us. Just like you saved Jeff Abercrombie's life earlier today, you saved our lives tonight."

David wiped his mouth with the sleeve of his coat. "Can't say I'm feeling very heroic."

"With you, me, and Andrew Turnbull dead, nobody other than Jeff Abercrombie would know Turnbull's secret, so they would've killed him too. The way I see it, you saved Jeffery Abercrombie's life twice, and now you can disseminate this knowledge unimpeded by sole proprietorships and patents."

"All right. I'm a goddamn hero. Now let's get out of here." With great difficulty, David got up from his rock. "But before we go, let me examine your ankle." With even greater difficulty, David sat down on his rock.

Mr. White used a tree for balance and lifted his left foot. David moved Mr. White's pant leg up out of the way and felt the ankle. Not swollen. When David pushed on the thick bones that make up the ankle joint—the lateral and medial malleoli—the pressure did not elicit pain. David flexed the foot up and down, everted and inverted it, rotated it side to side. Full range of motion with no pain. Using his fingertips, David pushed hard on the tibia, the larger of the two bones that make up the lower leg. No pain. He pushed on the fibula, the smaller of the two bones, and about three inches above the ankle he elicited a significant pain response.

Mr. White jerked his leg away. "Damn! That's it. That's where it hurts."

A slight grin creased David's lips. Finally, some emotion from the guy. "You have a broken fibula," he said. "Not a broken ankle."

"What's the difference?"

"Your ankle joint is stable. It hurts to walk because the ends of the fractured fibula are grinding against each other when you take a step. But the fibula is not a weight-bearing bone, so even though it's causing pain, there won't be any permanent damage. The tibia supports all the weight, and it's intact."

"So I just need to buck up and handle it?"

"Basically," David replied.

- 30 -

After a herculean effort, Petrovsky finally reached the road. He struggled to move air, every breath accompanied by a high-pitched wheeze, every few breaths punctuated by long fits of coughing that produced clumps of soot-tinged sputum. The stinging in his hands and face had intensified as he exerted himself and now bordered on the unbearable. He struggled to his feet and walked toward the battered BMW.

As he sat in the car trying to catch his breath, he debated if he should switch on the interior lights and look at himself in the mirror. The severity of his injuries were not going to alter his course of action, but he had to see the damage. He turned on the light.

The face staring back at him was horrifying. Patches of charred skin alternated with large blisters and areas resembling a severe sunburn. The hair on the front half of his scalp had been burned down to the follicles, the top of his head looking like three-day-old stubble on scorched white skin. He held his hands up to the light. His fingers were blistered, double in size, and had the appearance of sausages filled with bloody fluid. The palms and backs of his hands had swelled into tense, fluid-filled sacs on the verge of rupturing. His coat was blackened and burned but remained intact, undoubtedly protecting his arms and upper body. But the worst thing of all was the smell—burnt wool, burnt skin, burnt hair. He lowered the windows and breathed in the cold night air. Another coughing fit. More sputum. He spit into the gravel.

Loud wheezing from the side of the road signaled the arrival of the other two men. The BMW was now running, and they looked like the walking dead as they staggered through the headlights, their clothing tattered and burned, their faces charred and blistered.

Petrovsky called them over and told them to hold up their hands. Viktor's were burned the least.

"Can you bend you fingers?" Petrovsky asked.

"I think so," Viktor replied.

"Okay. Get in the front."

Viktor went around and climbed in the front passenger seat, Anatoly into the back, all three men wheezing and coughing.

"Open my laptop and go to the bookmarks," Petrovsky said. "You'll find one labeled Topo Maps."

A few moments later, Viktor had pulled up a topographical map of the region.

"Enlarge the area we're in and show it to me."

Viktor did so and turned the screen toward Petrovsky.

"We have to find where the ravine intersects the road. That's their plan. They'll come to the highway and follow it until they get help."

Petrovsky studied the map. "There," he said, more to himself than the other men. About a mile and a half from their location, the highway crossed over the ravine. McBride and Whitestone would be moving slowly, Petrovsky figured. He should be able to get there and intercept them.

"Aaaaahhhhh fuck," he screamed as he shifted the car into gear and gripped the wheel with his blistered hands. "I'm gonna get that book and put those fuckers in a deep, dark hole."

After another forty minutes of stumbling, cursing, grunting, groaning, and pain radiating everywhere, David said, "By the way, Fix-Your-Flat? Sitting next to a perfectly good spare?"

"Redundancy equals safety and efficiency."

"What're you, a Boy Scout? Always be prepared?"

As the word *prepared* left his mouth, David noticed two red dots dancing on his sternum, and two others fixed to Mr. White's.

"Freeze!" shouted a voice from the darkness. "Hands on top of your heads. Fingers laced."

They both complied, Mr. White wobbling and grimacing as he bore full weight on his injured leg, David's heart rate jumping into overdrive.

"Identify yourself," said the voice.

"84-5150-68-812," Mr. White stated.

Silence.

Moments passed.

David thought he could hear someone repeating the number sequence.

"What is this?" David whispered.

"The help," Mr. White replied.

"Around the rugged rock," called out the voice.

"The ragged rascal ran," Mr. White answered.

"Stand down," ordered the voice.

Mr. White lowered his arms and grasped David's shoulder.

"What's with the tongue twister?" David asked as he helped Mr. White regain his balance.

"If I had said 'she sells seashells' instead, that would have signaled I'm under duress, and they would have put eight or ten slugs through your heart."

Four ghostly figures, laden with body armor and night-vision goggles, emerged from the brush, their weapons now pointed at the ground.

"Are you being pursued?" one of them asked.

"No," Mr. White said.

"Is anyone injured?"

"I have a broken bone in my leg, but I can walk on it."

"We have vehicles waiting about a hundred yards from here. We can help you if you need assistance."

Mr. White allowed one of the soldiers, or special ops, or whatever they were, to support him as he navigated the final stretch of dry streambed. David fell into step behind Mr. White, with one of the spec ops guys walking alongside him. The third man led the way, the fourth brought up the rear. About ten minutes later they came upon a pair of black Humvees.

- 32 -

Petrovsky slowed the car and turned off the headlights as they approached the bridge that spanned the ravine. To his surprise, a pair of black Humvees were parked on the side of the highway just past the far end of the bridge. He pulled off the road about fifty yards away and parked the BMW out of sight.

He wondered if Richard Whitestone had been able to call for help. Matching Humvees, parked in the very spot where the ravine intersected the road? Why else would they be there? This was not a random occurrence, not out here in the sticks of Connecticut. Until proven otherwise, he had to assume Whitestone and McBride had called for assistance, and two vehicles meant at least four people. He was in no shape to wage a battle, so he would have to adopt plan B.

Another coughing fit erupted. He buried his face in the sleeve of his coat, trying to mute the noise. It seemed endless, more and more sputum, and each attempt to catch his breath made the coughs deeper and harsher.

When the fit abated, he sent Viktor to the trunk of the car to retrieve a pair of night-vision goggles. Viktor returned to the driver's window, goggles in hand.

"You won't be able to strap these to your burned head," Petrovsky said. "Can you just hold them like binoculars?"

Viktor gave it a try. "Yes. This will work."

"Okay. Go down the road and look at the Humvees. See if anyone is inside or standing around outside. Stay on the shoulder close to the trees so nobody spots you."

Viktor did so, and minutes later he returned, short of breath and wheezing after walking up the slight incline. "There is nobody."

"Good. Get two GPS trackers and plant one on each vehicle, but don't activate them."

"Don't act—"

"Do not turn them on," Petrovsky said.

Viktor took what he needed from the trunk and disappeared down the road. Fifteen minutes later he was back.

"All set?" Petrovsky asked.

"Yes," Viktor replied.

Petrovsky held up his hands and examined them, front and back. Some of the blisters had ruptured, and strips of skin were peeling away. He said to Viktor, "You drive."

As Petrovsky came around and slowly lowered himself into the passenger seat, another fit erupted. He leaned out the door, coughing and spitting into the gravel. Eventually, he caught his breath and leaned back in the seat. Viktor closed the door, went around to the driver side, and the BMW quietly pulled away and drove south toward I-95 and the Connecticut Turnpike.

Two of the special ops soldiers helped Mr. White climb into a Humvee. He thanked them and said, "Do you guys have an RF detector? Can you sweep both of these vehicles for GPS trackers?"

One of them said they did, and a few minutes later he was checking the undercarriages of both Humvees with a device much like the one Mr. White had used on his own car a couple of days ago.

"All clear," said the man who had performed the sweep.

"Very good. Thank you," replied Mr. White.

David said, "You really think Petrovsky was able to climb that steep hill, get in his car, drive down here and crawl around on the ground to plant GPS devices on two different vehicles?"

"No," Mr. White replied. "I think it's highly unlikely, but not impossible."

- 34 -

The front end shimmied wildly as Viktor took the damaged BMW up the sweeping on-ramp and onto I-95, heading west toward New York City. Petrovsky struggled to lift his head off the seat and ask Victor where they were.

"Interstate," Viktor said between wheezes.

Gasping for enough air to form words, Petrovsky told Viktor to pull into the next service plaza.

Over the past hour the wheezing had become constant, high-pitched, and raspy. Each breath was like trying to suck air through a straw, and the coughing fits were relentless. Same for the other two men, Anatoly barely alive in the back seat, Viktor fighting to remain alert enough to keep the car on the road. Ten minutes later they exited the turnpike at the Milford service plaza.

Petrovsky said, "Find -*gasp*- isolated -*gasp*- place -*gasp*- to park. Not -*gasp*- under -*gasp*- lights."

While Viktor was parking on the fringe of the lot, Petrovsky started coughing again. He hacked up a large glob of sputum and spit it into a handkerchief. It was now streaked with blood. He and Viktor exchanged worried looks.

Petrovsky had Viktor open the laptop and browser and told him which bookmark to select. Enough time had passed to allow Whitestone and McBride to get to the Humvees, and for the drivers of the vehicles to sweep for GPS trackers, if they were so inclined. When the website opened, Petrovsky took the device into his lap. His fingers unbending and oozing blister fluid, he struggled to enter his user name and password. Once logged in he clicked

"Serial Numbers," selected the two at the top of the list and clicked "Activate." He then navigated to a page titled "Live Tracking."

"There," Petrovsky pointing at the screen.

The Humvees had gone north into Massachusetts.

"Now we -*gasp*- track them -*gasp*- find where -*gasp*- they hide."

Mikhail Petrovsky coughed another glob of sputum into the handkerchief, this one mostly blood. He closed the laptop, dialed his phone and said, "Petrovsky -*gasp*- plus two -*gasp*- need help. Severe -*gasp*- burns -*gasp*- head -*gasp*- face." And he somehow found the strength to follow that with Milford service plaza, Connecticut turnpike, between exits 40 and 41. Then he passed out.

- 35 -

The Humvee pulled into the parking garage of the Upper East Side safe house and dropped David and Mr. White at the private elevator. Mr. White went through his biometric regimen—the retina scan, the cesium implant in the forearm, the thing about the ragged rascal—and the door promptly opened. Once inside the penthouse, they went straight to the kitchen. Mr. White leaned his crutches in the corner and carefully lowered himself onto a chair, grimacing as he did so. David grabbed two beers from the refrigerator, hobbled over to the table and put one of them in front of Mr. White. "Maybe I should go with a cup of coffee," he said. "I swallowed two Percocets a couple of hours ago."

"So did I," David said, "but if we don't drive or operate any heavy machinery, we'll be fine." He slowly sat down, also grimacing as he bent his swollen leg.

It was now 8:30 in the morning. The Humvees had picked them up around midnight, and after driving north into Massachusetts, they had been taken to an under-the-radar medical clinic where some kind of black-ops physician had X-rayed Mr. White's leg. The diagnosis? Nondisplaced fracture of the fibula. The treatment? A pair of crutches and a bottle of Percocet. They then met with a high-ranking member of the group for a debriefing. The whole situation had a paramilitary feel to it—an isolated compound out in the woods, none of the men wore any insignias or other identifiers on their fatigues—and David wondered if this outfit was sponsored by the United States government, or if its existence was even legal.

Either way, he now understood the enormous scope of Mr. White's resources.

The officer, if that's what he was, told Mr. White his team had located the crash site and were extracting the wrecked Mercedes. He added that no casualties had been found.

Mr. White offered no explanation of what had happened, nor had anyone asked. The officer seemed uninterested in the circumstances leading up to the crash or the events that followed. He seemed concerned only with Mr. White's—and by proxy—David's safety and eliminating all traces of the confrontation. In fact, during the debriefing David had not been questioned, or even acknowledged. Early on he had borrowed a stocking cap from one of the soldiers, had pulled it low on his head and had tried to remain as inconspicuous as possible.

David popped the caps off both bottles and took a long drink of his. The warmth of the early morning sun felt good on his back, but the throb in his leg was intensifying, and he noticed Mr. White struggling with every small movement. "Drink up," David said, pointing at the bottle of Heineken. "It will help with the pain. That, and some ice."

Mr. White had stocked the freezer with bags of ice two days ago when David first moved in. Mr. White propped his leg up on a chair, and David laid one of the bags on the area over the fracture. He then elevated his own leg and placed a bag on his thigh. Now that pain-relieving drugs were circulating, cold beer was being ingested, and ice induced cold was blunting the inflammation in his leg, David said, "Okay. Questions. Who were those guys, and what's that thing behind your ear?"

"They are ex-military, mostly special ops, who are unofficially under contract to the U.S. government."

"Unofficially, as in off the books."

"Yes," Mr. White said. "They are private security contractors. If the United States government, its military, or its security agencies have an unsavory or classified situation to deal with on domestic soil, these guys are called in."

"They're fixers for the federal government," David added.

"Exactly. If you have an incapacitated senator in a hotel room with a hooker, they will extract the senator and clean up the mess. If any member of the nation's security or federal law enforcement agencies are working undercover and find themselves in danger, a team can be deployed to locate and recover."

David shifted his weight and took a swig off his beer, his leg really throbbing now. "So last night you give them your secret ID number, and that identifies you as NSA on a classified mission."

"Not exactly. All they know is my number and duress question—the ragged rascal tongue twister. They don't know my name or the agency for which I work. I remain anonymous."

"Is the raggedy rascal your favorite animal?"

"What?" Mr. White replied.

"Nothing," David said. "The guys in the Humvees, how did they find us so fast?"

"These units are stationed all over the country, particularly in the Washington-New York corridor, where the majority of government personnel are concentrated. We can't deploy SEAL teams to deal with domestic situations, so we have these groups on call."

"And all you did was tap the thing behind your ear. Three short, three long, three short. Morse code for SOS."

"Yes. A central monitoring station received the distress signal and began tracking the GPS coordinates. As soon as we started moving down the ravine, the team was able to follow our direction of travel and identify the nearest road that would intersect our route."

"So what is it—the thing you were tapping?"

"It's primarily a GPS microchip that's been implanted on the knob of bone just behind my right ear. The chip has two modes—track, or send help. It's part of a DARPA project."

"DARPA?" David asked.

"The Defense Advanced Research Projects Agency. They are the research arm of the Department of Defense. They plan to implant these devices in ground troops, snipers, pilots—anyone that engages the enemy, even intelligence agents. The chip would be in track mode at the outset of a mission, and if trouble should arise, a distress signal can be sent."

Mr. White shifted in his chair and adjusted the bag of ice on his leg.

David took another healthy sip from his bottle of Heineken. "What do you think happened to Petrovsky and his men?" he asked.

"They must have climbed up to their car and gone for help," Mr. White replied.

"I doubt they would've been able to get up that steep hill, let alone drive a car."

"Perhaps Petrovsky has a support network of his own, akin to what we had."

"Maybe," David said, "but they would need a trauma center with a burn unit. They'd need intensive emergency care. Their injuries aren't the sort of thing that can be treated in someone's back office."

"I'll check back with the various hospitals this morning and see if any severe burns have been admitted. In the meantime, I think we can both use a shower and a nap. So get some sleep, use the rest of the day to organize the lab and review the books, and let's reconvene tomorrow and discuss our strategy for initiating the organ growing process."

"And getting my father out of that hellhole."

"Of course. Your father and my daughter are now our highest priorities."

- 36 -

Mikhail Petrovsky awoke to a vague state of black nothingness, then an onslaught of pain and confusion. His face and hands were stinging like a million pins and needles, his eyes were taped shut, and it felt like he had a garden hose passing through his throat and into his lungs. A machine pumped air in and out, expanding his chest against his will. He thrashed back and forth, trying to get his hands free so he could rip the tube out of his mouth, but they were tied down.

He couldn't see.

He couldn't speak.

He couldn't move.

But he could hear.

Alarms were pinging and chirping, and then the sound of a woman's voice. "Calm down, Mr. Williams. You're in the burn unit at Southern Connecticut Medical Center."

Petrovsky felt the woman stroking his forearm.

"I'm nurse Thompson. You've suffered severe burns of your hands and face, and your trachea and lungs are damaged as well. That's why you're on a ventilator, a breathing machine. Try to relax or the ventilator can't do its job, and your heart rate is too high. That's what those alarms are for. Do yourself a favor and calm down."

He couldn't calm down. The tube in his throat and the pain on his face were unbearable. He thrashed and pulled against the restraints. The alarms chirped and pinged, increasing in volume and frequency.

"How about a nice big dose of morphine," Nurse Thompson said, and about twenty seconds later, everything went black.

37

NSA deputy director Mitch Crawford had just returned to his desk after a morning briefing when his secretary buzzed him. "I have one of our liaison officers on the line," she said.

"With regards to?"

"An outside inquiry made last evening. An NYPD detective is investigating a case that may have ties to the agency."

"Put him through."

The officer introduced himself to Crawford and briefed him on the context of the inquiry.

"We have tens of thousands of employees," Crawford said. "It's very likely there are a few Richard Whites in the mix, it's such a generic name. This is related to the kidney snatcher thing going on up there?"

"Yes sir."

"And why are you bothering me with this?"

"According to protocol, when an outside agency makes an inquiry regarding possible data breaches or other types of illegal activity, those inquiries are to be passed on to the division or department—"

"I know the procedure, but I don't have a Richard White under my command."

"No sir, but you do have a Richard Whitestone."

"Yes, but why would he—"

Crawford paused.

The liaison officer waited, then said, "Sir?"

"Never mind," Crawford said. "What did you tell the detective?"

"As per protocol, I told her I'd look into it and get back to her."

"You stonewalled her."

"Yes sir."

"Very good. The inquiry is duly noted. I'll handle it from here."

Crawford hung up and buzzed his secretary. "Get me Ken Watanabe in forensics, please."

38

After a ten-hour "nap," David showered, dressed, warmed up some leftover Chinese food, then retired to the lab to review the composition books and develop a plan for moving forward with the organ-growing process. His first priority, making sure they had all the necessary equipment. His second priority, procuring a pig kidney for use as a scaffold, along with the other biologic materials needed. Third, getting Heather's stem cells ready, and fourth, gaining a full understanding of the use of gallium arsenide crystals and the role of low-level laser therapy.

David would begin the process by organizing the lab—putting everything in its place—and by doing so, would be able to determine if they needed any additional equipment or supplies.

Finding a medical-grade porcine kidney would be easy enough. The contact information for a supplier was listed in one of the lab books.

Heather's stem cell line was ready. They had a warm water bath to thaw the cells, and even though David had no experience with thawing human stem cells, the procedure was carefully outlined in the corresponding lab book.

Finally, and most importantly, the gallium arsenide crystals. This was the only aspect of the procedure David knew nothing about. But he had the book—*The Book*—that had left a trail of carnage in its wake and might have cost four men their lives.

The damage caused by the action of thumb on syringe was not lost on David. If he hadn't murdered Andrew Turnbull it would be business as usual—NuLife intact with a lab full of human organs, a lifesaving kidney for Heather Whitestone, Linda Turnbull unharmed, Jeffery Abercrombie going about the business of biochemistry, Mrs. Abercrombie at home doing whatever she did with her spare time.

But David did kill Andrew Turnbull, and in doing so had set into motion a cascade of events resulting in dire circumstances for a number of people, some innocent, some not. But all those affected were collateral damage of a larger battle, a war, and David didn't start the war. He reacted to it, and he wasn't going to allow himself to feel guilt or regret. He had always believed that regret was an exercise in futility. It accomplished nothing. It concerned itself with the past, with things that couldn't be changed. He was only looking forward now. He wanted to show the world how to grow a kidney, and he wanted to share the technology with academic medical centers and their research programs, and he wanted to block any individual or private company from cornering the market and holding the technology hostage. He looked over at Roosevelt Island, bid his father good night, lowered the blind and went to work.

39

David had worked late into the night organizing the lab and thoroughly reviewing the composition books. He was now at the kitchen table, bathed in early morning sun, sitting across from Mr. White. They both had bags of ice draped over propped up legs, Mr. White's crutches leaning in the corner, and both were working on an assortment of bagels and cream cheese that Mr. White had picked up on the way over.

"How did it go yesterday?" Mr. White asked.

"The lab is ready. I've made a list of the biomaterials we'll need, along with a few other items. If you get everything by the end of the day, I'll get started this evening."

David handed Mr. White the list. Turnbull had meticulously documented all the suppliers he had used for his research, making it easy for David to compile the names and locations of the supply companies and the quantities needed for each item.

"Veg-f," Mr. White said, reading from the yellow legal pad. "We discussed this at length during one of the research meetings. This is the stuff that helps blood vessels grow."

"Vascular endothelial growth factor," David added.

"Crea-tin? Createen?"

"Cre-a-ti-neen. It's a by-product of muscle metabolism and is filtered out of the bloodstream by the kidneys. We'll use it to quantify the filtering capacity of our lab-grown kidney. A normal creatinine clearance means it's ready for transplant. This is the single most important value we will measure."

"Gallium arsenide nanocrystals. Nano, as in a billionth of a meter?"

"Yes. A red blood cell is six microns or six millionths of a meter, about the same size as a capillary. If the gallium arsenide crystals are micrometers in size instead of nanometers, they will clog the capillaries and block the flow of the RBCs. This, of course, would be disastrous."

"Two units of red blood cells, cross-matched with Heather's blood." Mr. White looked up from the page.

"According to Turnbull's notes," David said, "it takes about two weeks for the vascular system to fully endothelialize."

"I'm not familiar with this term."

"The endothelium is the lining of the blood vessels. It provides a slick surface that keeps platelets and blood cells from sticking to the walls and forming clots. It's the *e* in Veg-f. Vascular *endothelial* growth factor. Once the endothelium is completely formed, we can perfuse the kidney with red cells, which greatly increases oxygen delivery to the developing tissues."

"How do I get two units of Heather's blood?" Mr. White asked.

"I assume you have a surgeon standing by, ready to implant the kidney when it's ready?"

"Yes."

"And this surgeon knows the source of the organ?"

"He knows it's the product of an experimental procedure. Nothing more."

"Then ask him to supply you with two units of packed RBCs that have been cross-matched with Heather's blood. We won't need them for a couple of weeks, so you have some time to work out the details."

As Mr. White scribbled notes on the legal pad, David shifted in his chair and repositioned the bag of ice, his leg particularly painful this morning. Earlier, in the shower, he had noticed an area of redness—cellulitis—around the entrance wound, and the thigh was swollen and tight. He was fairly certain an abscess was brewing deep in the muscle.

"Nutrient media and deionized water," Mr. White continued.

"For the organ-growing broth," David said, still trying to get comfortable.

"Composition book, marbled, black and white, times one."

"I'm going to document my experience with this process."

"And finally, a porcine kidney extracellular matrix?"

"The so-called ghost organ," David said, smiling at the apt description that had taken root in the research literature. He went on to describe how a pig kidney is exposed to a detergent bath, which removes all living cells, leaving a translucent or "ghost" version of the organ. The architecture of the kidney, including the blood vessels and glomeruli—the micro-organs that produce urine—are retained, but when the cells are washed away, this also removes the antigens that would trigger an immune response in the human recipient. "All you have left is a scaffold of connective tissue elements like collagen and laminin—the extracellular matrix—and when you infuse this scaffold with stem cells, it releases chemical messengers that induce the differentiation of the cells. The glomerular matrix will tell the stem cells to differentiate into glomeruli. The lattice of vascular structures will direct the cells to grow into arteries and veins. It's a beautifully elegant system, and since the ghost organ will have been repopulated with Heather's stem cell line, her immune system will recognize it as part of *her* and will not attack it."

"Sounds like a time-consuming process," Mr. White said.

"It is, but there's a lab near Boston that provides the matrix scaffolds of a variety of organs. This is such a prolific area of research, there's enough demand to support a small company."

"I'll call ahead"—Mr. White tapping the legal pad with his pen—"and make sure all these suppliers have what we need."

"A good idea. Now, what about my father?"

"I laid much of the groundwork yesterday. We should be ready to go in three days."

"Saturday?"

"In the evening when all the staff physicians and senior residents have gone home."

"Leaving the interns to cover the wards."

"Yes."

"Well thought out," David said. "And what about Petrovsky? Did you find out anything?"

"Admitted to the burn unit at Southern Connecticut Medical Center under a false name."

"Do you know his condition?"

"Third-degree burns on his face and hands, and he's suffered severe inhalation injury and is on a ventilator."

"What about the other two?" David asked.

"They were also admitted for burns on the face and hands, but they are not on ventilators."

David leaned back, sipped his beer and pondered for a moment. Then he said, "I have a kill-two-birds-with-one-stone request."

"And that would be?"

"The burn unit will be staffed by surgical residents. Find one that you can coerce, or blackmail, or whatever it is you do, and tell him or her I have an abscess deep in my thigh that needs to be drained using local anesthesia. I suggest you make this happen soon, or I'm gonna end up in the hospital."

"And the other bird?"

"While we're there I want to see Petrovsky."

Mr. White shook his head. "Quite risky. Any particular reason?"

"I don't know. I just feel like I need to lay eyes on the man." David paused for a moment, then said, "And besides, wouldn't it be a good idea to assess his injuries, see if he's off our backs for good?"

"I can always do that with a phone call."

"The eyeball assessment trumps the phone report every time."

- 40 -

Despite a broken fibula and a rental car that wasn't quite a Mercedes S500, Mr. White did, in fact, secure everything on the list over the course of one day. And as the sun was setting outside the laboratory window, the porcine ghost kidney lay in a stainless-steel basin, resting on a layer of laparotomy sponges that had been moistened with sterile saline.

"Here we go," David said as he opened the clasp on the IV tubing.

Heather's stem cells exited the vinyl bag, descended down the tube, flowed through the renal artery and gradually transformed the translucent organ into a reddish-brown, bean-shaped kidney that was indistinguishable from its human counterpart. He then opened a second bag that infused in a retrograde manner up the ureter. The cells flowing anterograde through the artery would, in theory, seed the vascular framework, giving rise to the arteries and veins. Those cells traveling retrograde through the ureter would repopulate the collecting system—the glomeruli and renal tubules—that filters the blood and collects the urine.

After the first two units finished, David infused the third, half anterograde, half retrograde. When the bag emptied, he turned to Mr. White. "We're all in."

"Yes. All in," Mr. White repeated in a somber tone. "If it doesn't work—"

"Turnbull's documentation is meticulous," David said. "All we can do is follow the recipe and hope for the best."

Mr. White gazed into the basin for a moment. Then, "Okay. What's next?"

"Into the cylinder. The kidney will be suspended in nutrient broth maintained at 98.6 degrees Fahrenheit, and the renal artery and vein, and the ureter will be secured to their respective cannulae."

"The three plastic tubes passing through the wall of the cylinder."

"Yes. The arterial cannula will deliver oxygenated blood, once the endothelium has matured. The venous cannula will remove the deoxygenated blood. The third one will drain the urine."

"When do you start infusing the crystals?"

"They're in the broth now, at twenty parts per million. These electrodes"—David pointing at two metallic strips inside the cylinder—"will generate a current that will induce the crystals to emit light in the near-infrared spectrum. In one week we'll start circulating the broth through the vascular system, and the gallium arsenide will be added to the perfusate."

"One last question, if you don't mind." Mr. White gestured toward the rest of the lab. "These are not exactly sterile conditions, and this kidney is ultimately going into Heather's body. How do you keep it from getting contaminated?"

"Supercritical carbon dioxide." David pointed to a pair of tubes passing into the cylinder near its base. Externally, they were routed through a pump, an oxygenator, and a filter sitting on the bench top. "This is a recirc system like you might use for your home aquarium. When the broth exits the tank, it will pass through a series of carbon filters that will remove all contaminants down to the size of a virus. Then, after the broth is warmed and oxygenated, it will be infused with supercritical CO_2 and paracetic acid before returning to the tank. The CO_2 and the acid will circulate around and through the kidney, killing any viruses and bacteria that have not been removed by the filters."

"Extraordinary," Mr. White said. "But one more question, if I may. What is supercritical CO_2?"

"What're you, an amateur chemist?"

"I'm just interested."

"When carbon dioxide is heated to 87.9 degrees Fahrenheit or greater, and subjected to a pressure of seventy-three atmospheres, it exists in a state that is no longer a gas, but not quite a liquid. It's described as a supercritical fluid. And for reasons that are poorly understood, CO_2 in this state, combined with paracetic acid, is toxic to bacteria and viruses. But since these are weak acids, they won't harm the kidney. Make sense?" David asked.

"More or less. Thank you."

"Okay. Time to put this baby into its womb."

With gloved hands and long instruments, David lowered the kidney into the nutrient media, slipped the artery, vein, and ureter onto their respective cannulae, and secured each with silk ligatures. The osmolarity of the solution provided a level of buoyancy that allowed the kidney to sit within the nutrient broth with no tension on the vessels or ureter. He then placed the lid on the cylinder, clamped it shut, pressurized the system, and turned on the electrodes. "I think this calls for a couple of beers. You mind?" David nodding toward the kitchen.

While Mr. White hobbled down the hall, David stepped back and admired the sight before him—the reanimated kidney gently swaying in the amber-colored nutrient media, the glass cylinder with its gleaming stainless-steel fittings and clear plastic tubes coming and going and passing through pumps and filters and reservoirs. He felt a little bit like Victor Frankenstein, creating new life out of tissues and cells and chemistry and electricity, and the thought that this organ had the potential to save a life was quite satisfying. He sat down at the desk, opened the marbled composition book he had labeled "Kidney 0" and jotted his notes for the day.

Day 1:

Nutrient media mixed per protocol, poured into glass cylinder, recirculated, oxygenated, and warmed to 37 degrees C. Flow rate maintained at 2 liters per minute.

Supercritical carbon dioxide (SC-CO₂) and paracetic acid infused into recirculating growth media to eliminate viral and bacterial contaminates.

Gallium arsenide nanocrystals added to recirculating media. Will be maintained at 20 ppm.

Sterile electrodes placed in tank and turned on, creating an electric field, which will induce the GaAs crystals to emit light at a wavelength of 870nm.

- 41 -

At 2:00 a.m. the following morning, David was awakened by violent, shaking chills. The sheets were soaked with sweat, a searing pain radiated through his injured thigh, and a putrid stench filled the room. He gagged and wretched and had to cover his nose and mouth with a pillow as he limped to the bathroom and switched on the lights. A thick fluid, the color of dirty dishwater, had soaked through the scrub pants he'd been using for pajamas. The watery-pudding consistency, cadaver-gray color, and rotting-flesh smell confirmed his diagnosis: an anaerobic abscess had formed deep in his thigh and had spontaneously drained while he slept. During his residency, David had smelled every odor the human body can emit—all manner of excrement, infected body fluids, infected body cavities, infected malignant tumors, stools that were more blood than stool, tubercular lungs surrounded by pus, muscle charred down to the bone, gangrenous toes, feet, legs and arms, you name it—but nothing topped the anaerobic abscess. He had once used a chest tube to drain an anaerobic empyema on the ward instead of taking the patient to the OR, or at least into a treatment room, and the backlash from the nurses and patients was so violent he was nearly fired. Even when draining these types of abscesses in a well-ventilated operating room, coating the inside of the surgical mask with wintergreen was a necessity.

Anaerobe bacteria are normal flora of the human colon, which means the sewer water David had waded through five days ago was teeming with them. And they thrive in low-oxygen environments, like deep in an injured thigh muscle where blood flow is poor and there's decaying, necrotic tissue to feed on. After dropping from the pipe, landing on his injured leg, and disrupting the partially healed wound while submerged in anaerobe-infested water, it was no surprise that his right thigh was now full of pus.

The concern—and it was an urgent concern—was whether or not *Clostridium perfringens* was one of the offending organisms. *C. perfringens* releases an alpha toxin that causes necrosis and putrefaction of muscle, fat, and skin, and the formation of gas bubbles within the decomposing tissues—a constellation of findings known as gas gangrene. Gas gangrene is destructive, it spreads rapidly, and can cause death in a matter of hours. Treatment consists of immediate amputation of the affected limb.

David examined his leg. Although a stream of pus was oozing from the wound, and the associated cellulitis had spread, he did not see the typical pitting or orange-peel appearance of the skin, nor did he feel crepitus—the crunching of gas bubbles—when he pushed deep into the involved tissues. Maybe *Clostridium perfringens* was not present, or maybe it hadn't gained a foothold yet, but it could rear its ugly microscopic head at any time, and the other anaerobes were more than capable of wreaking limb- and life-threatening havoc of their own. Either way, the wound required urgent surgical drainage and copious irrigation, neither of which were feasible in an Upper East Side penthouse. He expressed as much pus from the wound as he could, washed the area with hot soapy water, placed a clean dressing, then went into the bedroom and called Mr. White.

- 42 -

Day 2:

Recirc system working without incident. Temp maintained at 37° C ± 1°.
 Flow rate at 2 liters per minute.
Blood gas analysis of growth media shows slightly acidic pH of 7.38 and
 O_2 saturation at 100%.
GaAs crystals maintained at 20ppm.

David wiped the sweat off his forehead with a lab towel while finishing his morning examination of the kidney and jotting down his notes. Since 2:00 a.m. he had experienced two more temperature spikes, followed by shaking chills and full-body sweats, and his leg had continued to ooze pus. He had changed the dressing and examined his leg several times since the abscess first spontaneously drained. Thankfully, still no signs of gas gangrene.

But the recurring fever spikes meant bacteria were seeping into David's bloodstream and triggering his immune system to react by raising the core temperature, a defense mechanism designed to make conditions inhospitable to the foreign invaders. Sweating and chills were the body's way of cooling down after a temperature spike, and as long as the infection persisted, the cycle would continue until the immune system was overwhelmed, the organ systems became impaired, and multi-system organ failure ensued. The clinical term for this sequence of events was sepsis, and left untreated, sepsis uniformly ended with death. Unless the abscess in David's thigh was surgically drained, he would suffer organ failure in forty-eight to seventy-two hours and would die not long after that, provided *Clostridium perfringens* and gas gangrene didn't get him first.

David wiped his forehead again and checked the time. Going on 7:00 a.m. During the 2:00 a.m. call, David had impressed upon Mr. White the gravity of the situation. Mr. White had promised David he would do what he could, as quickly as he could, with regards to finding someone to treat his leg.

About twenty minutes later, David was changing the dressing on his leg when Mr. White entered the penthouse. He hobbled up the hallway—his crutches making the repetitive clicking noise that crutches make—and stuck his head though the open bathroom door. "What is that stench?" he asked.

"That's the smell of a pending amputation unless something gets done soon."

"Everything is a go. We'll get your leg taken care of, and you can get an in-person update on Mikhail Petrovsky. The kidney?" Mr. White asked. "So far, so good?"

"It's only been twelve hours, but yes, so far so good."

- 43 -

Following a two-hour drive, David and Mr. White were once again walking—both limping, actually—into a hospital, Mr. White in his spy-gear overcoat, fedora, and crutches, and David with his fake glasses, hoodie, and increasingly unruly goatee. He was moving slow, stippled with sweat, and his skin was pale and clammy. To any health care professional in the place, this was another instance of a father dragging his opioid-addict son into the ER for treatment, but they didn't check in at the triage desk. Instead, they stood off in a corner where Mr. White pulled out one of his throwaway cell phones and made a call. A few minutes later, a young man in scrubs and a long white coat joined them. He was thin, dark-haired, and brown-skinned—from India, David surmised. His name badge read Dr. Hari Thamaviran, Yale School of Medicine, Department of Surgery. A Yale surgery resident doing a rotation at Southern Connecticut Medical Center's burn unit, and the guy was not at all happy about being dragged away from his duties, in the middle of a busy day, against his will.

"This way," he said to Mr. White.

They followed the doctor through a series of hallways until they came to an automated double door with a sign overhead that read BURN UNIT. Thamaviran pressed a plate on the wall, the doors swung open. Before they entered he turned to David. "Don't touch anything. All these burn patients are immunocompromised. Those anaerobes draining from your leg, they could spread from surface to surface and wipe out everyone."

"Yeah, I know," David replied.

They walked past three glassed-in rooms and stopped at the fourth. "This is your guy," Thamaviran said.

"Can you run through his history?" David asked.

Thamaviran glanced at Mr. White. "My attending could walk down the hall at any time."

"Then be quick about it," Mr. White said.

Hari Thamaviran paused for a moment, clearly angered by the situation. Then, "This is Mr. John Williams, a forty-one-year-old white male, found with two other white males inside an idling BMW in a parking lot off the Connecticut Turnpike three nights ago. They all had severe burns to the head, face, and hands. They all presented with inhalation injury. Mr. Williams was intubated by paramedics at the scene. The other two did not require mechanical ventilation."

"What's the extent of his burns?" David asked.

"His face, ears, and the anterior half of his scalp are mostly second degree, with patches of third degree on the cheeks, forehead, and nose. His palms are third, the back side of his hands are second."

"What does his airway look like?"

"Daily bronchoscopy has shown persistent erythema and edema of the trachea and mainstem bronchi with areas of charring and mucosal ulceration. The lobar bronchi are uninjured."

"Gas exchange is good?" David asked.

"Yes. Blood gasses have been normal."

"Mental status?"

"We're keeping him snowed. When he wakes up he is quite agitated, thrashing around, pulling at his tubes, the usual stuff."

David stepped into Petrovsky's room.

"Please," Thamaviran pleaded. "Don't touch anything."

"Yeah, yeah. I know," David said. "I just need a couple of minutes."

The room was quiet except for the crescendo-decrescendo blowing of the ventilator. Mikhail Petrovsky's entire head was wrapped in Kerlix gauze, an endotracheal tube protruding from a gap in the dressings. His hands were also wrapped in Kerlix. Thick leather restraints held his wrists and ankles to the bed rails. A nasogastric tube passed through his nose, and a triple lumen catheter had been placed into the subclavian vein under the left clavicle. A two-liter bag of milky fluid—total parenteral nutrition, otherwise known as TPN—hung from an IV pole, its contents infusing through the subclavian line. Everything Petrovsky needed from a nutritional standpoint was in that bag—protein, fats, carbohydrates, vitamins, minerals. To heal large burns and fight off infection, the body required a ramped-up calorie count and a lot of protein. If you wanted to master nutrition in the critically ill patient, you rotated through the burn unit.

David moved closer to the bed, trying to figure out why he was here, why he needed to see Petrovsky. Maybe he was hoping to experience a strong emotional reaction—sympathy, or empathy, or even guilt—toward the man he had torched, but he felt none of these. He couldn't shake the images of Mrs. Turnbull strapped to a gurney, and Jeffery Abercrombie taped to a chair and badly beaten, and perhaps it was these images that made him hold the flame-spewing can on Petrovsky a little longer than the others. He didn't know. He had simply reacted. And now here he stood, his interest in the man who lay before him purely academic.

"What about the other two?" David asked as he exited the room.

"Not nearly as bad. Their burns are in the same distribution, but mostly second degree. If they need any skin grafts, it will be minimal."

"Has anyone else come to visit?" Mr. White asked.

"Detectives from the Milford PD and the state police narcotics task force."

"What's the consensus?"

"It's unclear. The burn pattern would suggest they had been cooking meth and their apparatus exploded, but they were wearing burned street clothes, not hazmat gear, and we did not detect the usual chemical residues on these guys consistent with a meth cook."

Another fever spike hit David—his face scorching hot, his forehead beaded with sweat. He had an overwhelming desire to just lie down and close his eyes.

Thamaviran must have picked up on the cues. "We better get to the procedure room before you hit the ground." He led David around a corner into a less-traveled area of the unit.

- 44 -

The room was small but had everything they would need—an exam table, sterile surgical instruments, vials of lidocaine, bottles of saline, dressing supplies. Once inside with the door closed, Thamaviran said, "I know who you are. Good surgeon gone bad. Shot in the leg two weeks ago, and now you have an abscess." He removed a basic surgical tray from a shelf and set it on a Mayo stand. "Now that you are pale and gaunt and have changed your hair, you don't look like the photo that's been on the news, but after studying your face, I put it together."

"Nice work, Sherlock." David nodded toward the hallway. "What's he threatening you with?"

"If I go to the police, he will manufacture evidence implicating me as a jihadist planning a terror attack. He knows the names of everyone in my family and will involve them too. Can he really do that?"

"Yes."

"But I am not even Muslim. I am Hindu, and an American citizen."

"Doesn't matter. He could implicate the Pope if he wanted to. He's very resourceful."

"Then let's get to it," Thamaviran gesturing toward David's leg. "The sooner you are out of my burn unit, the better."

David dropped his pants and lay on the table.

Thamaviran examined David's thigh. The lateral aspect was swollen, red, and hot to the touch. "You have a raging cellulitis," he said. Then he gently pushed on the area between the entrance and exit wounds.

David jumped, the pain exquisite.

"No question there is pus. This is the entry?" Thamaviran asked, pointing to the anterior wound.

David nodded. "Yes."

"It is clearly infected, but the exit looks fine, so I will go in anteriorly, drain the pus, and debride the superficial necrotic tissue. Also, you need antibiotics. If I saw you in the ER, I would admit you for a course of IV Augmentin."

"How about a gram of Rocephin in the butt?"

"Not optimal, but probably okay."

Thamaviran removed his white coat, put on a pair of gloves, and draped the area around David's injury with towels, not that this was a sterile procedure, but the towels would catch the pus. He then infiltrated the skin edges and subcutaneous tissues with local anesthetic. There was no need to go any deeper. All the sensory nerves resided in the skin. The intense pain in the thigh was the result of pressure—a collection of pus walled off deep in the muscle, the definition of a loculation.

"Ready?" Thamaviran asked.

"Yes. And don't stop, even if I'm jumping and squirming."

David grabbed the edges of the table to remind himself to not reach for the doctor's hands.

Thamaviran gently touched the opening of the entry wound with the tip of his right index finger and then pushed, not fast, but steady and deep, all the way to the knuckle.

David squirmed and grit his teeth and groaned as the surgery resident rotated his finger, back and forth, deep inside the wound to break up the loculations.

When Thamaviran removed his finger, a torrent of thick, yellow-brown pus boiled up from the cavity and ran down David's thigh to the towels. The smell was horrid, both men contorting their faces with disgust.

"Jesus, that's foul," David said.

"If my attending walks down the hall and smells this, we are fucked," Thamaviran added.

"Yeah, I know. I'm sorry."

"Let's just get this done. Relax for a moment, then I'm going to milk the path of the bullet."

David let his head fall back to the table, his forehead now beaded with sweat, his thigh on fire. If he were not running from the law, this procedure would have been performed in the operating room under general anesthesia.

"Are you ready?" Thamaviran asked.

"Yes."

The doctor positioned the heel of his palm on the posterior thigh, then pushed firmly into the muscle and up toward the entrance wound, trying to express any remaining pockets of pus.

David tensed. Another stream of pus oozed from the wound. Thamaviran wiped it away with a gauze pad, pushed one more time on the thigh, then irrigated the abscess cavity using a bulb syringe and sterile saline. He flushed until the drainage went from purulent, to blood-tinged, to clear, then debrided the edges of the entrance wound. And finally, he packed the cavity by pushing a strip of iodine gauze deep into the wound with a pair of long DeBakey forceps.

When the leg was dressed and a gram of Rocephin had been injected into David's left glute, Thamaviran filled a plastic bag with dressing supplies, bottles of sterile saline, vials of antibiotics, assorted syringes, lidocaine, and the basic surgical instruments needed to debride and pack a wound.

"I put three grams of Rocephin in here," Thamaviran said as he handed David the bag. "If you have a normal immune system, a gram a day for three days should clear up the cellulitis."

"Thank you," David said, and as he accepted the supplies he felt appreciative of, and humbled by, Dr. Thamaviran's thoroughness and compassion. He also felt a heavy dose of shame for having intruded upon the young man's life and putting his career in danger. This guy *was* David about three or four years ago, putting in the long hours, doing his best work, sacrificing God-knows-what for the chance at a privileged career, and in walks the fugitive David McBride and his henchman, Mr. White. And just like two dirty dogs, they were leaving their muddy prints all over Hari Thamaviran—muddy prints that just might blow his life apart. David hoped this wasn't the case, but based on their recent track record, he was not very optimistic.

"A surgeon is at his finest when he's draining pus," David said as he pulled up his pants.

"What?" Thamaviran replied.

"William Stewart Halsted, the father of American surgery. He said the surgeon is at his finest when he's—"

"I know who Halstead is," Thamaviran said, "but I've never heard that quote."

"In any event, thanks."

"You're welcome. Just call off your dog out there."

- 45 -

"How's the leg?" Mr. White asked as they drove down Interstate 95 toward New York City. "Are you out of the woods?"

"The pus has been drained. Got some antibiotics on board. If I change the packing three times a day and inject Rocephin into my butt once a day, I'll live."

"What about Petrovsky? Is he going to survive?"

"If he avoids an overwhelming infection, he'll live, but he's looking at a long recovery, lots of skin grafts, and he's at risk for developing tracheal stenosis as his trachea heals and forms scar tissue. He won't be a problem for us anymore."

- 46 -

Saturday morning, and by all appearances and assessments, the kidney was doing well. Mr. White was putting out bagels and the usual accoutrements in the kitchen, while David jotted his notes.

Day 3:

Recirc system flow rate at 2 liters per minute. Temp 37° C ± 1°.
Blood gas analysis of growth media: pH 7.38–7.36 and O_2 sat at 100%.
GaAs crystals maintained at 20ppm.

So far, the complex system of pumps, heaters, filters, and monitoring equipment were working without incident. Perhaps when all this was behind him, he could find a job as a saltwater aquarium technician. And the leg was doing much better. It had been forty-eight hours since the abscess was drained. The cellulitis was receding, the pain was minimal, and the amount of pus seen on the dressings each time they were pulled from the depths of the wound was diminishing. Perhaps when all this was behind him, he could find a job as a surgeon.

David went to the kitchen, sat down at the table and slathered a sesame seed bagel with jalapeno cream cheese. "Are we on for tonight?" he asked Mr. White.

"Yes. Everything is a go."

"What time?"

"I'll be here at five thirty."

Five thirty-five Saturday evening, and David was about crawl out of his skin. He peered into the mirror of the master bath as he donned his thick reading glasses and hoodie. Even with the obsidian black goatee and gradually-lengthening hair, it was not much of a disguise. But David wasn't worried about that. What had his nerve endings convulsing was the impending abduction of his father from a New York City hospital, out from under the protective gaze of nurses, interns, and the NYPD. Mr. White's plan was nebulous, at best—we're going to wheel him out the back door, was all he'd say—and if it went off the rails it would end very badly, with David in prison, his father committed to Coler for the rest of his days, Mr. White headed to a federal supermax facility, and Heather's three-day-old kidney left to fend for itself. To say the stakes were high was a gross understatement. David turned off the lights, joined Mr. White in the foyer, and together they headed down to the garage where a Stony Point Ambulette was waiting.

Unlike its larger, boxier brother, the ambulette was simply a van with all but the front seats removed. There were no monitors, oxygen regulators, or cabinets full of medical supplies. There was a blood pressure cuff and stethoscope, but otherwise, it was basic transportation for those sitting in wheelchairs or lying on stretchers. And, unfortunately, it was not a panel van. Instead, it had windows running the length of the vehicle that let the passengers look out and passersby look in. For that reason, David slumped into the seat and pulled his hood tight as Mr. White maneuvered the ambulette out of the parking garage and into traffic. Mr. White in his fedora and overcoat, David in his hoodie and glasses—the fugitive and the spy out for a Saturday evening drive.

- 48 -

On the Special Dementia Unit of the Coler Rehabilitation Facility, a gaunt, unshaved man in scrubs parked his gurney next to the nurse's station and leaned on the counter. "Mr. McBride needs to go for a cat scan of his brain," he said to the lone nurse staffing the desk.

She looked up from her keyboard. "Really? On a Saturday evening? His condition hasn't changed for days."

"Got the order right here."

He placed a sheet of paper on the counter.

The nurse glanced at it, then tapped her keyboard and peered into the screen. "That's odd," she said. "Dr. Woolsey ordered this himself. I can't remember the last time an attending put his own orders into the system. That's what the residents are for." She looked at the transport orderly. "Maybe I should call him to verify this."

"Yeah, I don't know," said the orderly. "All's I *do* know is we got the CT tech in house, and she wants to get this done and get herself back to Queens. Got a kid's birthday or something goin' on. And the doc? The tech says he's at the ballet, and his phone is turned off."

The nurse studied the requisition form, then the computer screen. "I mean, the order *is* right here in the system." She glanced at the orderly, studied him for a moment. "Are you new here?"

"Just started yesterday."

He showed her the ID card hanging around his neck.

"Okay. Let's go get him."

The NYPD officer sitting outside Hal McBride's room got up from his chair as the gurney approached.

"This man needs to go for a CT of his head," the orderly said.

"Yeah?" the cop asked, directing his question to the nurse.

"Yes," she replied. "Might be a good time for you to take a break? Get some coffee? Use the restroom?"

"I'll go with you. Can't let this man out of my sight."

The orderly grinned. "Yeah, yeah. Of course. This is the father of that kidney snatcher, CEO murdering, lady-beatin' dog killer, right? But I can't let you go in with the scanner. Too much radiation and magnetism flying around in there. With your gun and handcuffs and badge and stuff, you'll have to wait in the hall."

While the officer held the door, the transport orderly wheeled Hal McBride into the room that housed the CT machine. "I can take it from here," he said to the cop. "Gimme a minute, and I'll grab you a chair."

After the door closed behind him, the orderly parked the gurney next to the scanner, grabbed a chair from the corner of the room and carried it into the hall. "We'll be about forty-five minutes," he said to the officer.

The orderly turned the lock on the door as quietly as he could, making sure it didn't generate an audible click, then went to the far end of the room and propped open a second door. After maneuvering Hal McBride around the back of the scanner and out into the hall, he quickly moved down the darkened corridor toward the ambulance bay.

The ambulette crossed over the Roosevelt Island Bridge, which terminated in a 360-degree ramp that dropped them down to Main Street. They turned right and slowly drove up Main toward Coler. Despite the labyrinth of high-rise apartments lining the only north-south thoroughfare on the island, there were no pedestrians. Perhaps the cold, David figured, or the fact that this was primarily a residential area with only a handful of businesses. They passed a couple of small restaurants and a market, but signs of life were negligible, particularly for a Saturday night.

David had never been on the island, and even though it sat in the middle of the East River and was no more than a few hundred feet from Manhattan proper, it had always been an enigma.

In medical school he had become vaguely familiar with the island's dark history. Through much of the nineteenth and twentieth centuries, Roosevelt had served as a dumping ground for New York's sick, poor, insane, crippled, and criminally minded. A lunatic asylum, a prison, almshouses for homeless men and women, a charity hospital, and a smallpox sanitarium had called Roosevelt Island home at one time or another. In the mid-1990s a chronic care and rehab facility, known as the Coler-Goldwater Hospital, was formed by the merger of two institutions—Goldwater on the southern half of the island, and Coler at its northern tip. About three or four years ago Goldwater closed its doors, leaving the Coler Rehabilitation Facility as the sole survivor in a long lineage of Dickensian public institutions.

Main Street carried them north, past a large park on one side and the east channel of the river on the other. An abrupt left-hand turn, a small sign, and the sudden appearance of a sprawling complex of multi-story, red-brick buildings indicated they had arrived at Coler. Instead of following the road to the main entrance, Mr. White made another left, which took them through the parking lot of a residential building and down a single-lane service road to the west channel of the river. He parked in front of an abandoned church that was slowly being reclaimed by the surrounding vegetation.

"What are we doing here?" David asked.

"The ambulance bay is monitored by several cameras. Our in-hospital confederate will call when he's ready for us, and we'll get in and out as quickly as possible."

"And this place?" David gestured toward the pedestrian walkway that followed the river's edge. "Any cameras here?"

"No."

"Good, because after being cooped up in that penthouse for three days, and now waiting for SEAL Team Six to rescue my father, if I don't get out and walk a little I'm gonna lose my shit."

"By all means." Mr. White checked his watch. "I don't expect the call for at least ten minutes, and we are less than a minute away."

David went down to the path and leaned on the railing. A retaining wall elevated the walkway about five feet above the water, and small waves gently lapped against the rocks at the base of the wall. Across the river, the Upper East Side rose up like a great edifice of glass, steel, and masonry. The lights of the city radiated with warmth and life. The FDR thrummed with traffic, and even though it was muted, the clamor of Manhattan could still be heard. By contrast, the pencil-thin island on which he was standing, surrounded by dark, churning water, with its empty streets, leafless trees, and hazy yellow glow of argon streetlights had an eerie, post-apocalyptic feel. The juxtaposition bordered on the supernatural.

From behind David came the sound of a slowly approaching vehicle.

He turned.

An NYPD patrol car pulled up to the ambulette and stopped. In the dim light of the car's interior, the officer could be seen tapping the screen of a dash-mounted laptop—running the plates, no doubt.

David's adrenal glands sent a surge of epinephrine swirling through his veins, his heart thumping, his senses heightening. He tried to act casual as the cop climbed from his car and cautiously approached the driver's side of the van. Mr. White lowered the window. Standing just yards away, David could hear the exchange between the two men.

"Good evening officer," Mr. White said.

"Sir," the cop replied. "Break time?"

"We have a pick-up at Coler, and we got here a little early. Thought we'd come down to the river and take in the view. Better than sitting around in a boring hospital."

"A warm hospital," added the cop.

"Yes. It is a bit nippy out here."

"Thirty-seven degrees is more than nippy. Can I see some ID please?"

"Yes sir." Mr. White pulled out his wallet and handed over his driver's license.

The cop studied it with his flashlight, then gave it back.

"He with you?" the cop nodding toward David.

"Dammit," David whispered to himself.

"My son," Mr. White said. "Still willing to help out the old man."

"Okay," said the cop. "Have a good one, and stay warm." He turned to go, then stopped. "By the way, the patient you're picking up, why are they being moved on a Saturday night? These Coler patients are all chronics, and most of them leave in a box."

"It's a male with Alzheimer's. He's become violent over the last few weeks, and earlier this evening he knocked down one of the female patients and broke her hip. The hospital wants to put him in isolation, but the family said they'd move him in with them before they'd let that happen."

"All right, then. Safe travels." The cop returned to his car and drove away.

David joined Mr. White in the van.

"That could've spelled disaster," David said. "The plates, they're legit?"

"Yes."

"And the ID you showed him?"

"New York driver's license," Mr. White said. "Not me, but it would have checked out if he had run it through the system."

"How do you do all this—the van, the ID, some guy in Coler right now wheeling my dad out of his room while—"

Mr. White's phone rang. He tapped the screen and read a text. "He's ready. I'll explain my methods later."

They pulled into the ambulance bay and backed up to the loading dock. Mr. White climbed out and opened the rear doors, and he and the orderly pushed the gurney into the back. David secured it from inside the van, taking care not to show his face to the other man.

"Any problems?" Mr. White asked as he handed the fake orderly a thick envelope.

"Like clockwork."

"How much of a head start do you think we'll have?"

"I'd say the cop's gonna get restless and start poking around in fifteen or twenty."

"Okay. Nicely done. Thank you for coming on board with such short notice."

The man held up the envelope. "Happy to help."

- 50 -

While Mr. White pulled away from Coler, David climbed into the back to examine his father. He lay flat with a pillow under his head, a blanket covering him from the neck down, eyes closed, resting quietly. Under the blanket, a hospital gown. A pole attached to the gurney held an IV infusion pump. David checked the bag and the settings—Haldol, intravenous at five milligrams per hour. He then followed the tubing under the blanket and examined his father's forearm. The IV site was clean, and the skin around it was not reddened or inflamed.

David interrupted his exam and held on as the ambulette took the 360 degree ramp up to the bridge. Once on the bridge he checked his father's blood pressure. A perfect 120/80 with a pulse rate of 72. Now it was time to assess his level of consciousness. David gently jostled his shoulders and called out to him, "Dad, are you in there? It's David. Open your eyes."

No response.

David shook him a little harder and spoke louder.

Still no response.

The ambulette made a sharp right turn, down an off-ramp and onto Vernon Boulevard in Queens. When the ride settled, David pulled down the blanket, made a fist, and rubbed his father's sternum with his knuckles.

Nothing.

He repeated the sternal rub, hard this time, "Dad. Wake up. Open your eyes," and he dug the knuckle of his index finger deep into the sternum.

Hal McBride opened his eyes and moaned, and his hand came from under the blanket and grabbed David's wrist. Purposeful movement. He felt pain. He responded appropriately. A sign of high mental function. His gaze was glassy and unfocused, and he couldn't form words, but he was in there.

David took his father's hand into his own. "Dad. If you can hear me, squeeze my hand." And he did. His fingers closed around David's.

Following a command—a sign of even higher mental function. David closed his eyes tight and fought back the tears as he felt a surge of relief. "You're with me now," he said, softening his tone. "We're taking you to a place where I can help you get back to your old self. I have one more thing to do, and then I'll let you rest. I'm going to roll you back and forth a little bit. Just relax."

David flipped back the blanket and hospital gown, exposing his father's left side. Pushing on the shoulder and brim of the pelvis, he rolled his father onto his right side so he could examine his back, sacrum, and hip for skin breakdown.

Decubitus ulcers, or bedsores, were a common complication in thin, elderly patients who were bedridden. Any bony protuberance—the hips, the heels, the coccyx at the base of the sacrum, and even the tips of the scapulae—put pressure on the overlying skin, and if unconscious or immobile patients were neglected and not log-rolled from side to side every couple of hours, the skin would break down and become necrotic. With time, the underlying muscle and fat would also die, exposing the bone. If the dead tissues were not surgically debrided, systemic infection and sepsis would follow, and in a frail, malnourished person, death was not an unusual outcome.

David was immensely relieved to find nothing but healthy skin overlying the usual trouble spots. Hats off to the team at Coler for taking good care of Hal McBride, and for that, David would always be grateful.

With his exam completed, David climbed back into the front seat. They were heading up an on-ramp onto I-495 and the Queens Midtown Expressway.

Mr. White glanced over at David. "Is he all right?"

"As good as can be expected, considering he's drowning in Haldol," David said. Then, "Who was that guy at Coler?"

"Someone who is in trouble and willing to take a big risk for big money."

"How much?"

"Fifty thousand."

"What kind of trouble?"

"He's a nurse, and he's been stealing narcotics from the hospitals where he worked, with intent to distribute. He's also a carrier of hepatitis C, which he kept hidden from his employers. He is wanted in New York, New Jersey, and Connecticut."

"You figure that will keep him from calling Crime Stoppers?" David asked. "He had to know that was my dad, and he probably recognized me. He could be calling as we speak."

"He's facing serious charges that will add up to a long sentence, so I don't think he is in any position to be interacting with the police."

"How did you get my dad out of Coler?"

"I hacked into their system, found the name of the attending physician, and used that name to order a CT scan for you father. Our fugitive nurse posed as the transport orderly and wheeled him out the back door."

"Well, I thank you for that. I was more than a little skeptical." David looked out at the borough of Queens rushing by. There wasn't much to see. One- and two-story buildings, factories, warehouses, self-storage complexes. Then he turned back to Mr. White. "How do you do it—hack into hospital computer systems, personal computers, and God knows what else?"

"The NSA has the world's largest library of zero-day vulnerabilities."

"Laymen's terms?"

"Software bugs," Mr. White said. "Operating systems and software programs are made up of tens of millions of lines of code, and the possibility that one of the myriad code writers made a mistake is one hundred percent. A zero-day vulnerability is an error that has been found but not exploited—day zero, brand new, the clock is not yet ticking. Once a zero-day security flaw is exploited, meaning someone uses it to hack the software, the clock starts ticking. It has a limited lifespan before a patch is created to fix it."

"So you tap into the NSA's collection of zero-day bugs and use what you need to hack who you want," David said.

"Yes."

"I won't even ask if this is an abuse of your authority, but aren't you once again sharing classified information with a civilian?"

"No. The U.S. government's use of software vulnerabilities to collect data and spy on its adversaries is well documented, thanks in no small part to Edward Snowden."

"Ah yes, the devil himself," David said. "One last thing—where are we going?"

"Kings Park in Suffolk County. We're going to meet a doctor, a neuropharmacologist, who specializes in withdrawal, from anything—heroin, methamphetamine, cough medicine. You name it, he can get you off of it."

"Even Haldol?" David asked.

"Yes, even Haldol."

"He'll recognize me."

"His line of business relies on complete discretion. He has treated a number of high-profile individuals, and he's never failed to maintain patient confidentiality."

"But I'm a fugitive, not the governor's degenerate son. He'll be committing a felony."

"And he will be well compensated for assuming that risk."

"How much this time?"

"One hundred and fifty thousand."

David shook his head in disbelief. "Where is all this money coming from?"

"As soon as I became aware of Andrew Turnbull's demise and NuLife's impending implosion, I hacked into the company's accounts and emptied them."

"You sure you're not blackmailing this guy, because if you are, his standard of care for my father might be less than standard."

"No. There is no coercion here."

- 51 -

An hour later, the ambulette passed through a wrought-iron gate and drove about two hundred yards along a road bordered by dense woods. At the end of the road they came to a circular drive and a large, multi-story home—a mansion, actually. The white columns, green shutters, and warmly illuminated dormers belied the clandestine neuropharmacology apparently taking place inside.

The porch light turned on, and a man wearing a sweater over a collared shirt came out the front door. He had thick salt-and-pepper hair and a matching beard. Mid-forties, David figured. He walked around to the driver's side and greeted Mr. White through the window. "Richard, it's good to see you," the man said, as he reached in and grasped Mr. White's hand.

"Good to see you too, Vincent." Mr. White leaned back and gestured toward each man in turn. "David, this is Dr. Vincent Hoffman. Vincent, Dr. David McBride."

The two men exchanged greetings and shook hands.

"Why don't you pull ahead, and then back into the garage," Hoffman said.

Mr. White did so, and between the three of them, it took only a few minutes to move David's father from the van to a ground floor bedroom and from the gurney into a hospital bed. Hoffman put up the side rails, checked his new patient's vital signs, and reviewed the settings on the IV infusion pump. He then nodded toward the door. "Why don't we go into my study. Dr. McBride can fill me in on the history, I'll perform a physical exam, and we'll devise a treatment plan. Would anyone like a cup of coffee?"

David declined. Mr. White accepted.

Once they settled in the study, David recounted his father's medical history, which was significant only for the dementia. Hal McBride was otherwise healthy. David also gave an account of his dad's boxing experience as a young boy, as a teenager, and as a seaman in the navy, and the subsequent diagnosis of chronic traumatic encephalopathy.

The examination was brief but thorough. Hoffman listened to the heart and lungs and felt the superficial leg veins for evidence of thrombosis. He then examined the skin overlying all bony protrusions and checked the IV sites, old and new. There were no findings to suggest pneumonia, venous thrombosis, skin breakdown, or IV site infection—common complications of prolonged hospitalization. The staff at both Bellevue and Coler had done a good job of caring for a demented, bedridden elderly man, and that was no easy feat. Hoffman repeated the mental status exam David had performed in the ambulette and elicited the same responses. After more coffee was poured, the three men returned to the study. As they were taking their seats, David glanced at the wall of diplomas and certificates behind the doctor's desk.

"I suspect," Hoffman began, "that earlier attempts to wean Mr. McBride's Haldol involved loading with oral antipsychotics and then decreasing the drip over several hours, and when he awakened into a catastrophic reaction, they turned up the Haldol and called it a day."

"Without his medical records, we don't know," David added.

"That's the usual course of action, and this is where propofol comes in. Because it's rapidly absorbed and quickly eliminated, it is easily titrated. As the serum concentration of Haldol decreases, your father will wake up, and if he's agitated, I can increase the propofol just enough to calm him while continuing to lower the Haldol. In this manner, I can wean him off the drip as if landing a fighter jet on an aircraft carrier. Come in too steep and you crash into the deck. Come in too tentative, you miss the boat and have to circle around and try again."

"How will you monitor him?" David asked. "Using a general anesthetic like propofol in a non-hospital setting is risky."

"I use the Criticare system, which provides continuous monitoring of the electrocardiogram, respiratory rate, oxygen saturation, and frequent checks of the blood pressure."

"I think I should be here when he starts to wake up," David said.

"By all means. You're a crucial part of my plan. As he awakens, you are the first person he needs to see, the first voice he hears."

"I'm public enemy number one. How can we make this work?" David directing his question to both the doctor and Mr. White.

Hoffman spoke first. "I generally care for no more than three or four patients, so I maintain a small staff. I'll give the evening shift a few days off. You come at that time and stay as long as you'd like. I'll time the withdrawal of the drip to coincide with your presence."

"And the patients," David said, "what if they recognize me?"

"They won't. They're all in the late stages of their dementia."

"Okay," David said. "When do we start?"

"Tonight. I'll place a nasogastric tube and start loading Mr. McBride with oral antipsychotics, specifically risperidone and olanzapine. Once the proper loading dose has been achieved, I'll begin titrating down the Haldol."

"How long to load him?"

"Five oral doses—the first tonight, two tomorrow, two the day after. So I'll start weaning the drip the evening of the third day. Based on that schedule, why don't you go home tonight. You can come by tomorrow evening and check on him if you'd like, then plan to come and stay the night after."

"What do you think?" Mr. White asked David as the ambulette whisked the two men down I-495 toward Midtown Manhattan.

"About what?" David replied.

"The doctor, his methods. Are you comfortable with the situation?"

"Absolutely. My father will get one-on-one care in a quiet place, and there's the prospect of long-term care. So yes, I'm good, but I do have a question." David shifted in his seat and faced Mr. White. "Hoffman's diplomas were all from Yale—an MD-PhD degree, neurology residency at Yale-New Haven, a doctorate in neuropharmacology. This guy should be an academic powerhouse, but instead he's running a group home for Alzheimer patients."

The Saturday night traffic heading into the city was heavy. Mr. White kept his eyes on the road as he described the rise and fall of Dr. Vincent Hoffman. "After his training, Hoffman joined the Yale faculty and built a practice as an addiction specialist. Before long, he developed a reputation for breaking the most difficult addictions, and he attracted those patients who had been through the usual programs and protocols, yet still relapsed."

"Which is more than two thirds of all addicts who seek treatment," David added.

"Yes," Mr. White continued, "but using the same experimental techniques and drugs he was studying in his lab, he achieved a relapse rate well below the national average. And as his reputation grew, his clientele became increasingly high-profile—public figures, business leaders, and their wives, sons, and daughters—and these people demanded privacy, so he began treating them in his home. He had many successes, but as you know, all it takes is one failure and everything comes crashing down."

"Unfortunately, I know where this is going," David said. "He was practicing poly-pharmacology in a nonhospital setting, and someone died."

"A seventeen-year-old girl." Mr. White paused here, suddenly lost in thought, pensive even, as he navigated the road and the traffic. Then, after a few moments, "She was a heroin addict," he said, still staring straight ahead, "and her father was CEO of one of the world's largest banks, so you can imagine how important it was for the family to maintain privacy. Vincent was using the propofol regimen he described earlier, and despite meticulous monitoring of her vital signs, when he turned it off, she didn't wake up. She was brain dead."

"Jesus," David said.

They descended into silence again, Mr. White focused on driving, David assuring himself that his father was in good hands despite the horror story. But there was something about Mr. White's demeanor that suggested there was more to this than the tragedy of a life lost and a career ruined. Richard Whitestone was a wizard when it came to compartmentalizing emotion, but something about the death of this young woman had found a crack in the facade.

After a few minutes, David said, "You seem to have a personal investment in this story, more so than one would get from Googling it."

"I was a client of Vincent's when this happened. I was there."

"You? You were—"

"My son. I had a son. Heather had an older brother."

The pain on Mr. White's face was now obvious, the first real emotion this otherwise stoic man had displayed in front of David.

"He donated a kidney to his younger sister, and when it was time for him to go home, the doctors prescribed oxycontin for pain control. He quickly became addicted, started passing fake prescriptions, going to open houses and stealing from medicine cabinets, all of that. And when these sources dried up, he turned to heroin, which is cheaper and available on any street corner. Vincent was able to get him clean, but despite intensive follow-up, my son relapsed, one time, and once was enough."

David sat in stunned silence for a moment. Then he simply said, "I'm sorry."

- 53 -

As hoped, Dr. Vincent Hoffman brought Hal McBride down off his Haldol drip as though he were landing a fighter jet on an aircraft carrier. He avoided coming in too fast and crashing into the flight deck, nor was he too tentative, necessitating multiple flyovers. The landing was smooth, for the most part. There were a few bumps on the way down—confusion and disorientation, escalating to agitation—but they were easily quelled with a bump in the propofol infusion, thus avoiding full-blown catastrophic reactions. And now, one week after Hal McBride had been delivered to the wooded estate in Kings Park, he was sitting up in a chair, wide-eyed and alert, eating a grilled cheese sandwich. Unfortunately, his recovery was not complete. He was totally confused as to who he was, where he was, and what he was doing there. Nor did he recognize his son anymore, and he had no interest in the movie about the boxer. This was probably the new normal, Hoffman told David. With dementias, a severe psychological trauma—such as the type Mr. McBride had experienced over the past three weeks—often resulted in a digression of higher mental function, a progression of the disease, if you will. Sometimes they return to baseline, most of the time they don't. And with that, the last tiny pinpoint of love and humanity that resided in David's heart had been extinguished. Now, he truly had nothing.

Mikhail Petrovsky struggled to write on a clipboard with bandaged hands. His fingers were wrapped as one, his thumb surrounded by layers of Kerlix gauze, and he was propped up in a hospital bed. Following skin-graft surgeries to his hands, wrists, and face, and improvement of the inhalation injury to his trachea, he had been weaned off the ventilator and transferred from intensive care to a regular bed in the burn unit. Although his ability to breath had improved, his trachea and vocal cords remained too swollen to allow decipherable speech.

Standing on either side of Petrovsky were two new operatives—Sergei and Ruslan—the same men who came to the Milford Plaza, removed the laptop and other suspicious gear out of the BMW, then called 911. Anatoly and Viktor were gone, recalled to the home office in Moscow once they'd been discharged from the hospital. The firm threatened to recall Petrovsky as well, but he resisted, assuring his bosses that he had a solid plan for dealing with David McBride and getting the book.

The GPS device planted on the black Humvee had given them the location of McBride's safe house, and the new operatives had since been able to track the movements of McBride and Whitestone. Petrovsky did indeed have a solid plan. He just needed to get out of the hospital.

Holding the pen and clipboard as though his hands were lobster claws, Petrovsky scrawled, "Give me your gun," then showed it to Sergei.

Sergei gave him a quizzical look.

Petrovsky flicked his bandaged wrist, signaling for the gun.

Sergei motioned for Ruslan to close the door, then took out his Glock and gave it to Petrovsky. The bandages on his hands amounted to mittens, and he could barely grasp the firearm. He threw it onto the bed in frustration and grabbed the clipboard.

"Get me the fuck out of here!" he wrote, the tip of his pen cutting through the paper.

- 55 -

The sun was just peeking over the horizon when graveyard-shift patrol officers Vince DeVivo and Frank Cataldo of the 4th Precinct, Suffolk County Police Department, received a call over their radio: "Patrol 27," said the female dispatcher, "state your location please."

DeVivo clicked the mic. "We are driving north on Old Dock, approaching Sunken Meadow Road."

"Please proceed to 1620 Soundview. We have another report of zombies roaming the grounds of the Hoffman estate."

Cataldo shrugged and mouthed, "What the hell?"

DeVivo smiled. "Roger, dispatch. We're on our way. Did you try to call the doctor and tell him some of his patients are loose."

"We did, but there was no answer."

Vince DeVivo returned the mic to its clip and looked over at his rookie partner. "The Hoffman estate belongs to Dr. Vincent Hoffman. He runs a group home for Alzheimer's patients that sits on several wooded acres. Every now and then, one or two of his residents will wander out the front door and make their way down to the entry gate. School kids will spot them stumbling around in hospital gowns and call in with reports of zombies on the loose."

Five minutes later, patrol 27 pulled up to the wrought-iron gate marking the entrance to the estate, and sure enough, two stooping, gray-haired females, both clad in hospital gowns, were shuffling aimlessly behind the gate, while a third was trying to figure out the lock. And then patrolman Vincent DeVivo saw something that sent a wave of dread coursing through him like a current under his skin. All three of the women were covered in blood.

56

Like most mornings, Kate had the NY1 morning news turned on in the bedroom while getting ready for work in the bathroom. She was half listening to the television when something caught her attention. She stepped into the doorway to take a look. A parka-wearing female reporter was standing outside the gated entrance to a wooded estate:

> ... *just like something out of a George Romero zombie film, three elderly females wearing only blood-covered hospital gowns, trying to figure out how to open the iron gate you see behind me. At this point the details are sparse, but it appears the caretaker of these patients, Dr. Vincent Hoffman, has been found dead with a bullet wound to the head, and an elderly male patient has also been discovered deceased. I was unable to ascertain the cause of death of the second victim, but it seems likely that this is a double homicide.*

> The in-studio anchor: *You have referred to the male victim as a patient, and the females wandering the grounds as wearing hospital gowns. What kind of institution is this?*

> The reporter: *This is a group home for Alzheimer's patients. At one time, Dr. Hoffman was a respected neuropharmacologist specializing in addiction therapy. Following the death of a young woman under his care, he lost his license to practice medicine and subsequently opened this home for the custodial care of dementia patients.*

The anchor: *Have the police offered a motive as to why the doctor and only one patient were killed? Can we presume that the male victim suffered from dementia and would not have been a threat to intruders who, let's say, may have broken into the facility looking for drugs?*

Kate glanced at the banner across the bottom of the screen. It gave the reporter's name, followed by Kings Park, Suffolk County. She grabbed her iPhone and called desk sergeant Morales at the precinct. "Tell the squad I won't be in until later. I may have found Hal McBride."

57

Kate pulled up to the iron gate at the Kings Park estate and showed her ID to a fresh-faced, uniformed officer. As he waved her through she asked who was in charge, then followed the drive up to the house.

The home was large by Long Island standards—like something one would find along the North Shore or farther out in the Hamptons. A white clapboard colonial, two stories, green shutters on either side of each window, well kept, as were the grounds. The circular drive was jammed with vehicles—Suffolk County patrol, unmarked sedans, a CSU van, an ambulance. Kate parked at the end of the line and made her way to the front door, where another uniformed officer checked her ID.

"I'm looking for Detective McCarthy," she said.

"First hallway to the left. Down at the end."

As Kate walked down the long hall, she noted several bedrooms that were decorated in a distinctly feminine manner, as in elderly female décor. Hanging on the wall outside each door were glass-covered boxes of photos, trinkets, and other keepsakes—memory boxes—and above each of them, a large nameplate. Miss Shirley Faye Smith had occupied this room. Miss Vera Streeter, the next. What a shitty way to meet the end of your life—confused, disoriented, clinging to scraps of memory.

And then there was the other shitty way to make your exit. At the end of the hall, a large patch of blood stained the beige carpet, and the wall to the right was covered with crimson spatter, gray and white matter, and tiny bits of bone. There was no memory box or nameplate here, just two CSU officers, one snapping photos from all angles and another collecting blood and tissue samples with Q-tips and glass vials.

Kate displayed her shield. "I'm looking for Detective McCarthy."

The CSU guy with the camera nodded toward the room. "He's in there, but it's a mess."

Translation: we don't want you tromping around our crime scene.

"I'll just step inside the doorway," Kate said.

The CSU officers moved aside as Kate stepped over the stain and into the bedroom.

The place was a train wreck. The chest of drawers was over-turned. The mirror mounted on the back was shattered with large shards of reflective glass littering the floor. The paintings on the wall were askew, a corner chair upended, the bedding reduced to wads scattered about. Two men were working the room, another CSU officer dusting for prints, and the detective. Staying in the doorway to limit her disturbance of the scene, Kate displayed her ID and introduced herself to the man in the long, gray overcoat.

"Edward McCarthy," the detective said, carefully stepping through the debris and coming her way.

Kate offered her hand as he approached. McCarthy slipped off his latex gloves and reciprocated. "A long way from home, aren't you?" he said.

"There may be a connection between this"—Kate gestured toward the room—"and a case I'm working on."

"McBride?"

"You've been watching the news."

"The most wanted fugitive in the tristate area."

"Yes," Kate said, "and I think the man who occupied this room was McBride's father."

"There's a bombshell."

"Could be. Do you have an ID on the vic?"

"According to the doc's files, his name is Lloyd Parsons from Schenectady, but that means nothing. A lot of Hoffman's patients used aliases."

"Mind if I take a look at Mr. Parson's file?" Kate asked.

"Upstairs in the doctor's office. If this was McBride senior, what would a demented old man have to do with his son's involvement in the organ-stealing business?"

"Maybe the perps wanted him as a bargaining chip, leverage against McBride junior, or maybe this was a hit, retaliation of some sort."

"That would explain a few things. None of the other rooms were involved. Cabinets full of drugs and medical supplies were untouched. And the victim had severe bruising around the wrists and upper arms, like he was held down. Interesting enough, the vic's knuckles were scraped and cut as though he landed some pretty good punches."

"He was a boxer in the navy."

McCarthy nodded. "Makes sense."

"And the hallway?" Kate asked.

"I think the doc hears the struggle, comes down from his room upstairs and surprises the perps. They take him out with a single shot, middle of the forehead, large caliber, judging by the mess out there."

Kate assessed the various angles from the interior of the room to the door. It was clear the doctor was hit as soon as he appeared in the doorway. "A clean shot, considering the element of surprise, and they're struggling with this guy."

"Maybe they heard the doc coming or had just killed the old man when he appeared. But you're right, either way, a pretty quick draw."

"Presumed cause of death for the old guy?"

"His left temple bone was caved in. No other obvious injuries except the bruises, so I'm guessing death by pistol whip."

Not clean at all, Kate was thinking. There were at least two men, probably three, in the room, and they're struggling with a sixty-year-old man who is landing some hard punches. The doctor appears in the doorway, and he's taken out with a single shot between the eyes. Too messy. This was not a hit. This was an abduction gone bad.

They wanted Hal McBride alive, and that means they still want David McBride.

"I presume the M.E. has both bodies," Kate said.

"They left about fifteen minutes ago."

Kate made her way to the upstairs office and studied the Lloyd Parsons file. Other than the name, everything was a perfect fit for Hal McBride—age, height, weight, the diagnosis of Alzheimer's disease. The admission date and time coincided with the abduction of McBride from the Coler rehab hospital. It all fit, but to confirm her suspicion she needed to lay eyes on the body.

- 58 -

Twenty minutes later, Kate was standing over the pale, lifeless body of Hal McBride. The autopsy had not been performed, but the external injuries were obvious. Deep purple bruises ringed the thin skin of his wrists and upper arms. His knuckles were abraded and cut. The left temporal region of his head was badly contused and swollen. The medical examiner agreed with Detective McCarthy's assessment. Based on the surface exam, he told Kate, traumatic brain injury due to a blow to the head was his working diagnosis.

As Kate stood in the cold sterility of the morgue, she couldn't help thinking about David McBride's brutal response the last time someone close to him was killed. She figured now it was the Russian who was in the crosshairs, but how would McBride exact his revenge this time?

David was performing his morning evaluation of the kidney when he heard Mr. White enter the penthouse. It had been twenty-six days since the ghost kidney was infused with Heather's stem cells, and the organ was progressing as expected. It was making urine but not yet filtering creatinine or balancing electrolytes. It had form but no function.

It had also been awhile since David had seen his father. Weeks of severe psychological trauma had reduced Hal McBride to a simple organism that responded to basic stimuli with rote responses. When asked if he was hungry or thirsty, he would answer yes or no. When asked if he was comfortable, he would say yes. When asked if he knew where he was, he'd say no. Did he recognize the person— his son—standing before him? No.

David had done his best, visiting every day for the first week post Haldol drip, but this soon became unbearable. His father was awake and alert, but his mental status was that of a frontal lobotomy patient. So David took a break, a hiatus, and hadn't been back to see his father for a number of days, possibly more than a week. With the guilt building, he decided that this evening would be a good time to visit Kings Park. He finished his notes and went out front.

As soon as David saw the pained, sorrowful look on Mr. White's face, he knew the man was about to deliver news of tragic proportions. David's heart rate bumped up a few ticks as he was hit with a sinking feeling that something had happened to Heather.

"Should I open a beer?" David asked.

"I think you should sit down," Mr. White said.

David took a seat at the kitchen table.

Mr. White sat across from him and folded his hands. "It's your father. He was found dead this morning. I'm very—"

David did not hear Mr. White's condolences. He heard nothing as his mind whirled with confusion, then David, M.D. took over and imposed rationality. "Heart attack? Stroke?" he asked clinically.

"He was murdered."

Now his mind whirled with shock, disbelief, denial. But given a moment to fully process the information, he was no longer shocked, or even surprised. "Of course," he said quietly. "How? How did they do it?"

"Traumatic brain injury. They hit him in the head with a blunt object."

David went to the refrigerator. Returned to the table with a beer. Opened it and took a long drink. Stared into the black hole of the can for a few moments. Then David the son spoke. "I want two things. First, a proper burial for my father. I want to watch him go into the ground next to my mother."

"I'm afraid that's too risky."

"If you want me to finish Heather's kidney, you'll make it happen."

"What if I set up a funeral service and you watch the burial off site, on a closed-circuit feed from somewhere safe."

"I want to be standing graveside as the casket is lowered into the hole. I missed my wife's funeral. I will not miss my father's."

Mr. White pondered this for moment, then said, "What's the second thing?"

"Mikhail Petrovsky. I want him executed, like on-his-knees-hands-bound-bullet-to-the-back-of-the-head executed."

"That's—"

David raised his hand. "Call up one of your black-hat assassins, or mobilize one of those special ops teams that extracted us from the Connecticut woods. When they're done, I want them to text you a picture of his face. I want to see a gaping exit wound in his forehead, and I want to see his dead, lifeless eyes."

"Why don't we let law enforcement deal with Petrovsky?" Mr. White said. "Now that the kidney is nearing completion, I'll turn him in myself. If I go down with him, so be it."

David stood. "Make these two things happen, or there is no kidney."

- 60 -

Kate was back at her desk by midmorning. After grabbing a cup of coffee, she asked Tommy Li and Wayne DeSilva to join her. "I found Hal McBride," she said.

"Where?" DeSilva asked.

"He was in a group home for Alzheimer's patients out on Long Island. Now he's in cold storage at the Suffolk County morgue."

Both men leaned back in their chairs.

Tommy Li said, "The thing in Kings Park? Dead doctor and dead patient?"

"Yes," Kate replied. She shared her theory that the murder was an abduction gone bad. "I think the Russian wanted to use the elder McBride to draw out the younger McBride, probably to force a trade for the book."

"Now what?" DeSilva asked. "The Russian has nothing to bargain with, so the book, Richard White, and McBride will just disappear."

"Not necessarily," Kate said. "There may be one more chance to find David. Where is his mother buried?"

Both men shrugged.

"Well let's find out. Hal McBride was David's last human connection to this world, and now he's gone. I'm betting David McBride will want a funeral, and he'll want to be there. Find the mother's grave, and we might just find the son."

Wayne DeSilva: "We staked out his wife's service, and he didn't show."

"We hid behind trees and bushes like kids playing hide and seek. Maybe he was there, maybe he wasn't. This time we'll call up the big guns, every asset we can get our hands on. Nobody will get within a hundred yards of the casket without us knowing about it."

Tommy Li: "He's smart enough to know we'll be waiting for him, along with the Russian."

"Not necessarily. Hal McBride was admitted to the group home under an alias. David will anticipate Mikhail and may even use it as a chance to get revenge, but if we don't tip him off, he'll assume we don't know anything about his father's death, and he won't be anticipating us."

"What happens if there isn't a funeral? Maybe they just put the guy in the ground, no service, no nothing?"

"Then we'll never see David McBride again."

- 61 -

NSA senior analyst Jim Broderick was going through his morning emails when his secretary buzzed him. "The boss wants to see you," she said unceremoniously.

"The boss" was Major General Mitchell Crawford, an NSA deputy director and head of the Equation Group, which, of course, didn't officially exist. According to Kaspersky Labs, which claimed to have discovered Equation, the group was a covert NSA hacking operation that used zero-day vulnerabilities to install malware, spyware, and create backdoor entry points in both computer hardware and software, often before they even left the manufacturer. This, in theory, would allow the NSA to hack into nearly any computer in the world, including those used by common citizens, common criminals, terrorists, foreign governments, as well as the U.S. government. But the Equation Group did not exist, so all this was hyperbole.

Broderick rode the elevator to the twelfth floor and was shown into Crawford's office. Under normal circumstances, the major general would have risen and offered his hand, but this morning he didn't even look up from the file folder on his desk. He absently gestured toward one of two chairs and told Broderick to sit.

After flipping through several more pages, Crawford removed his glasses and looked squarely at Broderick. "You know what's in here?" Crawford asked, jabbing a stack of typed pages with his index finger. "This is a public relations shit storm on the level of Snowden and Stuxnet. This"—Crawford jabbing again—"is another case of an NSA employee abusing his security clearance. But this time it's for personal gain, unlike that asshole Snowden who half the population has branded a folk hero."

Crawford recounted a phone call the agency had received from an NYPD detective two weeks prior. The detective, he said, wanted to know if there were any high-level employees, analysts, or agents with the name Richard White, or something close to it. "She's investigating that kidney snatcher case that's been in the news, and she has reason to believe one of her suspects may be associated with the agency."

"We have tens of thousands of employees," Broderick replied. "The laws of probability would predict that there are a number of Richard Whites on the payroll."

"My thoughts as well, but then our Richard came to mind."

"Richard Whitestone?"

"Yes. He's been on leave for about six months now, dealing with his daughter, and as we all know, she'll die soon if she doesn't get a kidney transplant. You know? The whole desperate times, desperate measures thing?"

Broderick knew that his good friend Richard Whitestone would do anything to save Heather's life, but he would not step over the Thin Gray Line—the blurred boundary between legal and illegal, moral and immoral, right and wrong, the line that the espionage community straddled every day. And to compare him to the Snowden and Stuxnet debacles? The NSA's double black eyes? If this was true, it would indeed be a breach of the highest level.

"What makes you think Richard is—"

"It's all here," Crawford said, tapping this time. "I had one of our best forensics guys do some digging, and it took him two long weeks, but he finally uncovered numerous instances where Richard abused his authority within the NSA, as well as hacks and misappropriations of other intelligence agencies and their resources. He used assets that only Equation has access to." Crawford leaned forward, elbows on the desk, fine beads of sweat on his brow. "Can you imagine the fallout if this becomes public knowledge? Kaspersky and Symantec and all those other virus-hunting sons of bitches will have a field day exposing the Equation Group. And Richard?" Crawford leaned back and slowly shook his head. "He'll face a long list of serious charges, including spying on the U.S. government, and you know the kind of wrath that unleashes."

Jim Broderick slumped in his chair and rubbed his temples with his fingertips as if a migraine had taken root. "What do you want me to do?"

"The two of you are close. Find him, bring him to me, then expunge all evidence that he ever worked here."

Day twenty-seven for the kidney—growth, but still no function. Day number two since David's father's murder—the funeral and Petrovsky's merciless retribution pending. David was in the lab writing his daily notes when he heard the familiar sound of elevator doors opening, but he did not hear the familiar sound of bagel-filled paper bags rustling.

A moment later from the doorway of the lab, an unknown male voice. "Remarkable."

David turned, startled, epinephrine surging through his veins, a man in an overcoat standing in the doorway.

The stranger moved closer to the glass cylinder and admired the kidney suspended inside. "Truly remarkable."

"Who the hell are you?" David asked.

"Jim Broderick. National Security Agency." He showed David an ID. "And you must be the good doctor gone bad."

David handed the ID back to the man without looking at it. Fake NSA IDs were a dime a dozen. "How'd you get in?"

The man slid back his left coat sleeve and aimed his forearm at David.

"Ah yes, the radioactive wrist. But what about the other stuff—the retina scan and voice recognition, the thing about the raggedy rascal?"

"I went into the system and turned off the biometrics."

David paused for a moment, not surprised. "What do you want?"

"I'm looking for Richard."

"He's not here. He stays in midtown somewhere."

"You don't have an address?"

"Never been there."

"Next time you talk to him, have him call me." Broderick handed David a number-only business card, then nodded toward the kidney. "For Heather, I presume. Will it be ready in time? She doesn't have much longer."

"Are you part of Mr. White's...mission?" David inserting air quotes around mission.

Broderick grinned. "Mr. White. That's the same *nom de guerre* the NYPD is tossing around. Cute, but no, I have not been helping Richard. I've been sent here to shut him down and bring him in."

"And me? His accomplice?"

"You're a civilian. You'd be entitled to a trial in open court, and we can't have that."

"So this is a cover-up," David said.

"Yes. That's why I'm here, instead of U.S. Marshalls or the FBI." Broderick again gestured toward the cylinder. "How long?"

"If all goes well, a week, plus or minus."

"I can give you one week, but no more."

"That doesn't make sense. Why would you put yourself at risk, covering for Mr. White?"

"You'll have to ask Richard?"

"What's going to happen to him when all this is over?" David asked.

"He'll be debriefed, expunged, and sent out into the cold to fend for himself."

"No prison time?"

"Not unless your local law enforcement gets ahold of him. But that would not be good for the intelligence community, so we'll do what we can to prevent it."

"What if the NYPD picks me up, and I have this juicy story about a rogue NSA agent who broke all kinds of laws to save a girl's life?"

"I would strongly advise you to come up with an alternate version of the facts. The name Richard Whitestone will be meaningless. The name Jim Broderick is on the NSA website. And there are always countermeasures—quite severe countermeasures—that can be employed to keep that from happening."

After Broderick let himself out of the penthouse, David grabbed this week's disposable cell phone. "A guy named Jim Broderick was just here," David said to Mr. White. "He says they know everything, and he has to take you back to the NSA."

"I knew it was just a matter of time."

"He said he'll give us a week to finish the kidney. Why would he put himself at risk and cover for you like that?" David asked.

"He is Heather's godfather."

"What?"

"Jim and I were recruited out of Princeton together and brought into the NSA at the same time. He's like a brother to me."

"Has he been helping you?"

"No. He's clean."

"He says you're gonna be expunged. What does that mean?"

"I'll be scrubbed from the NSA files," Mr. White said. "No record of having worked there, no security clearances, no association whatsoever. I'll receive a new identity complete with a backstory and verifiable employment history, but other than that, I'll be on my own."

"And if for some reason I decide to sit down with a *New York Times* reporter or make a plea bargain with the NYPD?"

"Remember the red dots dancing around on our chests in the Connecticut woods?"

- 63 -

Sitting at the desk in his Second Avenue apartment, Mr. White studied both the Google Maps and Google Earth views of St. John's cemetery in Poughkeepsie, New York. It was a large facility with many crisscrossing, circuitous roads within its borders, but there were only three ways in and out—north, south, and east entrances. The Hudson River formed the western boundary. If Mikhail Petrovsky, his operatives, and the NYPD all showed up, and Mr. White had no doubt they would, getting David off the premises after the service would be near impossible. David's mother, Elizabeth, was buried near the middle of St. John's, which was helpful. Perhaps he could deploy several decoy vehicles, but still, when it was time to leave, the one carrying David would need to pass through a gate.

Unless...

Mr. White zoomed in on the western boundary. A set of railroad tracks ran between the cemetery and the river, and a layer of trees and shrubs filled the space between cemetery and tracks. The map also showed an abandoned factory no more than a hundred yards to the north. If he could send three decoy vehicles to the exits while a fourth delivered David to the back of the cemetery, David could climb through the shrubs, get picked up alongside the tracks and taken to the abandoned building. At that point, he could easily be moved out of the area and back to the city. Of course, Mr. White would need to go to Poughkeepsie and lay eyes on the cemetery, the defunct factory, and their surroundings, but it sounded like a viable plan. That left him with only a thousand other details to work out.

- 64 -

Six days after the death of Hal McBride, Kate got the news she was hoping for. A hole large enough to fit a coffin had been dug next to Elizabeth McBride's grave at St. John's cemetery in Poughkeepsie. That meant one of two things. Hal McBride was going to be quietly laid to rest next to his wife, or there was going to be a funeral service with the only remaining McBride—David—in attendance. Either way, Kate, the task force, and as many other warm bodies as they could amass would need to be there.

Inside a white panel truck parked two blocks away from St. John's cemetery in Poughkeepsie, New York, Kate took her seat alongside Lieutenant Rick Stubblefield, ESU Commander. The Emergency Service Unit was the NYPD's version of special weapons and tactics, and Stubblefield had been tapped to coordinate the interdepartmental McBride operation. On the other side of Stubblefield sat a young but very competent communications technician, and the three of them quietly peered into an array of high-definition screens overlooking Hal McBride's open grave, his casket, and the surrounding area.

The view on screen number one featured the first of several "bird cams" perched in a large pine tree near the gravesite. Other bird cams afforded wider views of the area and the nearby road where would-be funeral attendees will park their vehicles. The largest screen of the collection—the shining star around which the others orbited—would soon be streaming video surveillance from N23FH, the NYPD spy helicopter whose FAA registration number served as an homage to the twenty-three fallen heroes of the September 11th attacks on the World Trade Center.

Once McBride arrived, "23" would lift off from an airfield in Hyde Park, just north of Poughkeepsie, and take a position across the Hudson River approximately one mile due west of the cemetery. Even at that distance, the nose-mounted camera would be able to provide clear images of those standing graveside, without raising suspicions. It had been said that "23" could pick up the catcher's signals at Yankee Stadium from two miles out. Kate hoped this was the case and not just department lore. The arrangement of the graveside service had the attendees facing west, toward the chopper and its camera, with the bird cams at their backs. The helicopter was Kate's best chance to identify David McBride.

Undercover officers from both the NYPD and Suffolk County covered the cemetery grounds proper. Tommy Li was strolling around in forest-green coveralls with a lawn rake and a compost bag. Wayne DeSilva was wearing white coveralls and sanding old paint off a rusted wrought-iron fence. Dan Austin was inside the office at the main gate with a set of spike strips ready for deployment. Suffolk County—who were hoping McBride's presence would draw out Mikhail Petrovsky—had unmarked cars near the other two entrances, and several of their officers were wandering around under various guises. Three units from Stubblefield's Emergency Service Unit—twenty-four men outfitted with Kevlar body armor and assault rifles—along with two detectives from Homicide South, waited inside an unused warehouse a couple of blocks away. Once McBride was within the confines of the cemetery, they would secure the perimeter, and there would be no way out. In fact, it almost seemed too easy, leading Kate to believe McBride was not coming.

She leaned back in her chair and checked the time. Just after 10:00 a.m. As this was not a traditional funeral, there had been no announcement listing a start time, nor was the funeral director able to provide any details. He had simply been handed an envelope of cash, had been instructed to close for the day, and told to position the casket no later than ten. All Kate and her team could do was watch and wait, but they couldn't afford to wait too long. At the moment, the weather was cooperating. It was cloudy and cold—bitterly cold—but the cloud ceiling was high enough to allow a chopper to fly. Unfortunately, a powerful nor'easter was heading their way and with it, high winds and blowing snow—a chopper's worst enemy.

•   •   •

NSA drone #90125 hovered at a thousand feet elevation over St. John's cemetery. At two-and-a-half feet in diameter, and held aloft by four battery-powered motors, it was invisible to those on the ground on whom it was spying, and made no more noise than a large hummingbird. Sitting at his desk in the Lower Manhattan apartment, Mr. White studied the drone images on his laptop. He felt comfortable with his decision to manage the operation remotely. Should complications arise—and there was a high probability they would—he'd need to be far removed from the action to effectively deal with the consequences.

He checked the time—approaching 10:15 a.m. David was scheduled to arrive at 10:30. Hopefully, the team had assembled without incident and would deliver him on time. A significant storm was on the way, and with it, gusting winds that could carry the drone into the next county without warning.

Mr. White zoomed in and scanned the cemetery grounds. There was a multitude of workers and groundskeepers—too many, in fact—for an icy winter's day, but no mourners. He had insisted the funeral director keep the facility closed until further notice. Everyone down there was either law enforcement or Russian corporate espionage, which meant things were going to get complicated once David arrived. If any civilians were harmed during the unauthorized use of government assets, the fallout would be nuclear.

Mr. White moved the cursor from person to person and assigned them a red number, marking them as unfriendly. Upon arrival, David and each member of the team would receive a green number. He then maneuvered the drone around the perimeter of the cemetery. Unmarked cars were clustered at each of the three entrances. Two blocks east, a white panel truck sat curbside in front of a lumber supply company. The numerous antennae on the roof screamed NYPD command vehicle. And, it was likely that a larger force—probably ESU—had amassed in a nearby staging area. Mr. White closed his eyes and rubbed his temples. Getting David into the cemetery was not going to be a problem. Getting him out would take a herculean effort.

• • •

Mikhail Petrovsky settled into his chair and opened his laptop. With equal parts cash payment and threat of violence, he had taken over the AAA Pest Control Service right across the street from the cemetery. It was a satellite office of a larger operation and employed only a handful of technicians, which made it easy for the boss to give his guys the day off, citing some kind of systems failure, or whatever he told them. All that mattered to Petrovsky was that he had a base of operation close to the cemetery, and he could get his men near Hal McBride's gravesite with a reasonable cover story. St. John's had been using AAA for decades, so the presence of their vans and uniformed technicians on the grounds was not unusual and should not raise a red flag.

With his scarred, unbending fingers, Petrovsky clicked the link to the eyeglass cams sending images from the cemetery. He had three operatives on the grounds. Two of them had placed their glasses on the tops of gravestones within a hundred feet of Hal McBride's site. The third man was wearing his, allowing him to scan the area. Remarkably, Petrovsky had the ability to zoom in to 1000x magnification, so surveillance wasn't the problem. The problem, and it was a big one, would be grabbing David McBride out from under the watchful eyes of the NYPD and friends, who were swarming the place in their lame disguises, and Richard Whitestone, whose presence Petrovsky had not yet detected but was sure to be there in some capacity.

If only they hadn't killed Hal McBride. If only the demented old bastard hadn't screamed "they're killing me, they're killing me," he'd be alive, Petrovsky would've had a bargaining chip, and he would be on his way to Russia with the book in hand and David McBride in the ground. Instead, he was hiding in a cobweb-infested shack, breathing in rat poison, and trying to one-up the NYPD and the NSA. And he'd better pull it off. Oleg Vasiliev, president of Zelenograd Biomedical, was one of Vladimir Putin's oligarch cronies, which meant the biomedical company was essentially a state-run organization. Vasiliev—and by proxy, Putin—wanted to corner the world organ manufacturing market, and they wanted to do it without the hindrance of competition. Should Petrovsky fail to deliver the book, it meant a one-way trip to the gulag.

At 10:32 a.m. a procession of four black Humvees passed through the front gate of the cemetery. They followed a meandering road into the center of the grounds and came to a stop even with, but about twenty yards from, Hal McBride's grave. Sixteen men climbed out of the four vehicles, each wearing identical black overcoats, black stocking caps, scarves, and sunglasses.

Stubblefield to the communications tech: "He's here. Get the chopper in the air, and mobilize the ESU."

The tech into his headset mic: "Come in, Twenty-three. Suspect has arrived. Take up your position. ES units, secure the perimeter."

Ten miles north at Hyde Park Regional Airport, N23FH lifted off the ground and headed south by southwest.

Kate viewed the different bird cams. Number one showed the sixteen men walking toward Hal McBride's grave. Cams two, three, and four gave wider views of the area. As she studied the men, she could not determine which was David McBride. No facial features were exposed, and most of them stood about six feet tall, same as McBride.

Mikhail Petrovsky recognized the Humvees. They were similar to the pair that had been parked on the road the night he was burned. They must be part of a protection or extraction force organized by Whitestone. Petrovsky studied the men exiting the vehicles and assembling at the graveside, but it was impossible to ID McBride. Richard Whitestone had done a masterful job of disguising McBride and surrounding him with a human shield. Petrovsky's plan had been sketchy to begin with, but now, walking away with David McBride seemed impossible.

• • •

Five minutes later, the chopper arrived at its position one mile due west of the cemetery. It hovered at one thousand feet, facing east, and focused the nose-mounted camera on the group of men who had assembled next to Hal McBride's coffin. Kate looked at a photo of David McBride, then scrutinized the men—now in greater detail—but still could not single out McBride. "Can't tell them apart," Kate said to Stubblefield.

Stubblefield keyed his mic. "All units, we have sixteen men graveside, all dressed alike, about the same height and build, not enough facial features exposed to differentiate the suspect. I believe this is a shell game. After the service they'll return to the four vehicles and disperse in different directions. Let's move now before they get the chance. Suffolk County, make sure all exits are blocked. ESU, cover any gaps in the perimeter, service roads, etcetera."

Stubblefield linked to the chopper. "Twenty-three, do you copy?"

"Loud and clear, Command."

"Tag each of the sixteen men so we can track the suspect once identified."

"Roger that."

About five seconds later, a floating red number appeared over the head of each man standing graveside.

Mr. White spoke into his headset mic: "Guardian One, this is Ragged Rascal. Do you copy?"

"Loud and clear, Rascal."

"Unfriendlies are securing the perimeter. Give the chaplain the go-ahead, and tell him to be quick about it."

Guardian One turned to the man standing next to him. "It's time. Two minutes and we're out."

The chaplain took his place near the head of the casket. "Dr. McBride," he said, addressing David specifically, "My apologies for the brevity of this service, but as you know, we are under some time pressure here."

David acknowledged the chaplain with a slight nod.

The chaplain removed a small bible from his pocket and released the handbrake on the lowering device. Hal McBride's casket slowly descended into the grave. "A reading of Psalm 23," began the chaplain:

The Lord is my shepherd; I shall not want.
He maketh me to lie down in green pastures:
he leadeth me beside the still waters.
He restoreth my soul: he leadeth me in the paths
of righteousness for his name's sake.
Yea, though I walk through the valley of the shadow of death,
I will fear no evil: for thou art with me; thy rod and thy staff
they comfort me.

As the casket disappeared into the ground, David was overcome by the same dark, vacuous feeling he experienced as he watched Cassandra die on the side of the road seven weeks earlier. His soul, and the last remaining shred of his humanity, were ripped away that night. And after this—the brutal murder of his father—if there was even the slightest chance he would once again embrace the human race, that possibility had now been extinguished. He, himself, was no longer human. He was nothing more than a shell, a husk, a vessel that held only disdain and hatred for his fellow man. He reached under his sunglasses with a finger and smeared away the tears that had formed in the corners of his eyes.

"You're kidding me," Kate mumbled as one of the men moved to the head of the gravesite, took a bible from his pocket, and turned a lever that lowered the casket into the ground. Even the pastor, or chaplain, or priest—whatever the hell you call these guys—was wearing the same disguise as the rest of them. He opened the bible, addressed an individual member of the group and there it was, the tell Kate was hoping for—a slight nod from subject number six in response to the person conducting the service, and a moment later he rubbed his eyes.

"That's him," Kate said, pointing at the screen.

Stubblefield to the chopper: "McBride is number six. Keep him on camera at all times."

To the rest of the team: "We've ID'd McBride. Move in before they get to their vehicles."

Tommy Li to Command: "The exterminators are moving toward us with respirators on, and they're carrying heavy canvas bags."

Kate to Tommy: "Identify yourself, then use deadly force if you have to."

Tommy Li: "They're throwing canisters on the ground. Bug bombs—"

The bird cams flashed white.

The view from the chopper showed several clouds coalescing into one and enveloping the gravesite, the area around it, the Humvees parked nearby.

Kate: "Tommy. Wayne. Anyone. Come in."

Coughing and choking, the only response.

Stubblefield: "ESU. I need you graveside with respirators on. We've had a chemical attack of unknown origin."

ESU to Command: "Roger that. We're moving in."

Stubblefield to the chopper: "Twenty-three. Position yourself over the cemetery. We're under chemical attack, and we've lost the suspect."

The view from the drone showed a billowing cloud envelop David and the men.

Mr. White: "Guardian One, do you copy?"

Nothing.

"Guardian One, come in please. Do you copy?"

Mr. White lowered the drone to one hundred feet. The wind was rapidly dispersing the cloud, but it was also knocking around the drone, making it difficult to keep track of what was happening. His team was trying to get to the Humvees. A handful were crawling. The others were staggering. He could not differentiate who was who, but two of the men made it to the Humvee parked at the head of the line. The vehicle started rolling, then picked up speed, moving west toward the river, as planned. Then it turned abruptly, now chasing a white van with red markings on the side—the exterminators. The van moved east toward the main entrance, hopping curbs, driving on the grass, clipping headstones, the black Humvee in pursuit.

Tommy Li: "White van"—coughing and hacking—"they have McBride."

Kate checked the center screen, the feed from the chopper. The van was moving toward the east entrance with a black Humvee right behind it.

Kate to Dan Austin: "Dan, the van is coming your way. Deploy the spike strips."

Dan Austin: "Deployed. We're standing by."

The van approached the main entrance at high speed. It then veered south, down a road paralleling a hurricane fence that separated the cemetery from the on-ramp to State Route 9. The van swung wide right in a big arc, then hard left and smashed through the fence, speeding up the ramp with the Humvee right behind it.

Stubblefield to all channels: "Suffolk County and all other units, two suspect vehicles—a white van with a black Humvee in pursuit—are approaching the southbound lanes of highway nine. The suspect is in the van. Engage and follow."

Stubblefield to the comms tech: "Get the State Patrol involved in this."

The chopper quickly zeroed in on the van. About a mile south of the cemetery the Humvee rammed it from behind, sending it off the road, down an embankment and into a ditch. Kate watched as the driver exited the van and disappeared into the dense trees and brush that filled the space between the river and the highway. Two men from the Humvee moved toward the van with weapons drawn, but jumped back in their vehicle and sped away as two Suffolk County patrol cars approached.

Stubblefield to the comms tech: "Get paramedics down there now."

Then to Kate: "Go make your arrest."

- 66 -

After four hours of staring at David McBride cuffed to a gurney in the Bellevue ER, and waiting for the results of X-rays and scans to confirm what the paramedics had determined at the crash site—no serious injuries—detective Kate D'Angelo finally had her suspect behind the bars of the Manhattan South holding cell. Dr. David Mc Bride—kidney-snatching ghoul, good surgeon gone bad, executioner—was sitting on a bench with his legs straight, head against the wall, eyes closed, hands folded in his lap. His appearance had changed drastically from the NYU photo of a few years ago, and then the bleached spiky hair of the composite sketches from a month ago. He now had a jet-black goatee, bushy long hair of the same color, and he was quite thin and pale. In fact, the suit he had worn under the body armor was such a poorly-fitting, rumpled mess, he could easily pass for a homeless stockbroker.

David had been the most wanted man in the tristate area for the past seven weeks, and was now the highest profile collar of Kate's career, but seeing him sitting there was less than satisfying. The evidence clearly indicated that he had methodically and brutally murdered Andrew Turnbull, but only after Turnbull had forced him to steal human organs from homeless men and had played a part in the horrific deaths of Cassandra McBride and her unborn child. Kate would never classify premeditated murder as justifiable, but if there were a line between justified and unjustified, this case would stand with its legs spread right over it. In any event, society demanded justice, and justice is what they were going to get.

It was now four thirty in the afternoon. The squad room was overrun with detectives, Manhattan South's own, plus at least one from each jurisdiction involved in the case. If the ADA would show up, they could get started.

About fifteen minutes later, Lieutenant Hernandez entered the room with a nicely-aging brunette woman in her mid to late forties—Assistant District Attorney Anne Friedman, Deputy Chief of the Trials Division. The DA had sent in the big guns. Hernandez introduced Anne to Kate and Luis Sandoval, the leading homicide detective on the case. After pleasantries were exchanged, the ADA said, "Has he asked for a lawyer?"

"No," Kate answered.

"Has he made a phone call?"

"No," Sandoval said.

"Well then, time is of the essence. Let's get started before some third party rears its ugly head."

Tommy Li and Dan Austen cuffed McBride in the holding cell, led him down the hall to an interrogation room, then removed the cuffs and sat him down. Kate, Anne, and Luis Sandoval sat across from McBride. The remaining detectives, along with Lieutenant Hernandez, went around to the viewing room and watched through a one-way mirror.

Sandoval led off the interrogation. "Just so you're aware, Doctor, this interview is being video-recorded."

David looked up at the camera mounted in the corner. "Okay."

Kate gestured toward the ADA sitting next to her. "David, this is Assistant District Attorney Anne Friedman."

"Dr. McBride?" Anne said, looking up from a thick case file and peering at David over her reading glasses.

"Miss Friedman?" David replied.

"Okay," Sandoval said, "I'd like to document for the record that you have been read your Miranda rights."

"I have," David said.

"And you fully understand them."

"I do."

Sandoval leaned forward, rested his arms on the table and stared at his laced fingers for a moment, seemingly gathering his thoughts. Then he laser-focused on David. "When I build a first-degree murder case for the district attorney's office, I like to think of it as a three-legged stool. Each individual leg represents motive, means, and opportunity. The part where you sit, that's the evidence. If each leg is solid, and the seat strongly binds them together, the jury will come back with a guilty verdict. Now, we found Andrew Turnbull strapped to a gurney, killed by a lethal injection of succinylcholine, ten days after your wife was found dead only a few miles from his company headquarters. Motive. Means. Opportunity."

Sandoval stood and started pacing around the room, Kate wondering if there was a suppressed prosecutor trying to emerge from within the detective. He did look rather lawyerly in his vested three-piece suit.

"The evidence," Sandoval continued, "will solidly bind the three legs of our stool. We have eye-witnesses that saw you and a young woman escort a drugged Andrew Turnbull from the Elbow Room in Newark the night prior to his death. We have a GPS rendered map that delineates the route from the Elbow Room to the murder scene in Lower Manhattan. We have your fingerprints on the vial and syringe used to administer the succinylcholine. We found your prints on surgical instruments and equipment used to perform a sham operation on the victim, and we have DNA from discarded surgical gloves, masks, and hats that we predict will match yours. Motive. Means. Opportunity. Evidence."

Sandoval took his seat at the table.

"In addition," Kate said, "we've linked you to the forced removal of organs from at least two mentally ill homeless men, one of whom bled to death after the operation. And, we've recently been made aware of an institutionalized boy who appears to have undergone removal of a kidney for no discernable reason."

"Am I being questioned or arraigned?" David asked. "Sounds to me like the stool is done and it's just a matter of proceeding to trial."

Anne Freidman: "We'd like to hear all of this in your own words, Dr. McBride. We believe you were forced to steal those kidneys. This, and the loss of your pregnant wife, will have an impact on how we move forward."

"No thanks," David said. "I'm not interested in saying anything at this time."

He leaned back and folded his arms across his chest, but not in a defiant mode. To Kate, it seemed more like exhaustion.

"It's in your best interest to talk to us," Kate said. "We still have the assaults of Linda Turnbull, Jeffery Abercrombie, and Ruby Abercrombie to sort out."

"I'm not responsible for any of those. In fact, I saved Jeff Abercrombie's life."

"We know that," Kate said. "But we need you to help us find the Russian, Mikhail, and the mysterious Mr. White."

Anne Friedman: "Give us names and descriptions and any other useful information regarding the other players in this series of events, and the system will view you more favorably. Maybe you'll find yourself upstate in a private cell instead of out on Rikers Island with nothing more than a cot on the gymnasium floor, nestled among three hundred other prisoners."

Sandoval: "You heard of warehousing, Doctor?"

"Yes, but in what context?"

"In the context of overcrowded prisons. Rikers is so beyond capacity they have row after row of these tiny army cots lined up on the gym floors to handle the overflow. A cot's all you get. No cell. No privacy. No walls to protect you at night. Can you imagine what happens after lights out?"

"Look—," David started to say, but Sandoval interrupted him.

"You know what else is special about Rikers?"

David shrugged and shook his head.

"Ninety percent of the inmate population is black or Hispanic. Do you have any idea what's going to happen to a tall, skinny white boy such as yourself?"

"David," Kate said, "you're not a career criminal. You got caught up in some horrific circumstances and you reacted. We understand that, and we're on your side. Help us so we can help you."

"Okay," David said, "so the deal on the table is my confession, a guilty plea, plus everything I know about the others, and I go somewhere other than Rikers Island. No immunity, no reduced sentence, just a private cell versus the gym floor."

"Yes," Anne Friedman said.

David leaned forward, arms resting on the table. "What I really need is bail."

Anne: "Not likely. This is capital murder, supported by a large amount of evidence. That makes you a flight risk."

David: "I'm not going to run. I have nowhere to go. No way to live. Nobody to live for. I just need a few days to finish something important."

Kate: "And what is this 'something'?"

"I can't say." David turned toward Anne Friedman. "But please take me at my word. Convince the judge to grant bail, and I'll give you everything you want."

The ADA sat quietly, staring at David, her hands clasped with her index fingers forming a steeple. Then, "I'd like to confer with the detectives. Can we get you anything? Coffee? Soda? Something to eat?"

"No, thanks."

After coffee was poured, sweetened, and diluted with milk or cream, Kate, Luis Sandoval, and Anne Friedman sat down with Lieutenant Hernandez and the rest of the team.

Tommy Li: "He has no family, no friends, no money, and we've confirmed that he has no driver's license or passport."

Dan Austin: "But he has the help of this Mr. White, who seems to have significant resources. I mean, look at the paramilitary group that attended the funeral."

Kate: "If he wants to run, he will, and he'll have whatever help he needs. I'm against it."

Luis Sandoval: "Even without a confession, he doesn't stand a chance."

Anne Friedman: "There are always wildcards that surface during any trial. No trial means no acquittal, no hung jury, no mistrial because of some technicality."

Lieutenant Hernandez: "I agree with Detective D'Angelo. He's not a punk from the streets. He's smart, he's resourceful, and he has help."

After everyone used the restrooms, and checked their phones for emails and text messages, Kate, Anne Friedman, and Luis Sandoval returned to the interrogation room.

Kate put a can of Coke in front of David. "You need the sugar."

He popped it open and took a drink.

Anne Friedman: "In exchange for your full confession, as well as your complete cooperation in all aspects of this investigation, I will do my best to persuade the judge to grant bail."

Kate slowly shook her head.

Luis Sandoval leaned back and grunted.

"The bond will be high," the ADA said. "Do you have the means to pay?"

"I'll find a way."

"You will have to wear a GPS trackable ankle bracelet."

"I will."

"And if the judge denies bail?" Anne Friedman asked.

"Just do what you can."

As everyone filed out of the interrogation room, Luis Sandoval said to Kate, "I'll call transport?"

"No," Kate replied. "My guys and I will take him. After that show of force at the cemetery, I'm not taking my eyes off David McBride until he's booked."

The ride down Second Avenue this time of night was nauseating. Cars, trucks, buses and cabs lurching forward and stopping, lurching forward and stopping. Horns honking. Exhaust fumes seeping into the car despite closed windows, and it didn't help that David was sitting on his hands. He shifted his weight, trying to realign his arms and shoulders. The detectives had cuffed his wrists behind him, and the ride downtown to the Manhattan Detention Complex—more commonly referred to as the Tombs—was anything but pleasurable.

They came to the end of Second Avenue and proceeded across Houston, and the reality of the nightmare awaiting David began to set in. As a surgery resident, he had cared for many patients on the Bellevue prison ward who had been transferred from Rikers Island or the Tombs. Despite incarceration, inmates were able to get their hands on makeshift knives, clubs, and other weapons of human destruction. As a result, he had treated stab wounds, smashed faces, broken jaws, fractured skulls, ruptured spleens, and lacerated livers. And since a significant proportion of the city's incarcerated were IV drug abusers, he had drained his share of abscesses and empyemas from prisoners with AIDS, hepatitis, and multi-drug resistant tuberculosis. Now, as they turned off Chrystie and onto Grand, David was minutes away from stepping into a cesspool of violence and infectious disease from which he was unlikely to emerge unscathed.

The sedan drove south on Baxter Street in the shadow of the Manhattan Detention Complex and the New York City Criminal Courts Building, the latter a fifteen-story colossus of marble and limestone that seemed faded and worn with time and overuse. To the north of the Courts Building stood a newer, windowless structure of the same height. A pedestrian bridge connected the two. The lack of windows, along with the monolithic architecture and strands of coiled razor wire, indicated that the newer building was his destination. Across the street, the sidewalk was lined with bail bondsmen offices and one lone bar—The Whisky Tavern. David supposed the former were needed on the way into the Tombs, and the latter would be the first stop on the way out, for those lucky enough to leave in one piece.

After circling the block, the car stopped in front of a nondescript roll-up door. A rather unremarkable entrance for such a notorious institution. The door rose with a clatter, and the car pulled in. Once the door had rumbled to a close, Detective D'Angelo came around and let David out, thus initiating the prisoner intake process.

The setup was similar to the prison ward at Bellevue. After the detectives—D'Angelo and a guy named Tommy Li—deposited their firearms into a gun locker, a heavy wire-mesh door slid open. The three of them entered what amounted to a small cage, and as the door closed behind them, Tommy Li pushed the paperwork through a gap under a thick pane of glass. Once the papers were reviewed, another mesh door opened, and they moved progressively deeper into the bowels of the Tombs, stopping for fingerprints, mugshots, and the medical interview—*are you an alcoholic or IV drug abuser? You aren't going to withdrawal or go into DTs, are you?* Then came the full body search.

Kate D'Angelo removed the cuffs and waited outside as David entered a small room with Tommy Li and the same man who had conducted the so-called interview. The doctor—Michael Bates, M.D.—according to his nameplate, ordered David to strip.

"Okay, Dr. McBride," Bates said as he slipped a latex glove over his right hand. "Squat down and push like you're moving your bowels."

Squatting and pushing—the Valsalva maneuver—was not part of the standard rectal exam, but if someone had contraband hiding deep in their rectum, a good Valsalva would move it down to the anal sphincter, thus putting it within reach of the fingertip. David put his hands on a cold stainless-steel exam table, did a deep squat, pushed, then started to stand.

"Stay down there and push until I tell you to stop," Bates said.

David did as he was told—naked, squatting, pushing, the humiliation rising. This guy was about David's age, a couple inches shorter, and slight of build. In the outside world he would be David's equal, or perhaps even a colleague, but in here he was gruff, disrespectful, and trying to play the hard guy. David supposed he deserved the same treatment as any other lowlife, but having a wormy little man—who was carrying a chip for whatever fall from grace landed him in the Tombs—telling him to strip, squat, and push was humiliating nonetheless.

"Now stand up and bend over," Bates said.

David bent at the waist, rested his forearms on the cold table, and tried to relax. Bates was gonna go deep, and he wasn't going to be gentle. If David's anal sphincter was tight, he'd pay the price for days to come.

And without any warning, or finesse, Michael Bates buried his finger up to the knuckle.

"Christ," David said, looking over his shoulder. "A heads-up would've been nice."

"Yeah?" Bates said, taking off the glove with a snap and tossing it into the trashcan. "Is that how you do it in your practice, Doctor? Make sure your hands are warm, and you gently spread the patient's gluteal cleft, then quietly reassure them while you softly insert your finger?"

"Something like that," David said, now wishing he hadn't opened his mouth. "Are we done?"

"Why yes, Doctor," Bates replied in a sing-song tone. "You may get dressed now. I hope this experience has not been too distasteful. And leave your shoe laces and belt with me."

David said nothing as he put on his clothes. It would have been stupid to antagonize the guy who may be the first medical responder should things go sideways inside this freak show.

With the intake completed, the detectives escorted David down the hall to the holding cells. There were four of them, each facing the command desk. When David and the detectives stopped to hand off the paperwork, the inmates—about fifteen to twenty in each cell—used the occasion to gather at the front bars, hanging on them, hollering and catcalling the detectives and the corrections officers—when's my lawyer gonna get here, where's the pizza I ordered, I'm innocent, let me outta this shithole. And speaking of shit, somebody just took one on the floor.

Judging by the feculent stench wafting over the command desk, it seemed someone had, in fact, defecated without the benefit of a toilet. The hooting and hollering reached a new level as the inmates in the affected cell crowded into a corner. Detective D'Angelo looked at David as she removed the cuffs. "Take care of yourself in there," she said in a manner approaching maternal kindness.

"I'll do my best," David said.

One of the COs wrapped the bars with his nightstick, scattering the inmates, while another unlocked the gate and nodded David into the cell. He worked his way to the back corner, opposite from where the turd lay. A two-foot wide ledge, raised about eight inches, formed the perimeter of the cell floor. David sat down and leaned back against the cold concrete of the wall.

Even though nothing had been done about the turd, the prisoners—sixteen in addition to David—had settled down. Most seemed to take incarceration in stride, forming racially segregated groups of three or four, running their mouths about this and that as if they were hangin' in a parking lot drinking forties. David noted a couple of blank-eyed loners staggering about, one who reeked of booze and piss, one who didn't. The one who didn't reek, an emaciated white kid with waxy skin and greasy hair, had a pronounced tremor in both hands, a rigid gate, and beads of sweat stippling his forehead. David knew the look. Without a fix, he'd soon be in florid withdrawal.

Just as David was about to close his eyes, a lanky black kid broke away from his group and made a beeline for David. Sporting an ear-to-ear smile, he sat down next to him. "What you in for, Doc?"

David processed this for a moment, then he said, "If you know I'm a doctor, you know what I'm in for."

The smile disappeared, and the lanky body tensed. "I wanna hear you say it."

"Murder," David said with as much conviction as he could muster.

"And stealin' kidneys? And stranglin' little dogs?"

"The kidneys, yes. The dog, no."

The kid locked eyes with David, their faces no more than six inches apart, the smell of cheap vodka or gin rising up from deep within the kid's lungs.

"They say you pumped that CEO dude full of enough drugs to make his heart stop."

"Only after I strapped him down," David added, knowing weak and white weren't gonna fly in this place.

"Sounds like you figure yo'self for some kinda badass, but looks to me like you don't amount to much without your surgery tools and your syringes full of poisonous drugs."

"Maybe, maybe not," David said as his heart rate doubled and his anal sphincter tightened, and just as the stare-down began, the inmates shifted *en mass* from one side of the cell to the other—where the turd resided—yelping and hollering about some mother-fucker shitting himself and vomiting all over the floor.

David jumped to his feet and went to the vacated corner of the cell. As he'd predicted, the heroin addict had gone to ground. He lay on his back, vomit streaming from his mouth, his pants soaked with urine and diarrhea. David quickly rolled him onto his side, then grabbed the boy's arms and examined them. Needle tracks followed all the major veins from wrist to upper arm, and there were a number of scarred-over pockmarks from old abscesses. He was soaked in sweat, his forehead hot enough to fry an egg, and his breathing was shallow and coarse.

David went to the front of the cell. "We need some help in here," he yelled. "We have a heroin withdrawal with vomiting and labored breathing."

He peered out at the command desk. Deserted.

"Hey!" he screamed. "We need help. Man down."

A defensive lineman-sized corrections officer strolled over to the cell. "What's the problem?" he asked, clearly annoyed that he had to lift his fat ass out of the chair, or couch, or wherever it had been parked.

"The boy on the ground is withdrawing from heroin," David said. "He needs to go to the infirmary, and then probably to Bellevue."

"Listen, Doc," the officer said, "we see this every night. They sweat, they vomit, piss themselves and shit their pants, then they're fine. Nothin' to get excited about."

"Not this one," David said. "I think he aspirated vomit into his lungs. He's short of breath and probably should be on a ventilator. At the very least, he needs IV antibiotics."

"Just turn him on his side," and the guard walked away.

"Bullshit," David yelled. He grabbed the bars and screamed, "Dr. Bates, we need you. Bates! Get your ass in here!"

The nightstick came out of nowhere, smashing the fingers of David's left hand, and before he could react, the guard reached into the cell, grabbed his hair and collar and yanked him forward, jamming his face into the bars. In a low voice strained through gritted teeth, the guard said, "We don't need any heroes in here, so shut the fuck up and mind your own business."

The guard shoved David. He tripped over the heroin addict's legs, fell backward and smacked his head on the concrete ledge, snapping his neck forward. He didn't lose consciousness, but as he lay there staring up at the maze of air ducts and pipes that formed the ceiling, his vision was blurry and his ears were ringing.

David stayed still for a few moments, allowing his senses to clear. Fortunately, the other inmates were uninterested, nobody taking the opportunity to dig through his pockets, or worse. His hand throbbed, and the back of his head pulsed with a sharp pain, but it was his neck that concerned him the most. He flexed it slowly, moving chin to chest, then ears to shoulders, followed by ninety degrees of rotation left and right. With his right hand he pushed on the tips of the spinous processes and massaged the paraspinous soft tissues. No pain or tenderness with palpation or movement. His C-spine seemed intact.

His left hand was a different story. The fingers were already swollen and tight, and any attempt to move them resulted in excruciating pain. He worked himself into a cross-legged sitting position and rubbed the back of his head. No blood, but it was exquisitely tender to the touch. For Christ's sake, he'd been in the holding cell all of fifteen minutes and he'd already had his face smashed into the bars, his neck hyperflexed, and his fingers probably broken, along with his skull. And he might have suffered a concussion, judging by the intense headache setting in. Ironically, this was at the hands of the staff and not the prisoners. What the hell was next?

As if on cue the lanky kid was back, standing over him. "Now why you gotta go and get yo'self all busted up over some junkie?"

"If there's vomit in his lungs and he doesn't get proper treatment, he'll die," David replied, still rubbing his head.

"Says the guy who strapped a man to a bed and killed him."

"He needed to die. This boy," David nodding toward the addict, "maybe he deserves another chance. Maybe there's someone in there worth saving."

The lanky kid knelt down and got right in David's face, the smell of booze and unbrushed teeth turning David's stomach. "Piece of advice, Doc? You spend any time in the Tombs or they ship you over to Rikers, you find the biggest badass motherfucker you can, and you be his hero, 'cause a good-lookin' boy like yo'self with a skinny little ass, you gonna need a friend. Don't go wastin' your talents on a scrawny white junkie."

This time the conversation was interrupted by the delivery of blankets. The cell door opened, and a wad of scratchy-looking wool blankets was thrown into the middle of the floor.

"Best be fast, Doc," the kid said as he jumped up, "or you be havin' a long cold night ahead of you."

David was able to grab two. He balled up one of them and put it under the junkie's head, and used the other one to cover his body. The vomiting had stopped, but the fever and sweats raged on, and his respirations were raspy and labored. David put the palm of his uninjured hand on the boy's chest. He could feel the secretions rattling around in the larger airways. Maybe in the morning a different doctor would take over, someone with a conscience. Otherwise, this young man was dead.

A big, muscular inmate with sleeve tattoos covering both arms broke from the lanky kid's circle and came toward David. Without saying a word, he bent down and snatched both blankets off the junkie.

David, down on one knee, looked up at the guy. "Come on, man. Really?"

"Yeah, Hero. Really."

- 68 -

David was awakened by the sound of a nightstick dragging across the bars at the front of the cell. He lay balled up on the concrete ledge, no blanket, freezing cold and shivering, unsure of how long he might have slept. It couldn't have been much. The junkie had kept him busy through the night with more vomiting, diarrhea, raging fever alternating with shaking chills, and the near constant moaning that accompanies the abdominal pain typical of withdrawal. About an hour ago they finally hauled him to the infirmary, and only then did David get a chance to sleep.

When the inmates had backed away from the door, the COs came in with boxes of bear claws and those little cups of orange juice with the foil lids. David managed to grab one of the pastries and two orange juices, but the bear claw didn't stand a chance. Balanced precariously on his swollen left hand, it was an easy target, and one of the Latino inmates snatched it away as David walked by. Hopefully, the orange juices would hold him over until lunchtime.

After breakfast, one of the COs hollered out a list of ten names. David's was among them, the first of the morning groups to be arraigned. "Thank Christ," he said under his breath. He was just hours away from a hot shower, a warm meal, a cold beer, and a nap.

The inmates on the list had their feet shackled, hands cuffed in front, and cuffs chained to their waists. They were then lined up and ushered from the north tower of the Tombs, across the Bridge of Sighs—a small footbridge over White Street—and down to the ground floor of the Criminal Courts Building where they were placed in the Pen—the holding cell that adjoined Courtroom

1A, felony arraignments. It was a motley group, stooped over and stutter-stepping, everyone still in street clothes, which ranged from hoodies and baggy pants to David's suit he had worn to the funeral yesterday. Everybody was rumpled, everyone smelled, nobody's hair had been combed or teeth brushed. They milled around the Pen until their names were called. Groups of three or four disappeared into the courtroom. Some came back, some didn't. Those who returned were sent back to the Tombs, bail denied.

David was in the final group of four. They shuffled their way into the courtroom and were seated along the wall, off to the side of and behind the bench, where the judge was busy reviewing a file. The room was a noisy hive of activity. A ubiquitous chatter ebbed and flowed, rising from murmurs, to loud whispering, to blatant conversation. The bailiff, a thin, middle-aged man with close-cropped dark hair and a matching beard, had to repeatedly ask the well and the gallery to quiet down. The well, David surmised, was the area in front of the bench where the stenographer, the attorneys, and other ancillary staff were set up. The assistant DAs, their clerks, and stacks of files occupied a table to the judge's left. The table on the right was set up for the defense attorneys. A waist-high partition of dark-stained wood separated the well from the gallery—rows of benches filled with an assortment of individuals, some in suits, some in hoodies and baggy pants, mothers of the accused, friends of the accused.

The first person arraigned was a powerfully-built Latino about David's height and probably in his early twenties. He had a cold, hard stare and a jaw that seemed permanently clenched. Even though his arms and legs were shackled, David was unnerved by the guy. He exuded an air of simmering violence that could erupt at any time. David had seen more than a few noses shattered by vicious head-butts. Fortunately, the Latino had not been in David's holding cell last night, and this morning in the Pen he had kept to himself in the corner.

The Latino, Hector Gonzales, was called to the bench. An armed corrections officer walked him over and positioned him next to a lectern, facing the judge. Hector was joined by his attorney, a doughy-looking young man in a wrinkled, ill-fitting suit—a public defender, by all appearances. While the bailiff read the docket number and list of charges, the attorney placed Hector's file on the lectern and quickly flipped through it. When the bailiff finished, one of the assistant DAs stood—another young man in a rumpled off-the-rack suit. He introduced himself and spelled his name for the stenographer.

"Your Honor," he said, "the people will show that on February twenty-third of this year, Mr. Hector Gonzales engaged in a four-hour crime spree, during which he robbed two men at gunpoint, pistol-whipped one of them, then went to the home of his seventeen-year-old girlfriend"—air quotes inserted around girlfriend—"and raped her after assaulting her mother. He concluded the spree by robbing an elderly woman at knifepoint. We have blood toxicology positive for methamphetamine, we have a rape kit that provides a match for Mr. Gonzales' blood type and DNA, and we have numerous witnesses willing to testify."

The judge, a paunchy Asian American in his mid-sixties, seemed unimpressed. Without even looking up from the file on his desk, he said, "How do you plead, Mr. Gonzales?"

Gonzales, who had remained stone-faced and rigid through the recounting of his alleged egregious acts, said nothing.

His lawyer: "Not guilty."

The assistant DA: "Regarding bail—"

The judge: "Bail denied."

"Your Honor," the public defender said without conviction.

The judge looked up from his desk. "Bail denied, Counsellor," then, simultaneously pointing at the assistant DA and the public defender, "With that kind of evidence, I suggest the two of you put your heads together and come up with a plea deal that best serves the people of New York." He banged his gavel and handed the file off to the bailiff.

"Commit," said the bailiff, and the CO led Hector Gonzales out of the courtroom and back to the Pen.

During the lull, the murmurs of the well and the gallery quickly built to a loud chatter. Several members of the gallery took out cell phones. An armed, Kevlar-vested female court officer quickly descended on the cell phone users and threatened to confiscate their devices, brusquely informing them that their use was expressly forbidden. The bailiff once again demanded silence, this time threatening to call for a long recess if they didn't comply.

When the hubbub finally settled, the bailiff called for the next defendant. "Docket ending with six, two, nine, Dr. David McBride"—David, heart pounding, was guided to the lectern by the corrections officer—"charged with two counts of kidnapping, two counts of assault with a deadly weapon, two counts of robbery in the first degree, and one count of murder in the first degree."

David's lawyer, a sharply dressed middle-aged man with graying hair, met him at the lectern and opened the case file.

Assistant District Attorney, Anne Friedman, introduced herself and spelled her name.

The judge sat up straight and leaned forward. "Mr. Evan Beck," addressing David's lawyer, "it has been years since you've graced this court with your presence. And Ms. Friedman? You've traveled all the way down from the fifteenth floor for an arraignment hearing?" The judge focused on David. "Dr. McBride, you must feel very special. A highly regarded defense attorney who was once a formidable ADA in his own right, and the Deputy Chief of the Trials Division? I feel privileged to be in in such rarefied company."

The ubiquitous murmur again turned to a low chatter.

The bailiff: "Quiet in the courtroom!"

The judge: "Ms. Friedman, please begin."

The ADA: "Your Honor, the people will show that for a period spanning six weeks earlier this year, Dr. David McBride held a high-level position in a black-market organ-stealing conspiracy, that he took part in the abduction of two homeless men on two different occasions, and, using a makeshift operating room in a dirty, abandoned warehouse, forced these men to undergo surgery for the purpose of removing a kidney. He later had a falling out with a co-

conspirator and murdered this man by lethal injection after strapping him to a gurney in the aforementioned warehouse."

The murmur quickly rose to a chatter.

Someone in the gallery: "Dayum."

Someone else: "Cold motherfucker."

The bailiff: "Order in the court!"

The judge, once the room had quieted: "Dr. McBride, how do you plead?"

David: "Not guilty, Your Honor."

Anne Friedman: "In the matter of bail, we ask for a one-million-dollar bond."

Murmurs and chatter from the gallery.

Evan Beck: "The defense accepts. Dr. McBride has no criminal record, nor is he a risk to flee. He has no passport, no driver's license, nor does he have the means to get very far."

The judge: "He has the means to hire you, does he not?"

A burst of laughter from the gallery.

A single voice: "Roasted."

Another voice: "Get wrecked."

The judge pounded the desk with his gavel: "Order in my courtroom!"

The room quieted.

The judge: "Does Dr. McBride have any ties to the community?"

The ADA: "No, Your Honor. His father was recently murdered, and he lost his wife in a suspicious car accident about two weeks ago."

"I am aware," the judge said, looking directly at David, "and I'm sorry for your losses, Dr. McBride."

"Thank you, Your Honor."

"However, it is my understanding that prior to his death, your father was abducted from a New York City hospital, despite the watchful eye of the NYPD, and then placed under the care of a once highly regarded neurologist. Is this true, Doctor?"

"Yes, Your Honor."

"Were you solely responsible for the aforementioned events?"

"No, Your Honor."

"So, you had help."

"Yes."

"From a rather resourceful benefactor, perhaps? Maybe the same person who has helped you evade this country's largest police department, and also provided you with one of the city's finest defense attorneys?"

"Your Honor," Evan Beck interjected.

The judge: "Bail denied."

Anne Friedman: "Your Honor, we are quite confident the defendant will not flee."

The judge: "This is a capital murder case, among other things, and it is highly unusual for the DA's office to offer bail under these circumstances. Maybe you've struck a deal—bail in exchange for a full confession is my guess—I don't know, but I think Dr. McBride not only has the means to flee, but he also has the help to do it. Bail denied."

And a smack of the gavel made it official.

The murmur jumped to boisterous conversation.

"Commit," said the bailiff, followed by, "Quiet in the courtroom."

The command was largely ignored.

David turned to his lawyer, but before he could say anything the CO had him by the arm and was pushing him toward the door.

"Sit tight," Beck said. "We'll get you out. Just sit tight and watch yourself."

As David was delivered back to the Pen, he stopped short at the door as he was struck by a horrifying realization. Hector Gonzales, sitting like a stone in the corner, his eyes blazing and his teeth grinding—he and David would be returning to the Tombs at the same time, both remanded to custody. Would the COs put them in the same cell? Was Hector going to come down off of a meth high and descend into a violent rage? Would he give David a beat down just for the sake of it? Or worse?

69

And that's exactly what happened, David and Hector assigned to the same cell. First they stopped at a ground-floor holding room where, one at time, they were uncuffed, stripped down, and given orange jumpsuits to put on. With his left hand swollen tight, David struggled to work the zipper on his. One of the COs took over, zipping the suit for David.

"There you go, titty baby. Not much of a hero now, are you?" the guard said.

"No, not now," David replied, "but in my time at Bellevue, I patched up more than a few cops and corrections officers who came in cut up, stabbed, or shot."

"Shut it, Hero. That's one of them reticular questions you aren't supposed to answer." The CO, a huge white guy, got right in David's face, the agitation rising, and David certain he smelled booze. "Listen dumbass," he said. "You are white and you are educated, and we don't get too many like you in this joint. That means you're wearin' a big target on your back. Everybody in here would love to tear you down and put you in your place, so I suggest you keep your mouth shut and make yourself invisible. Got it?"

"Yes," David said.

From there they rode an elevator to Seven North—a cold, dimly-lit expanse of worn linoleum tiles, scuffed cinderblock walls, and thick steel doors. Compared to the mayhem of the holding cells, the seventh floor was eerily quiet as David and Hector shuffled the length of the floor. At the far end of the cell block, they were deposited into a six-by-eight cell. David's heart pounded wildly as the door slammed with a sickening, iron-on-iron, echoing clank. Without saying a word, Gonzales shoved David against the wall, pushed past him, then threw himself onto the lower bunk. He lay on his back, glaring into the bottom of the upper bunk, eyes blazing, jaw grinding. David climbed up top, lay down and stared into the ceiling, too afraid to move, or make a sound, or even take a loud breath, mortified that any little thing might set off his psychopathic cellmate and launch him into a violent rage.

They were let out for lunch—peanut butter on rock-hard Wonder Bread—and out again for dinner—mystery loaf, runny mashed potatoes, and sliced green beans, all bathed in watery brown gravy. And then a knife fight broke out right before lockup. The ESU turtles responded, searching every cell on the seventh floor for weapons and contraband, manhandling all the inmates in the process, including David and Hector. And finally, lockup and lights out.

About every hour or so, Gonzales let out a guttural scream and kicked the bottom of the bunk with both legs. David nearly plummeted to the floor each time. At 3:00 a.m. David had to pee, but he held it in, afraid to move, afraid to jiggle the beds. By 4:00 a.m. he could hold it no longer. He climbed down and quietly stepped to the toilet, which was no more than twenty-four inches from Gonzales' head. Even though it was dark, David successfully avoided hitting the water, finding the side of the stainless-steel bowl instead. A quiet piss, but not quiet enough. A rustling sound. David zipped up and turned around. A hulking silhouette stood before him. And then a blow to the solar plexus dropped him to his knees. Gonzales followed that with a kick to the chest, driving David's back into the steel toilet.

"Don't ever wake me up again," Gonzales said.

David lay on the piss-stained floor in a heap, clutching his upper abdomen, gasping for air.

70

Not long after another breakfast of bear claws and orange juice, two COs showed up outside David's cell, one white and one black—the white one the same guy who had zippered David's jumpsuit the morning before.

"McBride," said the black one. "Stick your arms out the slot."

David climbed down off his bunk and slipped his hands through a narrow gap in the door. The black guard cuffed him, and after telling Hector Gonzales to stay against the back wall, he unlocked the cell door with a set of cabled keys. "Step out and turn your back to us," he said.

David complied, and the white guard knelt down and shackled David's ankles. "What's this for?" he asked.

The white CO slowly stood and once again put his face inches from David's, David smelling Scope this morning instead of booze.

"What did you say?"

David looked down, wishing he'd kept his mouth shut. "I was just wondering what's going on."

"For a smart guy you're kinda dumb, aren't you?" The CO chest bumped David, nearly knocking him off his shackled feet.

Jesus. David wasn't sure who he should fear more, a psychotic Latino meth addict, or a steroid-addled white corrections officer with a chip on his shoulder.

The three of them headed for the elevator at the far end of the cell block. David fell in behind the black CO, his hands clasped in front of him as if in prayer, his feet shuffling along quickly so he could keep up with the man's long strides. The white corrections officer brought up the rear, jabbing David with his nightstick about every five steps and telling him to move faster.

The elevator carried them to the first floor, where David was escorted down a dark, dingy hallway to a small room. The walls were unpainted concrete, no windows, and a single light fixture of two fluorescent bars hanging over a stainless-steel table. A pair of U-bolts, spaced about twelve inches apart, protruded through the surface of the table. David shuffled over and sat down across from his attorney, Evan Beck. The black CO opened one side of the cuffs and locked it to one of the U-bolts. The white CO cuffed David's free wrist and secured it to the other bolt.

"That's not necessary," Beck said.

"Procedure," said the black corrections officer. "We'll be right outside."

"How are you holding up?" Beck asked.

"Well, let's see. Last night a knife fight broke out on the seventh floor. The ESU turtles shoved our faces into the walls as they frisked us and searched our cells for weapons and contraband. The guy one cell over refuses to use his toilet and crapped on the floor at least twice. My cellmate gave me a beat-down for taking a piss at 4:00 a.m. And, oh yeah, the white CO who just cuffed me to the table, he hates educated white men. Other than that, everything is good."

"ESU turtles?"

"The Emergency Service Unit. They respond to all violent confrontations, and they're so loaded down with body armor and riot gear, they look like turtles."

"Are you injured?"

David ran through a mental list of injuries sustained in the last thirty-six hours—a swollen, possibly broken left hand, a possible concussion and linear skull fracture, a blow to the upper abdomen, a steel toilet bowl to the thoracic spine, various bumps and bruises from the unrestrained van ride into a ditch. "Nothing permanent," he said.

"Very good." Evan Beck reached into his briefcase and came out with a white envelope. He leaned in close to David, and speaking just above a whisper he said, "I'm going to show this to you so you can read it. I don't know what it says. I don't want to know what it says."

Beck opened the envelope, unfolded the letter inside, and held it up for David. As David read the page, Beck spoke of expediting his trial date and trying to get him moved from the Tombs to a more suitable facility, along with a bunch of other legal doubletalk.

Typed in a large font, the letter said: *Find a way to get yourself transferred to the Bellevue prison ward. Fake an illness, get beat up, something serious they can't handle in the infirmary. We need you in a Dept. of Corrections van traveling to Bellevue—TONIGHT—the later the better. Understand?*

David gave a single nod and said, "Rikers Island. No thanks. I heard it's worse than this place."

"Okay. No Rikers. In the meantime, is there anything else I can do for you?"

"Just get me out of here."

71

After another dinner of mystery meat and slime, David found an unoccupied chair in the TV room and took a seat. He leaned forward, his heels drumming the floor, lockdown in about thirty minutes, time running out. He put his elbows on his knees, buried his face in his hands, then sat up, heels oscillating like a sewing machine. He had to get out of this place for any number of reasons—Hector Gonzales, the dickhead CO, Heather's kidney, he was white in a predominantly black and Latino detention center.

Mr. White had a plan, and all David had to do was get himself transferred to Bellevue, but this would not be easy. His options were limited to two: stage a fake illness convincing enough to warrant a transfer to Bellevue, or sustain a real injury serious enough to require transfer to Bellevue. Although David knew the signs, symptoms, and physical findings associated with a host of conditions that would mandate surgery, he wasn't sure he was a good enough actor to pull it off. In a place like the Tombs, the vast majority of patients seen in the infirmary were seeking drugs, with a transfer to Bellevue considered icing on the cake. Faced with this onslaught of malingerers, the doctors had fine-tuned their ability to determine who was faking and who wasn't.

That left option number two. A significant traumatic injury, either self-induced or inflicted by a fellow inmate. Other than jumping from a high concourse, which would cause more damage than David wanted to experience, there were no good options for the self-inflicted variety. He thought about amputating one of his own fingers with a cell door, but he lacked the fortitude to do this to himself. Besides, someone had tried it a few months ago. The doctor threw the finger in the trash, stitched up the stump, and sent the guy back to his cell with some Advil. The case was still under investigation by the Department of Corrections.

This meant there was one remaining option—provoke another inmate to hurt him. Find someone right here on Seven North, piss him off, and hope he didn't get beaten to death. A single blow to the face, jaw, or side of the head would probably do the trick. His concern was the unabated access to weapons—namely, homemade knives—this place afforded the inmates. He did not want to end up in a Bellevue operating room undergoing surgical repair of a perforated colon or a hemorrhaging liver laceration.

David checked the clock on the wall. It was now 8:42 p.m. Lockdown was at nine. Time to act. But goddammit, who in their right mind could subject themselves to intentional pain, suffering, and maybe permanent damage? But he couldn't stay in this place. Each time he'd been outside his cell today he was leered at, shoved, and elbowed. Hector Gonzales had become increasingly agitated, looking like he might go off at any moment. No way did David want to be within arm's reach when that happened. He leaned forward and buried his face in his hands.

From behind him, a voice he recognized. "Hey, Hero. You're in my chair."

It was the big black guy who stole the blankets from the junkie in the holding cell.

This was it.

Don't think about it.

Just do it.

"Hero! I said this is my chair."

David stood and faced the man. He was a mountain. David's heart pounding. Every muscle in his body taut. "Then why don't you take it you cunt."

A lightning-fast blow landed in the same place Hector Gonzales had hit him, upper abdomen just below the ribs, the diaphragm driven up into the lungs, his breath forced out of him.

David was doubled over, clutching his midriff, fighting for air when a second blow caught the right side of his face and jaw, and a third smashed into his left temple. Everything went black as his limp body sprawled across the dirty linoleum floor like a rag doll.

72

Darkness gave way to light. Silence filled with sound. Numbness became feeling. And then all the senses came alive at once. Something hard and blunt was digging into David's sternum. A thumping pressure, matched by a pulsating pain, pushed on his skull from inside out. His ears were ringing, his abdominal wall on fire, left hand throbbing, the metallic taste of blood in his mouth.

David opened his eyes to find a man in a white coat leaning over him, the man's knuckles burrowing into David's sternal bone. He tried to swat at the man, to get him to stop, but his wrists were cuffed to the rails of a gurney. The man straightened, taking his hand away from David's chest. "Welcome back to the land of the living, Doctor."

David squinted against the bright lights hanging above the gurney. Then he looked to his left and right—two rows of three beds, stainless-steel cabinets and countertops, exam lights over each bed. A young, emaciated white male was sitting upright in the far bed of the opposite row, one hand cuffed to the rail, the other holding a plastic kidney basin. David was in the infirmary, and Dr. Michael Bates was standing next to him.

"What happened?" David asked, slowly opening and closing his jaw, noting a sharp pain in the right temporomandibular joint.

"Well, you inexplicably called the biggest, meanest son of a bitch on Seven North a cunt."

"Apparently not a smart thing to do," David now examining his swollen hand.

"According to witnesses you were punched in the abdomen, and when you doubled over, you took a left hook to the right side of your face and then a right hook to your left temple. The hit to the side of the head sent you skidding across the floor, and after your unconscious body came to a stop, your new friend walked over and stomped on your previously injured hand."

"I remember now, at least the stuff before the concussive blow to the head."

A wet, raspy coughing fit erupted from the other inmate. He hacked up a golf ball-sized clot of blood and spit it into the kidney basin.

"AIDS or TB?" David asked, the kid too young for lung cancer.

"Both, with cavitary lesions in the upper lobes of both lungs." Bates paused for a moment, then, "You're a smart guy, so I'm having trouble understanding why you would say such a thing to someone twice your size."

"I don't know," David said, "maybe stress or fear. But I can tell you, while we're sitting here pondering my lack of judgement, I could be bleeding from a lacerated liver or ruptured spleen, or an epidural hematoma might be forming in my head."

"So you think I should send you to Bellevue for CT scans of the brain and abdomen."

"That's what I'd do."

"Of course you would," Bates said, "but how about I examine you first?"

Bates used the tips of his fingers to push deep into David's abdomen, trying to elicit a pain response. The abdominal wall musculature was tender from the punches, but there was no deep pain. David writhed and groaned anyway.

Bates looked at him with a skeptical eye, then carefully put pressure on David's left temporal bone, right mandible and temporomandibular joint, and the bones of the orbit and cheek. Again, David felt tenderness associated with soft tissue contusions, but not the pain of a fracture.

"An unremarkable exam. You have a few bruises. That's all."

"What do you mean that's all," David trying to sit up. He immediately fell back to the gurney as his contused abdominal wall lit up with pain. "I was knocked unconscious. That by itself justifies a CT of the brain."

"We'll keep you under observation and perform neuro checks every hour."

"I could be bleeding internally. You and I both know the physical exam is unreliable for detecting intraabdominal hemorrhage."

"Observation."

"What if I have fractures of the orbit, or the zygomatic arch, or the mandible?"

"You don't."

David held up his swollen hand. "What about this?"

"Ice and a sling."

"Come on, man. If you were working the ER at Lenox Hill, I'd already be on my way to radiology."

"We're not at Lenox Hill, are we?"

"Of course not, but the standard of care is the same whether you're at the Tombs or on Park Avenue."

"No, it's not." Bates started to walk away.

"Wait," David pleaded.

Bates stopped and turned around.

The other inmate coughed again, spewing aerosolized tuberculum bacilli and blood spatter into the air. David wondered why the kid wasn't wearing a mask.

"Look," David said. "I'm not after drugs or a stay on the Bellevue prison ward. I just want to go up there for a CT and some films of my hand, and they can send me right back."

"Not gonna happen."

David lifted his head off the gurney. "What's your deal? Your story? Why are you here?"

"It's none of your business."

"Was it drugs? Did you kill a patient or fail your boards? Something bad landed you here, and your wife lost all respect for you, maybe even ditched you, and now you hate the world."

Bates walked over to the gurney, jaw clenched, hands balled into fists. "My wife is dead, asshole."

David let his head fall back to the bed. "I'm sorry. I didn't—"

"You didn't what? Intend to exploit my personal hardship to buy your way out of here?"

"No. That's not it," David said. "I mean, we're both doctors. We've both suffered a great loss. I'm here because I murdered the man who caused my wife's death. A revenge killing. I'm sure if you could avenge your wife's—"

"It was metastatic osteosarcoma of her left femur. You can't take revenge on cancer."

"Jesus. I'm sorry. How old was—"

"Young," Bates said harshly.

"My wife was twenty-eight and pregnant," David said, "and I watched her take her last breath on the side of a deserted road with a steering wheel crushing her sternum, so maybe you can understand why I did what I did."

Bates' posture softened. He gripped the rails of the gurney, leaning on it slightly. "Maybe I can, but the law doesn't accept an eye for an eye."

"No, it doesn't. So what happened? How come you're here?"

"I don't want to talk about it."

"Come on. We're one and the same. Young doctors with bright futures and the world takes a big dump on us, and we both end up in the Tombs. Kind of ironic, isn't it?"

Bates' head fell forward, chin to chest, eyes closed tight. "Her left leg had been amputated mid-thigh, and she had metastatic lesions in her spine and her lungs and her brain."

"Incurable," David said.

"And painful." Bates lifted his head and looked at David. "I was stealing IV Fentanyl from the hospital to help with her pain, and then I started injecting myself to ease my pain. I got addicted, and caught, and if I wanted to practice medicine in the State of New York I had to agree to rehab and a five-year stint with the Department of Corrections."

David slowly shook his head. "I'm sorry, I mean really sorry. We're both facing a lifetime of painful and tortured memories, but that's why I'm here, right here, right now, in the infirmary. I took a life, but I've been given the chance to save a life, a young woman, but she won't survive another week if I'm stuck in this place. Please, transfer me to Bellevue. You're my only way out."

"I'll be implicated."

"No, you won't. Just document my injuries in the record. Sending me for a CT scan and X-rays is the standard of care. Nobody will second-guess your judgment."

Michael Bates sat down on an exam stool, shoulders slumped forward, eyes closed, a deep furrow in his brow, and he suddenly looked old and tired.

"She's young, Michael. Like your wife. Like my wife. And we are the only ones who can save her. You and me. If I don't get transferred tonight, she's dead."

Bates remained lost in thought for a few moments, as if he hadn't heard David's plea, then he slipped his cell phone out of his back pocket. The lock screen was a photo of a smiling young woman. He stared at it, tears forming in the corners of his eyes, then he stood up, walked over to the desk, and picked up the phone. "This is Dr. Bates in the infirmary. I have another transfer to Bellevue. Significant head and facial trauma."

73

Corrections officers Koslowsky and Rizik loaded David and his traveling partner, Jeremy Butler, into the back of a Department of Corrections ambulette.

"Head injury protocol says to keep this one's gurney at forty-five degrees," Koslowsky said to Rizik. "And prop his up too, so he doesn't choke on his own blood," Koslowsky gesturing toward Butler.

With both gurneys secured to the floor and both inmates cuffed to their side rails, the COs climbed into the cab and started the van. The roll-up door that provided vehicle access to the Tombs rumbled open, and they pulled out and turned right onto Centre Street.

Even at nine o'clock on a Saturday night, traffic was bad. Traffic was always bad south of Houston, day or night, because of the narrow, mostly one-way streets intersecting at all kinds of odd angles. Once they hit First Avenue it would be a straight shot up to Bellevue, but from the Tombs to First was always a pain in the ass, unless someone was bleeding to death and they got to ride in a real ambulance with a siren.

At the corner of Centre and Grand an NYPD traffic cop stepped out in front of the ambulette and waved his arms. Koslowsky stopped and rolled down the driver's side window as the officer approached. "I see you guys are DOC," the cop said. "You transporting?"

"Yeah, to Bellevue, head injury and coughing up blood."

"Then get off Centre. There's a real mess a couple blocks up at Spring. Take Grand over to Forsythe, and north to Second Avenue."

Forsythe was a funky street, narrow and one way, always lined with parked cars, and it had this skinny park on the left that ran for about ten blocks. Nothing but drug dealers and homeless in there, and the street itself was full of stop signs and lights. A real pain in the ass.

"Why not just go north on Chrystie or three blocks over to Allen and up to First?" Koslowsky asked.

"Both of them are torn up the closer you get to Houston. The detours will take you longer than if you just go up Forsythe."

"We didn't see any of that earlier today," Koslowsky said.

"They unloaded the jackhammers this afternoon. Didn't take 'em long to bust up all the northbound lanes on both streets."

"The fuck!" Rizik said, leaning toward the driver's side. "Why don't you guys stagger this shit so you don't have so many roads torn up at the same time?"

"I'm NYPD, not public works, you dick."

"Yeah, yeah. Whatever," Rizik leaning back into his seat.

"All right," Koslowsky said. "Forsythe it is. Thanks, officer."

At Forsythe the ambulette took a left and hadn't even traveled a block when a white panel truck pulled out from the curb and cut them off.

Koslowsky laid on the horn and flipped the bird out the window.

The truck just puttered along, crossing over Broome, then it came to a sudden stop.

Koslowsky honked again, head out the window and yelling this time, when the back door rolled up and six heavily armed men in helmets, goggles, and body armor jumped out and stormed the ambulette.

Koslowsky shifted into reverse and stomped on the gas, slamming into another panel truck that had pulled up behind them.

Rizik grabbed the radio, yelled at dispatch that they were under attack and gave the location.

The commandos surrounded the ambulette. The one closest to the driver's side used the butt of his rifle to smash the window, filling Koslowsky's lap with chunks of glass. Then he pointed the muzzle at Rizik. "Drop the radio and get out!"

The two men complied, climbing out of the van, hands up.

"Drop to your knees, fingers laced behind your heads."

As Koslowsky and Rizik did what they were told, two other commandos went to the back of the ambulette and opened the door. "Whoa. What's going on here?" one of them hollered, taking a step back.

During the melee, Jeremy Butler had coughed up blood all over his orange jumpsuit, enough to cover his chest and lap. And this was bright red blood, not maroon clots—massive hemoptysis in medical terms, which meant he was bleeding to death.

"Which one of you is McBride?" said the commando.

"I am," David trying to wave his cuffed hand.

"Who is this?"

"Jeremy," David said. "Don't touch his blood."

Sirens a couple of blocks away and approaching fast.

One of the other commandos came around to the back with a set of keys. He climbed in, uncuffed David and said, "Let's go. We have to move quickly."

"Uncuff him," David nodding toward Jeremy.

"That is not part of our mission."

"Just do it," David said.

The commando unlocked the cuffs.

David wrapped Jeremy with a couple of blankets. "When the cops get here they'll call a real ambulance, and you'll be taken to Bellevue. Hang in there, okay?"

Jeremy nodded, tears forming in the corners of his eyes, then he coughed another five or six hundred milliliters of bright red blood all over the blankets.

David was ushered past the white panel truck where two black Humvees were waiting. He was helped into one—Mr. White already in the back seat—and once the rest of the team had jumped in, the vehicles drove a half block north, turned right on Delancey and went up and over the Williamsburg Bridge, disappearing into Brooklyn.

74

For the second time in the last few weeks, David and Mr. White were delivered to the parking garage of the safe house, in the early morning hours, by a black Humvee. After the commando raid on Forsythe the night before, Mr. White had insisted they return to the spec ops medical facility in southern Massachusetts to have David's injuries evaluated by a physician.

During the three-hour drive, David's mental function had remained unimpaired, and his headache had diminished from a pulsing throb to a moderate ache, so he declined a CT scan of his brain. He knew the early signs of both epidural and subdural hematomas and had exhibited neither, so he was comfortable with his decision. He did, however, submit to X-rays of his face, jaw, and left hand. The films were normal, no fractures, just significant contusions and swelling. The treatment for the hand? A sling and ice, as Michael Bates had indicated. While they were there, the doctor performed a follow-up X-ray on Mr. White's fibula. The bones were aligned nicely and had essentially healed. The whole trip had been a long run for a short gain.

As the Humvee left the garage, they approached the private elevator. Mr. White aimed his right wrist at the cesium detector on the wall.

The door promptly opened.

Mr. White glanced at David, a look of alarm on his face.

"Your buddy Jim Broderick disabled all the biometrics when he came to see me," David said. "He didn't tell you?"

"No, he didn't."

"Well, it *is* faster this way."

Once inside the penthouse, they sat at the kitchen table, David sipping a beer, Mr. White a cup of hot tea.

"Must have been a rough couple of days," Mr. White said after a few minutes of silence.

"You could say that," David replied, taking a drink of his beer.

"I'm sorry I was unable to arrange a nonviolent way to get you out of the detention complex. I just didn't have the time to find the right people."

"You mean no sons of immigrants whom you could blackmail."

"Something like that. But seriously, are you okay?"

"You heard what the doctor said."

"No, I mean are you okay mentally, not just physically."

"My jailhouse virginity is intact, if that's what you're getting at."

"Your wit seems to be intact, as well."

"Look," David said, "the place is a hellhole, but I survived. Let's leave it at that."

"Fair enough," Mr. White replied. "Where do we go from here?"

"First of all, for obvious reasons I haven't showered since being booked into the Tombs. Secondly, I didn't really get much sleep. So why don't you go home and get some rest. I'd like to get out of these"—David tugging on the orange jumpsuit—"and clean up. Then I'll check the kidney. If there is anything dramatic to report I'll give you a call, otherwise I'm going to take a long nap. Okay?"

"Sounds good," Mr. White said.

- 75 -

After a long, hot shower—where David did his best to scrub away all the grease and grime and fear and abuse and humiliation and TB spores and AIDS viruses that *was* the Tombs—he put on clean scrubs and headed for the lab. Even though the sun was just peeking over the horizon, the room was still dark, so he flipped on the light hanging over the glass cylinder, and the desk lamp in the corner near the computer monitor. He was happy to hear the familiar hum of the pumps and filters. The system had been unattended for close to seventy-two hours, but based on the various sounds, it seemed everything was in working order.

The first thing David checked, as had been his routine for the past few weeks, was the urine collection bag. To his surprise, and excitement, it did not contain the usual scant amount, but instead held nearly three liters. And the color, a light yellow, indicated it was neither too concentrated nor too dilute. The time had finally come to check the glomerular filtration rate, the magic number that would determine if the kidney was functioning. To do this, David needed only three values: the serum creatinine level, the urine creatinine level, and the rate at which the urine had been produced. Easy enough.

Five minutes later he had his numbers and was about to enter them into the computer when he heard a noise out front, maybe the foyer, or the kitchen area. He walked over to the door, aimed an ear toward the hallway, but heard only the hum of pumps and filters. He went farther down the hall and listened again, wondering if Mr. White had returned for some reason. Still nothing, so he went back to the lab, sat down in front of the computer and performed the calculation. And the result was perfect. The glomerular filtration rate was 100 milliliters per minute. Anything over 90 was normal.

After double checking the math and getting the same answer, David swiveled his chair toward the glass cylinder and admired his creation as it gently swayed in the amber nutrient broth. This organ was now capable of regulating blood pressure, serum electrolytes, and the body's pH and fluid balances. It would filter the waste products of metabolism and secrete hormones needed for red blood cell production and maintenance of bone density. And when transplanted into Heather Whitestone, it would save her life and restore her to a vibrant, functioning human.

David grabbed his phone and dialed Mr. White. Straight to voice mail. "It's me," he said, barely able to restrain the giddiness in his voice. "I just calculated the glomerular filtration rate, and it's perfect. We now have a fully functioning kidney. Call your guy in DC and have him schedule Heather for her transplant."

"He's not going to get that message."

David spun around. A dark silhouette stepped through the doorway and into the halo of the track light. Mikhail Petrovsky. Holding a gun. A laser site trained on David's heart. Petrovsky's hands and the front of his overcoat were soaked with blood. But that was the least horrifying of the grotesque scene before David. Petrovsky looked like a monster. His hair had been burned away to mid-scalp and replaced with uneven plaques of scar tissue. His face was a patchwork of skin grafts and scars, the tip of his nose gone, his eyelids scarred down to slits, the cartilages of his ears no more than stubby remnants of what they once were.

"Admiring your work, Doctor?" Petrovsky asked.

David had no words, and only a single thought came to mind: he wished he had killed the man instead of turning him into a deformed freak.

"So this is it," Petrovsky turning to the cylinder and marveling at the organ inside. "The holy grail of transplant medicine. A marvel of human ingenuity. And it works?"

"How'd you get in here?" David asked as Petrovsky's bloody hands and coat revealed the only sickening possibility.

Petrovsky reached into his coat pocket and came out with a severed hand, which he tossed onto the benchtop. "Had to make sure and take plenty of wrist in order to get that implant."

"Where's Richard? What have you done to him?" David pressed his palms into his temples. "Jesus Christ, you sick fuck."

Petrovsky nodded toward the black-and-white marbled composition book sitting on the counter. "And there it is, the famous book that has caused so much grief for so many."

"Take it and get out."

"We are way beyond handwritten notes and carefully crafted diagrams. I'm here to collect a debt. You're a firm believer in an eye for an eye, right?"

Petrovsky reached into the other pocket of his overcoat and came out with an aerosol can of cockroach spray and a lighter. "It's not the foamy stuff you sprayed us with, but it will do. If the flames don't kill you, the poison will."

He set his gun on the benchtop and tried to spark the lighter, but his fingers were thick and clumsy, stiffened by scar tissue. He clicked once, twice, three times.

David lunged for the gun.

The lighter ignited.

The aerosol can spewed its pungent contents.

David ducked just as the poison turned to flame, the fireball singeing the top of his head.

A flash and the earsplitting crack of a gunshot.

Petrovsky's legs buckled. He hit the ground.

Mr. White staggered into the lab and fell to the floor.

David grabbed Petrovsky's gun from the bench, kicked the roach poison and cigarette lighter out of reach, then kicked the Russian. No response.

He went over to Mr. White and rolled him onto his back. His eyes were closed in a tight grimace. Both the radial and ulnar arteries were shooting pulsatile streams of blood from the stump of his right forearm.

David ran to the bathroom and grabbed the dressing supplies left over from his leg. He returned to the grisly scene, placed a stack of gauze pads on the end of the stump and tightly wrapped everything with a role of Kerlix gauze. Consistent pressure on the arteries would stem the bleeding, and given some time they'd spasm, form clots, and seal themselves off.

Mr. White opened his eyes. "Don't bother." A paroxysm of wet coughs interrupted. "Open my coat."

David did, and he found a blood-soaked shirt underneath. He ripped open the shirt, exposing a stab wound just to the right of the sternum. If Petrovsky's knife hadn't penetrated the heart, it very likely hit a pulmonary artery, or vein, or both.

Mr. White coughed again, sending clots of blood onto his face and chest. A grave injury David was all too familiar with. In addition to whatever had been lacerated—heart, pulmonary artery, pulmonary vein—the right mainstem bronchus or the trachea had also been violated, allowing the passage of blood into the tracheobronchial tree and out the mouth with each cough. Fatal without immediate surgery.

"Richard," David said, cradling Mr. White's head in his arms. "We've done it. The kidney is functioning. It's ready to be transplanted into Heather."

Mr. White managed a weak smile. "I knew you'd do it. I always had faith."

Another spasm of coughs sent a stream of blood roiling out of Mr. White's mouth. His body jerked and bucked as he choked and gasped, unable to move air through his obstructed trachea. He was suffocating.

David turned Mr. White's head to the side and pounded on his back, hoping the blood would drain and clear the airway. There was nothing else he could do. He was helpless without a suction device, a laryngoscope, and an endotracheal tube—his knowledge and experience useless without the most basic instruments.

Another cough, the effort feeble, no movement of air. Mr. White stiffened for a moment and then his body fell limp. David felt for a pulse, pushing his fingers into either side of Mr. White's neck, but he found nothing, as expected. He gently lowered Mr. White's head to the floor and looked over at Petrovsky. He had worked his way to his hands and knees.

"Where's my Glock?" Petrovsky said. He was slowly crawling along the border of light and dark, sweeping the wood floor with one hand while holding his neck with the other. Bright red blood streamed from between his fingers. Mr. White had shot Mikhail Petrovsky through the carotid artery.

Petrovsky gave up the search and propped himself against the wall, still holding his neck, blood pouring from beneath his hand.

David knelt down next to him and shoved the barrel of the Glock deep into his throat. Petrovsky tried to speak, his words frantic and garbled, his head thrashing from side to side. Then David stood, focused the red dot of the laser site in the middle of Petrovsky's forehead and fired.

A thunderous boom pierced David's ears and left them ringing. Pulverized brain, bone, and blood sprayed the wall behind Petrovsky. The smell of spent gunpowder filled the air. His head fell forward.

David stared at Petrovsky's lifeless body for a moment, then aimed the laser sight at his heart and fired two more shots in quick succession.

76

In the forty days David had lived in the safe house, he'd never heard a single noise indicating the presence of anyone living one floor down. The walls were thick, and the floors solid, so he was not worried that the sound of four gunshots had carried beyond the confines of the penthouse. Nevertheless, he was ready to get the hell out of the place. He cleared his mind of the carnage that lay at his feet and focused on the task at hand—a task for which he and Mr. White had carefully planned.

First, he went to the bathroom, stripped out of his bloody clothes, took a hot shower and scrubbed his body from head to toe, and he kept scrubbing until the bloodstained water circling the drain turned clear. After drying off, he used a pair of scissors to cut off his hair and goatee, then finished the job with a succession of razors, shaving his face and head until both were bare. Now dressed and feeling clean—not cleansed, but at least clean—he went to the bedroom, pulled the sheets from the bed and used them to cover the bodies in the lab. David then went to the kitchen, and from the freezer he removed a one-liter bag of saline solution, a one-liter bag of preservative solution, and a bag of crushed ice.

Back in the lab he donned a surgical hat and facemask, retrieved sterile gloves, specimen bags and instruments from a cabinet, then turned off the pumps, filters, and monitoring equipment. After climbing a step stool and unclamping the lid of the glass cylinder, he slipped into the sterile gloves and used long forceps and Metzenbaum scissors to reach down into the cylinder and snip the ureter, artery, and vein of the kidney.

With the kidney freed of its attachments, David gently lifted it from the tank and set it into a sterile basin filled with iced saline solution, which would provide topical cooling of the organ. To flush the broth from the vascular structures and cool the deep layers of the organ, David cannulated the renal artery with a catheter and infused the liter of cold preservative solution.

When the bag was empty, David removed the cannula and trimmed the ends of the artery, vein, and ureter, just as he had done as a general surgery resident two years ago, and just as he had unwittingly done for Andrew Turnbull a few weeks ago. Only this time he was preparing the world's first bioengineered kidney for transplant into a human recipient. This was an achievement unparalleled in the history of medicine. This was an achievement that should be lauded around the world as a great triumph in the battle against end-stage organ failure—mankind at its best. Instead, the genesis of this organ had cost lives, caused immeasurable human suffering, and had drawn out the dark, ugly, brutal side of men the way only greed can—mankind at its worst. Smart and stupid at the same time.

With the prep work done, David placed the kidney into a sterile specimen bag, filled it with iced saline and sealed it, put that bag into another for added protection, then set in on top of the ice in a six pack-sized cooler.

In the bedroom, he stuffed his meager wardrobe into a duffel bag, along with the iPad and the two composition books—Low Level Laser Therapy, and Kidney Zero—and one hundred thousand dollars' worth of crisp hundred-dollar bills banded into ten stacks.

In the bathroom, David took a moment to check himself in the mirror. Since his arrest and seventy-two-hour detainment in the Tombs, he had slept very little and eaten next to nothing, and the stark result was staring back at him. His skin was drained of color. His eyes were recessed deep in their sockets and surrounded by dark, finely wrinkled skin. His cheekbones were sharpened and his temples sunken due to poor nutrition and dehydration.

But this was okay. This was a departure from the healthy David McBride the public had seen in the papers and on the TV. This was the gaunt, bald, post-chemotherapy David McBride who was going to take the subway to Penn Station and board an Amtrak train to Washington, DC. He went to the closet, grabbed the fur-lined canvas coat he had acquired from Homeless Larry on Fourteenth Street and slipped it on. With a scarf wrapped around the lower half of his face, the hood covering his head, and his eyes framed by fat-rimmed reading glasses, it would require an astute observer to recognize him. He took one last look, from the front, from the sides, and returned to the lab, confident in his appearance.

Richard Whitestone had planned for every contingency. Sadly, that included handling his dead body. David knelt down next to him, reached under the bed sheet and gently felt the skin at the base of his right ear. The DARPA-designed GPS chip, which was the diameter of a cocktail straw and about half an inch in length, was somewhere near the right mastoid process. David found it and tapped it nine times—three short, three long, three short—SOS. He then used a Sharpie to write Jim Broderick's contact number on the sheet.

Before turning to leave, David paused for a moment. His eyes filled with tears as he felt the same rage and emptiness he had experienced when Cassandra died on the side of the road that night, and when he'd heard about his father's brutal murder. At least Richard Whitestone left this world knowing his daughter would be saved, his mission successful, and that gave David a small measure of solace. Ice chest in one hand, duffel bag in the other, he turned and headed for the elevator.

77

After riding the 6 train to midtown and the E train across town, David once again found himself traversing the corridors of a bustling Penn Station as a fugitive. He had made the subway ride unnoticed, hunkered in a corner with his coat, scarf, and glasses providing a serviceable disguise, but passing through Penn Station was a different story. Just like the morning after the subway tunnel showdown with the Russian, David's face was plastered on the front pages of all the area newspapers, which were displayed outside the myriad Hudson News stores populating the station. But this time it wasn't a two-year-old ID-badge photo. It was the mugshot taken at the Manhattan Detention Complex three days ago, when he had thick black hair and a bushy goatee. The most sensational of the headlines was, of course, courtesy of the bottom-feeding *Daily Mirror*: "Dog-Murdering, Woman-Beating, Organ-Snatching Ghoul Escapes from the Tombs!" He'd just have to keep his head down, not call attention to himself, and hope for the best.

Hiding behind his coat, scarf, and glasses, David approached an Amtrak ticket window and paid cash for a ticket on the noon Acela Express. With a top speed of 150 mph, he'd roll into Washington DC's Union Station by 3:00 p.m. And the faster the better. The kidney was on ice, but the sooner it was sewn to an artery and blood flow was restored, the better the postoperative function and long-term prognosis. Ticket in hand, he stepped away from the counter and flipped open his TracFone. The signal was poor. He'd have to go up to street level.

The escalator carried David, his duffel bag, and cooler up to Seventh Avenue. He stood near the curb and dialed the phone while looking over at the Hotel Pennsylvania, recalling the hot bath in room 1308, the cleansing of a gunshot wound to his own leg, the bloody bathwater running down the drain. He had first laid eyes on Kate D'Angelo the following morning as the NYPD piled into the place searching for him, the disgraced physician turned organ-snatcher.

"Hello," said a nondescript male voice.

"It's David. The kidney is ready. I'm taking the noon express and will be there in three hours."

"Why you and not your senior partner?"

"He'll be unable to make the trip."

"Is his condition terminal?"

"Yes."

A pause, then, "I'm sorry. When you arrive, go to the food court and order a cup of navy bean soup at Panera Bread."

"Okay," David said, "and I'll need a place to stay for a few days."

"Anything else?"

"How's the patient?"

"Deep coma. Doctors say she's down to her final hours, a day at most. They made her a DNR."

Do Not Resuscitate. If she has a cardiac or respiratory arrest, no attempt will be made to save her. Standard practice for terminally ill patients whose underlying disease can't be treated. But now she is treatable, the cure sitting at his feet. "Have the order rescinded immediately. Full resuscitation if she codes."

David checked his watch, then dialed another number on a second TracFone. The other end picked up on the second ring. "Thirteenth precinct. Morales."

"Detective Kate D'Angelo, please. Tell her it's David McBride calling."

"Uh yeah, sure, *Doctor*. But I'm gonna have to put you on hold. There's about eight other McBrides ahead a you."

"Tell the detective someone took a dump on the holding cell floor in the Tombs."

A click. Music that was more static than music. Then, "Well, well. Hello, David. Ready to turn yourself in?"

"I thought you might like to know that all of the principle players in this series of unfortunate events have been summarily dispatched."

"With the exception of yourself," Kate said.

"Of course, but I'll be disappearing soon, so your case is essentially closed. I just didn't want you to tie up your manpower any longer than necessary."

"On behalf of the NYPD, we thank you for your thoughtfulness. We need more fugitives like you. But in all seriousness, David, I want you to know I've always been on your side. Let me bring you in, and I'll do what I can to see that you get treated fairly."

"Sorry, but I have something important to take care of that is much larger than me or my inevitable date with justice."

"If you run, we'll find you."

"I'm not worried about that. Once I've done what I need to do, fate can take over."

- 78 -

Three hours and thirty minutes later, David was eating navy bean soup in the food court at Washington, DC's Union Station when a man wearing an overcoat and fedora walked up to his table. He greeted David warmly as if they were old friends, handed him a thick manila envelope, picked up the cooler and disappeared into the crowd.

- **79** -

David's hotel was within walking distance of the station. Everything needed for check-in was inside the envelope—directions, a DC driver's license with a pseudonym, and a credit card in the same name. The hotel itself was small, identified only by a brass nameplate mounted outside a revolving door. The lobby was utilitarian and staffed by a single person, a young woman who intentionally avoided eye contact with David. Six floors with only four rooms per floor meant minimal contact with other humans. It was the kind of place where one could come and go unnoticed, all by design, it seemed.

David entered his room, put out the Do Not Disturb sign and locked the door behind him. The only significant sleep he'd had in the past three days was on the train, about two-and-a-half hours. He tossed the duffel bag into a chair, slipped out of his coat and shoes, lay on the bed and everything went black.

Sixteen hours later he awoke with a head full of cobwebs and a body full of kinks and tweaks. He stretched, sucked down two cartons of orange juice from the mini-fridge, and jumped in the shower. Following the shower, he shaved his face and scalp, got dressed, and sat down with the TracFone. Time to make the call.

As he punched in the number, he was surprised to find his hands shaking and his heart racing. Considering the death, carnage, and mayhem he'd both seen and perpetrated over the past couple of months, a simple call to check the condition of a patient should be no big deal. But it was precisely this patient and her condition that was the genesis of the death, carnage, and mayhem. If he had failed, if she was now beyond saving, all this tragedy and all the lives that had been irrevocably altered would have been for naught.

The phone rang once. Twice.

"Hello," said the same male voice.

David's heart was pounding so hard his voice caught as he spoke. He swallowed, then said, "How's she doing?"

"Very well. She was transplanted about three a.m. No complications."

The kidney had been exposed to a nineteen-hour ischemic time—nineteen hours on ice—David quickly calculated. Acceptable but not ideal. And this was a bioengineered organ, so there was no way of knowing how it was going to respond to such a long period of ischemia. "Is the kidney making urine?"

"Between a hundred and a hundred and fifty milliliters per hour."

David relaxed into the chair, overcome with relief. That kind of urine production exceeded his greatest expectations. Of course, it remained to be seen if the kidney was filtering the nitrogenous wastes and other toxins contributing to Heather's uremic coma, but the first hurdle had been cleared, and the next twenty-four hours would determine if she was going to get over the second one.

"Can I call you later for another update?" David asked.

"Anytime, day or night."

"And one other thing, if you don't mind."

"Sure."

"Where is she?"

"Washington Hospital Center."

"Can you get me a surgical hat and mask, and a long white coat and ID badge, and drop them by the hotel?"

"End of the day work for you?"

"Yes."

David tossed the phone onto the bed, let his head fall back onto the chair, and rubbed his face with his palms. He needed two sausage-egg-and-cheese bagels and some orange juice.

80

Now that he was 230 miles south of New York City, David was confident his altered appearance would allow him to blend in with the rest of the faceless, self-absorbed rabble that populated major American cities. The organ-snatcher story had gone national— international even—but the intensity of the coverage dwindled to morbid fascination once outside the tristate area. Nonetheless, David kept his face covered and glasses on as he ventured into a nearby deli.

Back in the hotel room he sipped his orange juice, bit a bagel, and sat down at the desk to go through the manila envelope he'd been given at the train station. Contained within were two additional envelopes, one letter-sized with a note that said "Read First," and a larger one with "Fallon, Nevada" written on it. As instructed, David opened the letter first.

Dear David,

> *If you are reading this, it means I've met my end and you have delivered Heather's kidney to my associate. It also means Heather will soon, or perhaps has already been, transplanted. If that's the case, you have done everything I've asked of you, and for that you have my undying gratitude.*
>
> *The last time we addressed your future, you were unsure which direction it would take. Should you decide to turn yourself in to law enforcement, Evan Beck will represent you, and I have set up an escrow account that will cover his fees. However, if you would like to start a new life as a new person, everything you*

need is right here in the envelope labeled Fallon, Nevada. Fallon is a small (very small) town and may not be your ideal place to start over, but it is way off the beaten path, and the surgical practice there will allow you to fulfill your dream of practicing general surgery. I sincerely hope you choose this option. In a cruel twist of irony, it was your surgical skills that brought you into this nightmarish situation, and if you so choose, it will be these same skills that will deliver you from it.

With great esteem and appreciation,
Richard Whitestone

"Well, Mr. White," David said to the empty room, "I'll accept the Fallon offer, because there's no fucking way I'll spend another minute behind bars with the likes of Hector Gonzales, overdosing junkies, the ogre that gave me a concussion, and people who think shitting on the floor is normal behavior."

David set the letter aside and opened the larger, fatter envelope. It contained a U.S. passport, a Nevada driver's license, the deed to a house, and the title to a car. The name on the documents: David S. Aaronson. And under that same name, an M.D. degree from The University of Nevada School of Medicine, a certificate of completion from the general surgery residency program at UC San Francisco, board certification from the American Board of Surgery, and a Nevada state medical license. And the crowning jewel? His copy of a signed contract giving him a 50 percent stake in Fallon Surgical Associates with a stipulation that full ownership will be turned over to him in three years.

David was stunned. He was acutely aware of Richard Whitestone's vast resourcefulness, but this was ridiculous. A state medical license? A medical school diploma? Residency and board certifications? And God knows how he wrangled away half of somebody's surgical practice. David could only hope the proprietor of Fallon Surgical Associates was a single practitioner on the verge of retirement who was offered a fair buyout, and not some poor lug coerced into an early exit by Mr. White's trademark bag of threats.

Mr. White also provided contact information for a plastic surgeon the intelligence agencies used when hiding high-risk individuals. He added a note that said, "A few nips and tucks will go a long way toward protecting your new identity." And finally, the documentation for an escrow account that held two million dollars.

David leaned back in the chair and stared at the ceiling, dumbfounded by the set of documents sitting before him. It was going to take some time to process everything. The idea of becoming a completely different person was unsettling, but now that he thought about it, Andrew Turnbull had already taken care of that. David McBride died on that dark road in northern New Jersey along with Cassandra. And if there had been a shred of the old David remaining, it was extinguished when his father was beaten to death. So, yeah, he supposed David Aaronson had already made his debut, and all David McBride had to do was get out of the way.

81

As the idea of growing a human kidney in a glass cylinder had inched toward reality, David had compiled a list of university-based labs that were working in the field of tissue engineering and organ fabrication. After a thorough review, he had settled on five programs he thought would benefit the most from Turnbull's breakthrough. The plan? Send each of them the composition books, including the two describing the low-level laser techniques and David's experience with kidney zero. And in a few weeks, he'd follow-up with a report detailing the success—or failure, should that be the case—of kidney zero and the patient in which it was implanted.

But first things first. He had worked through the morning and into the early afternoon digitizing the LLLT and Kidney Zero volumes at a FedEx-Kinkos, and had downloaded the files onto his iPad and converted them into iBooks. He was now ready to send the complete set out into the world, but considering he was about to shake the foundations of medical science and change the world, he thought it appropriate that the books begin their journey in a bar, much the same way Watson and Crick had deciphered the molecular structure of DNA in a pub and had drawn their rendition of the double helix on a cocktail napkin.

David found a softly lit Irish pub and headed for a booth in the back. The crowd was scant, a handful of men sitting at the bar, several couples in booths, most everyone dressed in business attire. Happy hour was approaching, and he figured these fortunate souls were getting an early start. The conversations were muffled, and the U2 ballad "One" drifted from the sound system. David removed his heavy coat, slipped a knit cap over his bald head and adjusted his reading glasses, sitting down just as the server approached.

She set a cardboard coaster on the table. "What can I get for you?"

"A Guinness Stout, please," David said with a partial glance in her direction. "And do you have any Midleton behind the bar?"

"Yes, but it's pricey."

Indeed it was. Somewhere north of one-fifty for a 750ml bottle, but it was one of the finest Irish whiskies out there. "That's fine," David said, slipping a crisp C-note onto the table. "I'll take a double, neat, along with the beer."

As she walked away, David turned on the iPad, linked to the bar's Wi-Fi signal, and opened the browser. Having set up a dummy email account specifically for this task, he clicked it open and reviewed the message he had previously composed:

Dear Esteemed Colleagues,

Attached to this email is a collection of research materials that will change both medical science and the world. Each of you are striving to create bioengineered human organs in your laboratories and have met with varying success. The information contained within the attachments will enable you to clear the final hurdle and grow adult-sized organs ready for transplantation. Pay particular attention to the techniques in the volume labelled "LLLT." In the book titled "Kidney Zero," I have documented my experience growing the world's first transplant-ready bioengineered kidney, which just yesterday was implanted into a human recipient. Both the recipient and myself prefer to remain anonymous, but I will provide you with periodic updates as to how the patient and her new kidney are doing.

This is not my original work, but I pass it on to you for the betterment of science and mankind. The techniques I have provided here are not intended to be hoarded for the sake of professional glory and institutional profit. My intention is that they be shared with the research community and those patients

*with end-stage organ failure are the ultimate beneficiaries.
Please honor my efforts by further perfecting these techniques
and making them widely available to all in need of replacement
organs. In providing you with this technology, I have placed my
trust in your hands. Please treat it with honesty and integrity.*

*My best regards,
Unsigned*

David entered the five email addresses, all of them with the *.edu*
domain—Harvard, Wake Forest, Boston, UCLA, UCSF—and then
attached the iBooks. He did not hit send immediately, but instead
waited for the server to return. A few minutes later she did, and
once she was out of earshot he hoisted the tumbler of Midleton and
said, "In honor of Andrew Turnbull. You were an absolute sociopath, and I'm glad you no longer walk the earth, but you were also a
genius, and I hope your brilliance saves many lives."

He sipped the whiskey and hit send.

With a few healthy sips, David polished off the Midleton and
waved the empty glass at the server. He then took a long swig of
beer, and as the velvety Guinness cascaded down his esophagus he
reflected on what he had just done. He had taken one of the greatest achievements in medical history and freely shared it with the
research community. Andrew Turnbull would not have done that.
The Russian biomedical company would not have done that. They
would've kept the technology locked away so they could monopolize
the market and hold the insurance companies and private payors
hostage. Perhaps he wasn't a gray person after all.

And then he considered what lay before him. Yes, he was
finally going to realize his dream of practicing general surgery. That
was all he had wanted for the past two years. But he'd be doing it
alone, without his wife, without his child, without his father, without friends or family in a small town he knew nothing about in a
part of the country he didn't understand. What kind of existence
would that be? And for how long? This ugliness he'd been a part
of for the last couple of months would eventually catch up to him.

What then? Spending the rest of his life locked up with the Hector Gonzales of the world? Another double Midleton arrived. David downed half of it, asked for a third, along with a second pint and promised the server he'd slow down from here on out.

Now halfway through the second pint of Guinness, and taking his first sip of the third Midleton, one of U2's more moving songs, "Walk On," wafted from the speakers:

> *And if the darkness is to*
> *keep us apart*
> *And if the daylight feels like it's*
> *a long way off*
> *And if your glass heart should crack*
> *And for a second you turn back*
> *Oh no, be strong*
> *Oh oh*
> *Walk on*
> *Walk on*

And all at once, two months' worth of pain and heartache and loneliness came blasting to the surface. His diaphragm lurched, and his abdomen bucked as he started to sob uncontrollably. He tried to stifle it, pulling the knit cap off his head and burying his face in it, but his entire body quaked with spasms. He got the sense someone had briefly walked up to the table, but he was powerless to stop the sobs and kept his face hidden.

After what was probably no more than a minute or two, but seemed like ten, he regained control and composed himself. The server showed up a few moments later with a glass of water and a menu.

"Is everything okay?" she asked.

"A rough couple of months," David replied, "but I'm good now. Thanks for your concern."

The server nodded at the menu. "You should probably eat something."

David smiled. "Yes, I probably should."

82

David awoke into an unfamiliar blackness, not knowing where he was for a moment, but his throbbing head, ashtray eyes, and phlegmy throat quickly oriented him. Midleton Irish Whiskey and poor impulse control were the culprits. His recollection of the night's proceedings was hazy at best—a trifecta of drinking, in a public place, to the point of a blackout. Numbers one, two, and three on the list of things fugitives should not do. He supposed two months of anguish, pain, and sorrow had finally come calling. The cops were not beating down the door, so no harm, no foul.

He lifted his head to check the clock. The throbbing intensified to a pounding, like someone was smacking his cranium with the ball end of a ball-peen hammer. He dropped his head back to the pillow but managed to catch the time on the way down—11:30 a.m. Since he was not on any kind of a schedule, he thought the better part of valor would be to lie still for a few minutes, then try to get to the Advil. And he needed water. Rehydration was the key to blunting the effects of a hangover. Guzzle some fluids, pop 800 mg of Advil, or 1000 mg of Tylenol, or both and get back into bed. That's what David did, and he woke up two hours later feeling decent. A long hot shower elevated him from decent to nearly cured, and after two sausage-egg-and-cheese bagels he felt almost human again.

Now that he was back to baseline, more or less, it was time to check on Heather. As he dialed the TracFone he did some quick math. It was three in the afternoon, the kidney now thirty-six hours post implant. If it was filtering, the lab values would reflect that. If the lab values had not changed, the kidney was not filtering and never would. Game over. And once again, David's hands were shaking, and his heart was pounding, which was resurrecting his headache.

"Hello," said the contact.

"I'm hoping you have good news," David said.

"I have excellent news. Blood urea nitrogen and creatinine have decreased by half, electrolytes are stable. She was weaned off the ventilator twelve hours after surgery, and today she's awake and coherent. She is still sleepy, but easily arousable and oriented to person and place."

David slumped into the chair, fighting back a wave of emotion. "I'd like to come see her."

"Did you get the package?"

David glanced at the brown paper bundle tied with a string. Surgical scrubs, a white coat, a hospital ID. "Yes. It's here."

"She's in the step-down unit, room 314."

83

David stood next to Heather Whitestone as she slept peacefully, her bed raised forty-five degrees to help her lungs move air, a monitor silently tracing the rhythm of her heart, a nasal cannula delivering a few extra liters of oxygen with a soft, bubbling hiss. She was thin and frail, but absolutely beautiful in her serenity. Her hair was long and straight and black, much like Cassandra's, and she bordered on petite, just like Cassandra.

Heather awakened and looked up at David, her eyes sparkling with sleepy tears. "Hello," she said softly. "Are you my surgeon?"

Standing there in a white coat, green scrubs and cap, and a surgical mask partially covering the lower half of his face, David looked like he could have been her surgeon. "No," he said, smiling warmly and taking her hand in both of his. "But you could say I'm part of the team."

"Well…thank you for everything you've done for me," and she drifted back to sleep.

David's heart swelled with pain and love, and loneliness and hope. And his eyes filled with tears as Heather's sleepy smile reminded him of the dreamy expression on Cassandra's face the night she lay dying on the side of the road. He lingered a few moments longer, holding Heather's hand in his, afraid to let go, knowing that when he did his heart was going to break all over again. But he had to, and as he placed her hand at her side, the chambers of his heart weakened and dilated, and his breath became trapped in his lungs. He turned and walked out the door, tears streaming down his cheeks.

Acknowledgements

Learning how to write and publish a novel is a long and arduous process, requiring many contributors along the way. The following individuals deserve my immense gratitude:

Franco Audia, Patti Arthur, Christine Grace, Karin Wigley, and Kathleen Isdith for their early reads and feedback.

Homicide detective, Sgt. Mark Worstman, Seattle Police Department.

Tom Hyman at Kirkus editorial services.

Kate Race at Visual Quill for her cover and marketing platform designs.

Chris O'Byrne and the staff at JETLAUNCH.net for their design and distribution expertise.

About the Author

Richard Van Anderson is a former heart surgeon turned fiction writer. His surgery training took him from the "knife and gun club" of LSU Medical Center in Shreveport, Louisiana, to the famed Bellevue Hospital in Midtown Manhattan. His education as a writer includes an MFA in creative writing from Pine Manor College in Boston, Massachusetts. He currently lives in Seattle, Washington with his wife and two sons.

To learn more about Richard Van Anderson the author, visit rvananderson.com.

Connect with Richard on:

Facebook
Twitter
Google Plus
Goodreads

And finally, the best way for a book to find its audience has always been, and still is, word of mouth recommendations. If you liked the story, please consider telling others about it, either person to person, using social media, or (and this is the most effective way) posting reviews at your favorite review site. Thank you.

Made in the USA
San Bernardino, CA
05 January 2018